THE
Sharpest
PETAL

Book Cover by Kier Smelcer, @foxlore_art on IG

To all the women who wanted the assassin in a book to be more like you, this is for you.

Prologue

As I'm standing at the end of the aisle staring at the love of my life, I realize that everything in my life has led up to this moment. Today, I finally get to marry the man who will be with me throughout the rest of my life. We weathered the storms that life threw at us and made it to this moment together. Where we belong.

The ceremony is everything I could've hoped for. The palace garden is set up for all of our friends and family, and anyone who wants to join us from the surrounding kingdoms. Charlie's eyes sparkle in the light with tears when I walk out the doors. I reach the end and can't stop myself from pecking him on the cheek before the officiant even starts. Getting lost in Charlie's eyes, I forget the world around me until I am snapped out of it by the officiant clearing his throat.

They're waiting for me.

The officiant repeats himself, "Do you take this man to be your husband?"

"I do," I say with a smile, then Charlie leans in and kisses me, in a way I've never been kissed before.

Immediately following the wedding ceremony is the coronation, crowning us rulers of the kingdom. Fulfilling a dream I never knew I had.

Then we dance the night away until our feet give out, and the lights and ballgowns blur together. The only time we stop is to entertain guests. When I finally pause for refreshments, a king and queen from a neighboring country bombard me with questions about how my husband and I met.

"Queen Anna, please tell me how you met! I've been waiting all night to hear the story," the queen asks me with a smile.

"Well, when he had a ball looking for a wife, I showed up. I knew from the moment I laid eyes on him that we would be here one day," I tell her, smiling at Charlie, who is across the room talking to another set of royal monarchs.

Telling this version of the story has become second nature to me. There are very few people aware of what actually happened, and they are all from our kingdom.

"Tell me the full story! I want all the details," she says. "I *love* love."

"There really isn't much to tell," I lie, kissing her cheeks so she can head out for the night. "It's just not that interesting."

What they can't know—in fact, what no one can discover—is that I accepted a job I never should've taken, and it led to meeting the love of my life. I might have almost destroyed the kingdom, but now I will do everything in my power to save it. It is my home now. Where I belong.

This secret is one that I will protect with my life, because no one can learn of our weakness. In the end, it's not always about love; it's about survival. We will be the strongest kingdom on the continent. No one needs to know the rest.

The secret I'm hiding? I tried to kill the prince. Now, I will do anything to protect him.

Part One

Chapter One

Anna

My kingdom—Weide Saliba—has an underground network of people who do jobs that are a little less than legal. How much trouble you get into entirely depends on whether you're caught.

My vocations, for example, are assassin and bounty hunter. Yes, I'm a female, and yes, I am very good at my job.

At this point in my life, I have captured and eliminated many high-ranking nobles for crimes against the crown. Technically, I work for the king, but that's between you and me because if the civilians knew what their ruler was asking for, there would be a rebellion.

Don't get me wrong though, as soon as I receive word about a crime against the crown, I immediately jump on it...for the right price. I'm sure they deserve their fate.

I don't enjoy my employment, but due to my father's illness, my mother cannot work. Someone has to be home to take care of him, which means that, like a lot of people in this network, we're desperate for money.

When I hear whispers of a potential job in the evening, I wait until the early morning hours to walk into an abandoned barn where my prospective employer is hiding. While the space has housed no animals for years, the scent of old dung makes me grimace. I wrap a black scarf tighter around my face both to conceal my features and keep out the stench.

"There you are," a voice rasps behind one of the old wooden doors.

I approach, but can only glimpse the green eyes of whoever is delivering this information, and a job letter written in code, through the cracks between old planks. I'm assuming this individual is some kind of messenger for my real boss, and I say nothing to protect my identity. But as the person explains the details, the hair raises along the nape of my neck.

What's the job, you ask?

"Kill the prince *before* he finds a wife."

Kill the prince.

Kill the prince.

Before I can ask why the king wants his heir dead, the messenger whispers, "The prince's misdeeds must never see the light of day. Complete this termination, and you save your kingdom."

Foreboding makes my stomach clench.

Only someone as desperate as me would attempt an assassination like this, and once I realize the reward money will be enough to take care of my family for years, I jump on it immediately.

Prince Charles Greystone is no easy mark for my five-foot-two self considering he stands ten inches taller than me. Not to mention the fact that he is very well built. Sadly, that is all I know about him, so putting my plan into action will take a lot of effort. There is no quick sneak-into-his-house-and-end-him option, like with the last traitorous noble I eliminated.

For this task, the messenger told me about a ball the royal family is hosting, and provided a stipend along with a map of the palace and surrounding grounds to help me purchase the materials and have the intel I require to infiltrate it. They assume I know what he looks like, even though I'm not completely sure. If he's ever visited the village, I've never laid eyes on him. I just know what I've heard from other people, like his height and build, which doesn't help much. However, I always complete my jobs, so this one cannot be any different.

Still, the realization that I must end the future king makes me shiver. The crown has hidden his 'misdeeds' very well, and

I can't help but wonder what atrocities he's committed. I tuck the letter and map into hidden pockets lining the inside of my trousers.

As I walk down the familiar roads to my small village, and away from the musty abandoned farmhouse, I see it all with new eyes—the eyes of someone hoping for a change that the money from this job can give my family.

I live in a small village, close enough to the castle that it is easy to get to, but far enough away that we don't receive any of the benefits of being a neighboring town. When I was young, I used to love my village, but the older I get, the more I dislike it. Not the village itself, but how we are treated. We live in rundown shacks that are barely standing. Most of our homes have roofs in need of repair, with water constantly dripping into them when it rains. But a few rooftops are completely falling apart. The road is so dusty that all the shacks and shops are always covered in grime.

The aroma of fresh-baked bread, wafting through a window, calms my senses. My favorite smell. Slowing my pace, I peek in the window to see what kind of loaves the baker has today.

"Good morning, Anna! Only small loaves today, but I do have pies!" she shouts when she sees me peeking in.

Smiling, I wave at her. "Not today! I'll try to stop tomorrow though," I shout back, while continuing my stroll. Soon, I near my destination, and I slow my pace to admire the roses from the florist next door. I pass the pretty flowers and open the seamstress' door. As I step inside, the bell on top of the door jingles.

"Good morning," the seamstress calls from her workstation.

I walk up to the counter, looking out the windows that bring in the natural light as I dig in my bag for a gold coin. I place it on the counter along with a list of things I need for my mission.

"Good morning, I need the stuff on this list if you can help me?" I ask her. This is my first time here. Normally, my mom just makes all of our clothes by hand. The shopkeeper gives me a strange look before heading to the back of the shop, gesturing for me to follow her. As she throws dresses and fabrics in every different shade of yellow and texture imaginable into my arms, I realize how heavy clothing can be. By the time she finishes grabbing things off the list, my arms feel like they're going to fall off.

"Go behind the curtain and try everything on. Come out with every change so I can take notes on any adjustments that need to be made," she says before practically shoving me into the dressing room. I try all the items on, following her instructions of letting her see every dress and pair of shoes.

Each dress I put on is unlike anything I've ever worn before. While I'm used to cheap fabrics, the fine silks are soft against my skin. As I run my fingers through all the fabrics, feeling the softness on my skin, she sits at her messy desk writing notes down, which I don't understand, periodically getting up to place pins or move something around, before we finally finish the last garment. "I will have this all ready for you to pick up first thing tomorrow."

"Thank you," I say softly before giving her another coin for making my items a priority. She'll probably be up all night to get this much work done.

Leaving the dress shop, I make a note of everything I need to pick up tomorrow so I don't forget anything, before heading to my next stop. Needing a tiara of some kind, I stop at the silversmith's to see if I can get one custom made so it's not like anyone else's there. Lewis, one of the connections I have from the network, is already at the anvil when I walk in. I describe to him what I want with the promise that I'll be back to get it shortly. No one can find out what we're up to. He promises he'll make it as cheap and lifelike as possible.

Only one more item remains on my list. The apothecary is my last stop.

Pushing the heavy door open, I walk inside my second home and take a deep breath, bringing back all the fond memories. I grew up coming here with my mom while she worked, and I eventually took over when my dad started getting sick. Unfortunately, an assistant position at an apothecary doesn't pay enough to support a family. I try to still help out when I don't have a more pressing job to do. As the floor creaks, announcing my arrival, Lyla comes out from the back.

"Good evening, Anna! What are you looking for today?" she asks, knowing if I were here to help, I would've arrived earlier.

"Hi Lyla, I need some yarrow for my father," I tell her, looking around the shop at all the different herbs she has. I grab the green leafy stems I need for my father along with the potions required for my vocation. Dropping it all on the counter, I lean over, reaching underneath for dark elixir bottles. "I also need a few of these."

She gives me the side-eye, like she always does when I ask for the poisons she makes for emergencies. "You know you're the only one that knows about those. I never even told your mother."

A lie. Why would she keep them in stock and hidden behind the counter if only I used them? But I nod and pretend I believe her.

"I know Lyla, and I hate to ask. But this situation is complicated," I whisper, pleading for her to trust me. I try not to ask for her to make a new batch to keep in the shop in case I need more later. The truth is, I don't want to use methods like this, but for my current job, I'm going to have to make an exception.

Lyla glances around the shop, even though no one else is here. "Fine," she says so softly, I can barely make out the words, "but you owe me. I don't want any money, but you better be prepared to help me out during the busy season next month. My last assistant was useless."

"Deal!" I say with more excitement than I mean to. She grabs the glass vials and puts them in the bag with everything else as I hand her a coin.

"Take it," I urge. "For the yarrow. It's complicated, but this is going to work out."

She accepts it with a smile before kissing me on the cheek and shooing me out the door.

"Be careful!" I hear from behind me as I walk away laughing.

The trip home from the apothecary is short, even with my stop at the silversmiths on the way, and when I arrive, I plod up the stairs to my makeshift room in the loft since my hands are full. After I drop everything on my bed, I grab the herbs for my father, careful not to disrupt the vials of poison, and head down the stairs. I hold out the fronds of greenery to my mother.

"Thank you," my mother says as she sets them aside.

I nod and grab a spoon to help her finish up dinner. As I stir, I say, "First thing in the morning, I have to grab some stuff from the seamstress before my assignment. It's for another noble, so I have to go to the castle and will be gone all day."

My sister, who is sitting at the table sewing, pipes up before my mother can, always ready to help whenever needed. "I can grab it for you, Anna, while you start getting ready! Then I'll be back to help you."

I turn over my shoulder and smile at my sister. Amelia—we sometimes call her Amy for short—is a beautiful girl who takes more after our mother than I do, and she has also always been my best friend. Every time I have a job I have to dress up for, she is there to help me out, knowing I'm the strong one, and she's the gentle one, but in the best way.

"Thank you, sis, I would appreciate it," I respond as I dish our meals.

After dinner, I say my goodnights, heading up to bed to attempt to get some sleep for tomorrow. I've never felt so nervous about a job like this one. This is high profile, high price, and high risk.

Falling asleep is harder than it normally is. The voices in my head are impossible to silence. *What if a guard catches me? What will my family do then?* Spending most of the night tossing and turning, brain on high alert, I eventually quiet the voices for a few hours. Enough to not be exhausted, but not enough to feel rested.

The next morning, I wake up and stretch, preparing myself for the long day ahead. I get up and head over to my mirror, debating how to get ready. Picking up my powder, I decide to start there since that is what I struggle with the most. A few minutes into it, my sister peaks her head in and starts giggling.

"What's so funny?" I ask. turning to look at her for a brief second before turning back to the mirror.

"You always do this," she says as she steps in holding my dresses. She sets them down on the bed and reaches for my makeup, taking it out of my hands. "Those colors look terrible on you."

Reaching for a different set of powder, she sits down next to me to make me look better. When she's done, I turn and look in the mirror and see that instead of using gray, she applied a dramatic eye makeup with different shades of brown to elevate my look. I smile in the mirror seeing how well my blue eyes pop while she dabs a rosy tint to my cheeks and lips. Then she stands up and comes around behind me, taking over styling my hair. She puts my tiara on first before braiding my hair down the back and twisting it up into the prettiest updo. Tears well in my eyes as I look at myself, feeling more beautiful than ever.

I might be able to pull this off thanks to my sister's talent.

"What exactly is this job, sis?" she asks me while she finishes putting pins in my hair, the concern evident in her voice. Despite my efforts to keep her innocent, my sister is aware of my actual profession, and she hates that I put myself in danger to do it. But she understands how desperate we are for the money.

I swallow the truth and try to come up with something that will frighten her less. "I just have to capture a noble and turn them into the crown. They can't do it on their own without it being too suspicious."

"Promise me you'll be careful?"

I turn to see her grabbing my dress and setting it into the bag I'll use to keep it from getting dirty on the way to the palace..

"Promise."

She stays with me while I finish getting ready. As I put on my riding clothes, she starts humming my favorite song. She takes the closed bag out of my hands, going to place it behind Epona's saddle while I finish collecting my things. I strap my dagger—a three-inch blade with a black cloth handle covered in flowers—to my thigh along with my pouch for potions and the map, so that once my dress is on, they'll still be accessible. I grab my cloak and throw it on, using the hood to cover the tiara in my hair.

I hug my family goodbye and mount my black horse as quickly as possible before urging her into a trot, starting toward the castle. I stay off the main road and carefully ride in the woods, circumventing the villages as much as possible. This adds time to the journey, but I do not want to be noticed. Unfortunately, the closer we get to the castle, the richer the villages and the wider the roads, which also means less tree coverage and more residents.

After the two-hour ride, I arrive at the castle outskirts, but manage to remain hidden within a cluster of trees at the top of a hill. I take my dress off the saddle, pulling it over my head and lacing it up as quickly as possible. The pale yellow dress with tiny white flowers on the bodice—that coincidentally match my dagger—looks more beautiful than I could've imagined. The skirt feels voluptuous and soft—softer than I've ever felt in my life. After going over every inch of the dress, I jump into motion. Knowing the main gate is out of the question, I need to find another way inside. So I watch the castle for an hour, learning the guards' routines. I notice a guard who slips around the corner for a few minutes every half an hour, leaving the staff entrance unguarded, and realize that will be my best bet to get in unnoticed.

I sneak as close as I can while I wait for my chance to slip in. Finally, I make my move, dashing through the doorway and quickly pulling the map out of my thigh pouch so I can make my way to the ballroom.

Chapter Two

Anna

WHILE SNEAKING INTO THE castle was easy enough—though that guard should be relieved of duty for negligence—sneaking through the castle is *much* harder. There are so many twists and turns I can't tell if I'm even in the right hallway. When I arrive at some stairs, I know I've messed up, so I take a few minutes staring at a map that seems to be outdated and try to figure out where the ballroom is. I turn from the stairwell, ready to make another attempt at finding my destination when I hear voices and panic. I plaster myself to the wall, holding my breath and peering toward the speakers.

Down a hall to the left, I see a maid and a guard arguing. "We need to get back to the ballroom before we get caught."

"The prince will never notice that we're gone, and the queen couldn't care less what we do," he says, trying to pull her into a doorway.

"We have ten minutes before my sister notices," the maid says. When I squint to see better, I notice they're more enchanted with each other than they seem to be with anything else going on.

I quietly sneak past the hallway they're in—which is difficult when wearing yellow—and try to get back to the ballroom before they snap out of whatever they're in the middle of doing. As I turn around the next corner, voices and the scuff of boots warn me I'm not alone. *Again.*

Throwing my dress up, I struggle to hold it and slide the map back into the pouch on my thigh before they reach me. My heart rate speeds up, and my palms get sweaty, smudging the map. Right as the guards turn the corner, I drop my dress just in time. Had I been any slower, they would've gotten a front row-seat to my riding clothes, immediately giving away that I shouldn't be here.

"Thank goodness you're here," I say, wiping my hands on my dress.

"What are you doing in the middle of the hall?" the first guard asks me, the two behind him laughing quietly, probably assuming I cannot hear them.

An excuse pops into my mind. "Well, I was looking for the privy, but this castle is so confusing. I got lost. I have been wandering out here for what feels like forever before I heard you coming and knew I'd be rescued!" My voice comes out rushed, but my breathing finally slows when I realize how easily that lie fell off my tongue.

Behind the main guard, the younger guards mumble under their breath, "Are all princesses this dumb?"

"Quiet!" the other whisper-hisses.

I pretend they said nothing.

As the guards turn around, they wave at me to follow them, hoping I'll be obedient, which I am for a second.

"Please make sure you stay in the ballroom this time. The privy is right outside the door. I don't understand how everyone misses it." Annoyance is evident in his voice.

"Absolutely, it won't happen again." I assure him as we round the last corner to the ballroom.

I knew I was close. Thankfully, there are no issues with the guards after this considering they just escorted me inside.

Standing at the edge of the dance floor, I wait to see who everyone is dancing with, assuming it will be the prince. The prince I'm supposed to kill. The royal heir committing heinous crimes my informant couldn't even utter.

Since I arrived late, it appears most of the princesses have already waltzed, pranced, and sashayed with His Highness. I should be able to cut in soon. I subtly push my breasts up, making my cleavage a little more prominent in my dress, and put on my best smile before leaning on the pillar I'm standing beside.

A kind footman offers a tray of refreshments. I accept, putting the narrow glass up to my mouth and savoring a sip of strawberry wine, my favorite. At least, now it's my favorite. As I take my place leaning against the pillar again, I overhear something I know wasn't meant for my ears.

"Oh my goodness, the prince was so dreamy," a princess with a gold tiara over her long blonde hair says, fanning herself. "I definitely think that, out of all of us, he's going to choose me based on how our dance went."

"Oh really? It looked rather awkward from out here," another high-ranking young woman says with a scoff. The voice's owner is hidden behind the bulk of a pillar, except for a few tresses of mousy brown hair. I suppress a giggle.

"Plus," Mousy Hair continues, "he doesn't have to choose one princess to court. It's up to him to find the right match, so he can court as many people as he wants."

This tidbit of information piques my interest. That could cause a problem.

Shaking off their conversation, but tucking what I learned into the back of my brain, I step toward the dance floor, hoping someone will ask me to partner with them for a slow waltz, so

I don't look so out of place. Perhaps this daffodil-hued gown wasn't the best idea.

As I'm scanning for the prince, I make contact with the most beautiful pair of chocolate brown eyes I have ever seen, and the world around them disappears. As the song comes to an end, I snap out of my gaze, heat rising on my cheeks when I realize the eyes are getting closer. It feels like an eternity, but when he finally reaches me, I curtsy, reaching for his outstretched hand, assuming he's inviting me to dance.

"I don't think I've seen you before," the owner of those beautiful eyes says as he pulls me in for a dance

Attempting to shake off whatever thoughts are running through my head, like the fact that he is the most handsome man I have ever met in my life, I need to focus on the task at hand. However, when he smiles at me, I melt to the floor. That smirk could make women do whatever he wants. He is so much taller than me, his brown linen shirt, tucked into his forest green pants, fitting him snugly under his mantle, and his sandy blonde hair makes me want to run my fingers through it.

"My parents tend to leave me out of these things," I say, letting the sarcasm come through just slightly, "but I wanted to meet the infamous prince before he settles down, since apparently that's what this ball is for." Looking around, I still don't see any princesses dancing with the same person; they all seem to dance with anyone who asks them.

The handsome stranger in front of me grins down at me, taking me into the next spin across the dance floor. "You haven't met the prince yet? I'm surprised, as I thought all the princesses danced with him already."

"Not me. It seems to me he left his own ball early!" I respond, trying not to sound too annoyed about not being able to find him.

But I am annoyed.

And this man is distracting me.

"I'm sure he's around here somewhere. However, it doesn't seem like you're interested in being his wife."

"I'm mostly here to verify the rumors." I mention a few, but hold back on the worst ones. "I've heard he's a playboy, more concerned about himself than anyone else. Too cocky for his own good. I want to know if what the people are saying is true. Which...since he isn't here...it seems to be." As I finish the stranger spins me again, the song ends and another one begins, I go to step away but he pulls me back towards him, and starts the dance again, causing me to laugh.

"Well, I can tell you for a fact he's around here somewhere, just waiting for the right woman so he can make his decision on who to court."

Although the conversation comes to an end, we continue to dance. When I realize his hand is resting on my lower back, my face warms.

He grabs my hand, causing a laugh to slip from my lips as he spins me, putting my very full skirts on display. My riding clothes remain well hidden beneath the layers of fabric.

The music quiets, and the stranger pulls me off the dance floor, giving me a break to drink something. Every time I try to scan the room looking for the prince, I get sucked into those beautiful brown eyes that are looking at me like I am the only one in the room, and that is when I realize that if I wasn't here to kill the prince, I might just like this man.

I observe my surroundings in case I need a quick escape. Standing by one of the pillars, I see three more spread throughout the room, all having different lights spread between them. When the smell of bourbon and cinnamon hits me, I smile. The smell reminds me of my father. The intermingled fragrances here are just slightly different. I relax a little thanks to the homey smell, and count the windows, accepting that the prince isn't here and I should leave, but also wanting to enjoy my night.

"Save another dance for me," the stranger says when the song comes to a close.

I nod my agreement before wandering away, continuing my search for the elusive evil prince. But my job is now an excuse to wait for the handsome stranger, needing to dance with him again, and be in his presence. When I see him still looking at me from across the room, I smile, the butterflies in my stomach never calming down while I await his return.

I take the time away to get refreshments, swaying in place to the string instruments playing. My eyes scan the room for him. I don't know what it is, but I feel drawn to him. As I finish my drink, I glance up from my glass and once again meet those eyes, and a palm held out to me. I take his hand, deciding one more dance cannot hurt.

"Thank you for inviting me to dance with you. This night has been enjoyable, even if the prince left early," I mumble the last part with an eyeroll, assuming this noble is going to defend the prince again.

If he does, I don't notice because I'm looking out the window and realizing that the sun is already going down. I need to leave. But I continue the waltz, not letting the sunset ruin my mood.

"I'm glad it was enjoyable, but it's not over yet." He twirls me, likely expecting me to giggle after last time.

"Well, the dukes hosting me are expecting me to return to my lodging, so I need to leave after this dance. I don't want to worry them."

"Will you meet me again? Tomorrow? Please, princess?" he pleads.

"I'll try," I respond hopefully, assuming this is my way back into the castle since I wasn't able to complete my job. I need to assassinate the prince as soon as possible so I can collect the rest of my payment. "Maybe you'll be able to introduce me to the reclusive prince so we can put the rumors to rest for him?"

"Actually, Princess, I think we put them to rest already."

I look at him, confused, until the pieces slowly fit together in my mind. Tall, handsome, danced with all the princesses before I got there...he kept backing the prince up.

"I don't think I ever caught your name..." I say, staring at him. Anxiety clenched my stomach. Could he be?

"My name is Charles, Prince Charles Greystone. And you are?"

At this moment, all the thoughts running through my brain stop. I've been waiting for him to make an appearance, and this whole time he's been right in front of me. My heart races and my breathing picks up. I already told him I was leaving for the night, so I can't put my plan into action now, or he'll be suspicious. What am I going to do? I've never had an issue like this before. I always know what my targets look like, and this is why. Why couldn't the person who hired me give me a description? Or why couldn't he have deigned to visit the villages so I could have *seen* him before?

Why did I even take this task? He doesn't look evil. I should have pushed the informant for more details. Finally, I realize the prince is still staring at me. I need to say something.

"I guess you'll just have to wait and find out," I say, winking at him before I turn around and walk away, wiping my sweaty hands on my silky skirt as I escape.

Chapter Three

Charlie

AFTER A LONG EVENING of dancing, I am reminded why I loathe attending balls. Usually, my father doesn't force me to come unless absolutely necessary. Since this ball is for my hand in marriage, I can't avoid it. All I have been able to think about this whole time is how terrible I am going to be at being king and hoping the healer finds a cure for my father. I am not ready to take over this kingdom.

As I finish up a dance with what I assume is the last princess here, I look across the room and discover the most beautiful pair of ocean blue eyes I have seen. The song drifts to an end, and the royal girl clutching my arm tries to keep my attention for the next waltz, but I am too distracted by the mystery woman to hear what she says. I remove myself from the princess' grip, walk over, and reach my hand out to the blue-eyed beauty to catch her attention.

"I don't think I've ever seen you before," I say to her. She snaps out of whatever trance she's in.

As she rolls her eyes, I realize she doesn't know who I am. How refreshing.

"My parents tend to leave me out of these things, but I wanted to meet the infamous prince before he settles down, since apparently that's what this ball is for."

I laugh at the sarcasm in her voice. That was all the confirmation I needed.

"You haven't met the prince yet? I'm surprised, as I thought all the hopeful queens danced with him already." I try not to make it obvious who I am, but I want to see how far I can take this. When I notice some of the other princesses glaring at us, I assume it won't be long.

"Not me. It looks like he left his own ball early!" she says with a scoff, but I'm too distracted by her eyes to even care. Obviously, she isn't interested in me, so why is she here?

"I'm sure he's around here somewhere. However, it doesn't seem like you wish to be his wife."

"I'm mostly here to verify the rumors. I've heard he's a playboy, more concerned about himself than anyone else. Too cocky for his own good. I want to know if what the people are saying is true. Which, since he isn't here, it seems to be."

We spin, and as we twirl, she looks around again, always scanning the room like she's looking for an escape. Why?

"Well, I can tell you for a fact he's here somewhere, just waiting for the right lady so he can decide who to court." I know deep down that this woman will be my future queen. She is so different from the princesses I have met tonight. I'm tired of the desperate conversations where they'll say anything to appease me. The more conniving ones unnerve me. This princess is who I need. Intellect observes me being those gorgeous blue irises, but something about her is carefree.

I want someone who will be crazy with me when it's just us, while also standing by my side to help rule the kingdom. Someone who is kind, smart, and funny. My future queen must love my people, including the villagers, more than the prestige of being a ruler. This princess...she is all these things. Call it intuition, perhaps?

As the song ends, she tries to step away, but I pull her closer, putting my hand on her lower back. When her cheeks turn red, I know I'm getting somewhere. She finds me attractive even though she's ignorant of who I am.

We continue into another waltz, spinning around the room, and I hope she feels this connection between us. As we dance, she searches the crowd, and I assume she's looking for—me. But I want to know why. If she believes the ridiculous rumors, why is she here? And how does she not recognize me?

When the second song comes to an end, I lead her off the floor to procure some refreshments and wander away to socialize with my guests. But I try to keep an eye on my mystery woman while I'm at it. When it seems she is ready to dance again, I am right there, hoping she won't partner with anyone else. As I draw near, I reach my hand back out, and a smile spreads across her face as she accepts my silent request.

"Thank you for inviting me to dance with you. This night has been enjoyable, even if the prince left early," she says softly.

I laugh internally, amused that she isn't aware of who she's dancing with. Despite her glancing about the room, she seems to have missed the death glares from a few princesses.

"I'm glad it was enjoyable, but it's not over yet," I say, twirling her and hoping she giggles again. It is the most musical sound. I want to hear it over and over.

"Well, the dukes hosting me are expecting me home, so I need to leave after this dance. I don't wish to worry them."

My heart stops. She can't go yet. She doesn't have any idea who I am. We're still getting to know each other. It's too early. "Will you meet me again? Tomorrow? Please, princess?" I don't realize how desperate I am for her to reunite with me again until I hear the pleading in my own voice.

She gnaws on her lower lip, looking like she's debating something in her head. As anxious as I am about her leaving,

I find her thoughtful expression endearing, the cutest thing I have seen tonight.

"I'll try," she finally says. "And maybe you'll be able to introduce me to the prince so we can dispel the rumors for him?"

"Actually, princess, we can put them to rest already," I say, hoping she will figure it out without me telling her.

Her eyebrows scrunch together before her entire face widens with understanding. She clears her throat. "I don't think I ever caught your name?" she questions, her gaze holding mine, waiting for an answer

But I don't know how to respond, so finally I just say it. "My name is Charles, Prince Charles Greystone. And you are?"

When I finish my sentence, I pause, expecting her to provide her proper name so I can refer to her as something beyond "mystery woman." I wait and wait, staring at her, hoping she'll say something.

At last, she snaps out of her daze. "I guess you'll just have to wait and find out." She winks before turning around and scampering off, leaving me gaping at where she was standing, shocked because she's the only potential wife who has ever run away from me.

I don't know how long I stand there, confusion written all over my face, I'm sure. I go over the whole night in my head, trying to figure out where I went wrong. Maybe I should have told her earlier? Maybe I should have just stuck to one dance? No, none of those things explains her erratic behavior.

Eventually a servant walks by me, and I grab a glass of wine before waving at Avery, my guard, that I'm heading up to my room. I'm still in disbelief that someone walked away from a prince the way she did. There are plenty of princesses who will want me, but I'm so drawn to her. I've never felt this way before. I don't know what it is about her, but I am certain we belong together.

Chapter Four

Anna

RACING OUT THE DOOR, much to the guard's surprise, and back to my horse, I try to calm my wild heart. At least no one followed me, though I'm beginning to wonder about the castle's security.

Grabbing Epona's reins, I slowly walk away from the tree and find a fallen trunk to help me mount her in my dress. I wrap my cloak over my beautiful gown as I step onto the log. *How did I miss it? I should have noticed the way the actual princesses were looking at me. I can't believe I could be so stupid.* Distracted by my thoughts, I almost face-plant while attempting to mount my horse—not able to focus. Taking a deep breath and wiping my hands on my cloak's rough fabric, I try to climb astride the nickering beast once again, this time successfully. Urging Epona into a trot, I glance back at the castle one last time, letting the weight of the evening settle on me.

I can't believe this entire night was a waste when I should've completed the job. As I reach the first village, I slow, taking in the views. This calms my racing thoughts, at least a little. The mountain range under a full moon is the second most beautiful thing I've ever seen. I can slightly see the trees, tiny dark specks covering the bottoms of the mountains.

The peaks look snow-covered, but it's hard to tell from this far away, especially in the dark. The stars illuminate the river that flows down the mountain. I wish I could live there instead of in my run-down village. I love my family and my fellow villagers, but sometimes I wonder what it would have been like to be born into a noble bloodline. To have never had to take such a risky occupation for the sake of my loved ones.

I stop just inside the settlement line to admire the breath-taking views one last time before I continue my trip home, wanting the night to be over with. *You should be returning with the task completed.* Again, I hear the voice in the back of my mind, berating me for failing.

I just have to let him court me; there's no other way, I tell myself, hoping I will be able to come up with a foolproof plan. *How am I going to kill someone I obviously like?* Realizing I'm arguing with myself, I shake my head and laugh. I really have gone crazy...

Continuing the rest of the ride home is a blur with too many thoughts swirling in my brain for me to focus on my surroundings. That is until I hear the sounds of leaves rustling. My heart stops and I hold my breath, looking around to see if I might find anyone. When I realize there is no one around, I let out a breath and keep moving, but then the sound comes again. I pull on Epona's reins, halting her so I can get down. As I reach for my dagger, I survey the area once more. Not seeing anything, I take this opportunity to stretch my legs and walk for part of the trip.

The closer I get to home, the more stressed I become. I have so many questions running through my mind. What am I going to do to earn this money? Why would anyone want to kill the prince when he is so sweet? Is this just a trick he's playing to find a wife? I nod to myself. Yes, that has to be it. There is no reason, if he was truly kind like this, that someone would want to assassinate him. All those rumors have to be true, or else he wouldn't be a target. "Once the job is complete, I won't need to think about any of this stuff anymore," I mumble under my breath. Shaking my head, I continue on my way. I'm lying to myself, and I know it.

I spend the walk through the last village before my own rethinking my plan. *I never told him I would see him tomorrow, but I did tell him I would try. However, with how I left, I feel like it wouldn't make sense for me to want to encounter him again. I need to craft an excuse for leaving so abruptly. Maybe I can say I was embarrassed for the things I said about him?*

I rub my neck, but nothing relieves the ache of my tangled thoughts. He seemed so genuine. What horrible acts has he done? *I feel like I have to return to him, but then how am I going to?* I swallow, but my throat is tight. *I have to kill him.*

I don't even know why he wants to see me. Maybe I can convince him to have tea and slip the poison in his drink? Or should I try to have a picnic and a walk and make it look like he fell and hit his head? I squeeze my eyes closed at the thought of those beautiful brown irises glazed over. Dead. I continue planning, as if figuring out the best way to take his life will make this situation easier.

There are so many options of things I can do, but I'm just unsure. Maybe I should wait and see what he has planned, and decide how to finish...the job...in the moment. You've got this, Anna. Then I look up and realize I have already made it through the village and can glimpse my shack of a home. I tie Epona up outside with food and water and head inside.

As soon as I enter, I slip into my room as quietly as possible. It is well after dark, and I know my family is asleep. I slowly remove the pins from my hair, grateful to my sister for making sure it stayed in the whole night. One after another, I take them out until my arms are so tired I can barely hold them up. Then I climb into bed, eyes closing the moment my head hits the pillow. The exhaustion from my day helps me fall into a near-instant deep sleep.

Chapter Five

Anna

I WAKE SLIGHTLY EARLIER than normal, which is hard considering I'm already an early riser, to my heart beating out of my chest. It takes a few minutes for me to reorient myself.

"Oh, I had a nightmare, I guess." I lay under my blankets staring at my ceiling, noticing how dark it is, which means I probably don't need to be awake right now. "I suppose I'll take this time to come up with a plan," I mumble to myself before climbing out of my warm bed.

Still in my sleep dress, since the village isn't awake yet, I quietly go outside to give Epona some more food and water. She needs it before our long ride to the castle. Sitting outside for a few minutes, I stare at the sky as it slowly gets brighter.

No plan forms in my mind. Just remnants of that nightmare, though I can't remember it. The fear it left still makes my middle ache. With a deep breath, I finally decide it is time to head inside to get ready for my day with the prince.

I pick out my nicest blouse and trousers, hoping the outfit is appropriate since I'm still supposed to be a princess, before grabbing my corset as well. *Princesses cannot ride horses in dresses—there is no way.* Then I grab my doublet so I don't get chilly on the ride to the castle. I walk over to my small mirror in the corner of my room to sit down and put on some powder and do my hair. I won't be doing anything extravagant since Amelia isn't awake to fix it. With my hair in two braids down my back and the silver tiara I wore last night pinned to my head, I give my makeup one final look before deciding it's good enough.

Grabbing my dagger off my nightstand, I strap it to my ankle. I do this often, so I know it's small enough for it to still be hidden, but it's a little harder to get to. Then, I put on the outfit I selected a few minutes ago. Once my boots are laced up, I grab my doublet and head out the front door, softly telling my mom, who is now awake and putting the teakettle over the smoldering fire, that I'm going for some fresh air so she doesn't stress. Thankfully, her back is turned, and she doesn't notice how I'm dressed. It's safer for her to not be aware.

Before mounting my horse, I do one last check, patting my outerwear to ensure my vials of poison are inside the secret pockets.

I can do this. I always get the job done.

And I will finish this. With a deep sigh, I climb astride Epona and begin the trek back to the castle, wanting to hurry so Prince Charles doesn't think I turned him down. We canter the whole way, only slightly messing up my tiara, before I slow my mare so I won't look suspicious. We need to make sure they believe I'm coming from close by, where a princess or high-ranking lady would stay, or my entire plan, or lack thereof, will fall apart.

"Good morning," I say to the guards at the door with a smile, even though secretly my heart is beating out of my chest with nerves. *You've got this, Anna.* "I am Princess Anna, here to see Prince Charles. He should be expecting me."

One thing my vocation has taught me is that pretending to the point where you almost believe it yourself is the best way to get others to trust you.

"You really think showing up like that is lady-like?" the guard mutters before wandering off, I'm guessing to find the prince. After a few minutes he returns, waving at me like I'm an inconvenience.

As he leads me to the courtyard, I smile when I see Prince Charles through the glass doors, sitting at a small table with a second chair. I walk towards the door, pushing it open, pausing when I remember what the guard said to me. With my foot already on the other side of the threshold, I turn over my shoulder to face the same guard.

"Judging a princess for wanting fresh air and using the skills she's trained for years to achieve is a punishable offense in my kingdom. I suggest you keep your opinions to yourself next time."

He pauses, and the blood drains from his features. He bows slightly before mumbling an apology. Then he scurries away before I can go through with my threat, which is a little disappointing since I need to do something to get rid of these nerves.

Ignoring the pins and needles crawling up and down my skin, I step out onto the covered courtyard path. I can see the candles that were blocked before. The whole path to the prince is lit up with flickering votive candles. I walk closer to the table that Charles is sitting at, my vision blurry through the tears forming in my eyes. It would be so easy to slip the poison into his drink, but I can't.

I've never met anyone like him.

As I reach the prince, he jumps up and goes around the table, pulling my chair out for me. I sit down, surveying the setup, appreciating the candles all over the surface making the lighting perfect. Rose petals rest all over the place   settings. The pang in my chest reminds me why I'm here. I cannot lose sight of what's important today. Glancing into the corner as I recline, I see the guard who is always with Charles, watching us and waiting. Relief pulses through me. I can't poison him or use my dagger if we're being watched.

I just have to get him separated from his guard. I slap the thought away until I remember why I'm here. There is no choice, not unless I want to disappoint my employer, possibly end up with a price on my head, and leave my father to slowly fade away without his medicines.

Trying not to appear suspicious, I spend the day talking to and getting to know Charles, keeping things as real as possible so my lies don't fall apart. The longer we talk, the harder it becomes to remain devoted to the job. He is a genuine person, and not at all the spoiled boy the public thinks he is. Worse, I see no evidence of cruelty, which means he cannot have committed terrible crimes.

He tells me he has spent a lot of time traveling to other countries since he's been an adult. The king was completely healthy, thriving in fact, until one day he wasn't. And now the pressure to not only prepare to rule a kingdom but also the expectation to marry immediately and take over because his dad won't be here long has him concerned. When that happened, all of Charles' hopes and dreams came crashing down.

When he's done recounting his childhood, he asks me about mine. I try to be as vague as possible while still telling the truth. "My father is ill, a lot like yours, but he isn't dying yet. When he got sick, it was really hard on my older sister and me because our mom has to spend most of her time with him now." In an attempt to be careful with my words, I murmur, "I love both my parents. But I wish there wasn't so much pressure on my sister and me because of it."

"I understand that," Charlie says, nodding his head. While it's not a lie, it's also not the whole truth. The strain on us is to pay for food, clothing, my dad's medicine, not get married to secure the kingdom like he thinks I'm implying. I sit there quietly, trying to think of more to say but still not wanting to give too much away. After a few minutes of silence, Charles pushes his chair out, the sound of the wooden legs scraping on the garden stones. "I know we're still getting to know each other, but I would love it if you would join me on a walk around the castle. Some quiet time away?"

The way he says it makes my skin itchy, not because of *why* he says it but because this is my opportunity.

"Maybe another time. I think this whole conversation has been very overwhelming, so it's probably a good place to end the day." The sentence comes out before my brain can even process what I'm saying.

I'm so stupid. This is the perfect time.

The disappointment on his face is evident, but he gives me a stern nod, anyway.

Take it back, go with him and complete the job. For some reason, I cannot bring myself to take back what I said. Instead, I let him pull me out of the chair and lead me towards the front door of the castle.

"So, mysterious woman, before you leave for the day, will you finally tell me your full name?" he asks as he swings the door open and waves at the stablehand to grab Epona for me.

"It's Anna, Anna Marie." I give him my middle name instead of my last because, again; the less information I give him, the better.

"Well, Princess Anna," he says in an unexpectedly sultry tone that makes me want to melt into him, "I would love to officially court you."

And with that, my brain catches up once again. *No feelings, Anna. Knock it off!*

"I would enjoy that, but I need to think about it. Thank you for showing me that rumors aren't always true, though," I say with a giggle, allowing him to bend down and kiss my hand.

"Okay, I will give you a few days before expecting you back at the castle, or I will take that as a no. Thank you for getting to know the real me."

As he finishes his sentence, the stablehand arrives with Epona, who whinnies at me, hinting that it's time to go.

"Okay, I will see you in a few days," I say, heading down the stairs and mounting my horse, easing her into a trot toward home.

Well...now what am I going to do?

.

Chapter Six

Anna

FOR ONCE I DON'T wake up before the sun. However, that also means I didn't wake up before my sister. As I feel the end of my bed shifting, I slowly open my eyes to find Amelia sitting at the end of my bed. I stretch out, slowly pushing myself into a sitting position. That is, until I see my job letter in her hand, causing me to freeze. How did she find it? I thought I'd stuffed inside my mattress along with my other job materials that no one but me can ever see.

"What. Is. Your. Problem?" Amelia whisper-yells at me.

I flinch, but her low tone clues me in that our parents don't know.

"Sis," I say with a sigh, debating how bluntly to put this. "We need the money." Amelia is the only one who knows what I actually do for work, the assassin part of it at least. I can't tell mom and dad or they'll just worry about me instead of focusing on dad's health.

"But the prince, Annabelle?! Do you understand how dangerous that is? What if you get caught?"

I did not expect her to figure out my target, though. That's a problem.

"How did you find...never mind...I don't have a choice, Amelia! Plus, I am fine, see?" I say, dramatically gesturing at my unharmed body so she sees I am perfectly fine. *Physically, at least.*

The worry on her face remains as I say that, as she slowly puts the pieces together. "Did..." the tears slowly form in her eyes, "did you do it?"

I open my arms up to her, hoping she'll come lay in bed with me. Once we are both under the covers, I snuggle into her, needing my sister's embrace, just like when we were kids, and she'd hold me on the couch. I sigh. "No, I couldn't do it."

She looks at me with a shocked expression.

"I know we need the money, but I don't know why anyone would want him dead. He's sweet, funny, down to earth, and so handsome...but I know that I have to do it. I have to protect us, and, like I said, we *need* the money."

"Maybe that's a good thing. You can be done with this dangerous game, and we can work together to figure something else out for money."

Now I'm the one with tears forming in my eyes. "I have to. The king will put a price on *my* head if I fail." I wonder how Charles would feel if he knew the father he's so worried about wants him dead.

"We have to get you out of the network," she insists.

"You're right," I whisper, my words sticking a little in my throat. I hold Amelia tighter, wishing it were that simple. I would love to find different work, but I can't imagine another job for a young woman in this kingdom that would allow her to support a family of four. Let alone something...ethical. Even with us both working, it will be practically impossible.

After sitting there for a few minutes in total silence staring at the wall, I get up. I want to play along with this plan for my sister, hoping to get ready and see if there's something else we can do for work. As I stand, however, she giggles behind me. "What's so funny?" I ask, looking back over my shoulder at Amelia, where she still lies in my bed. *Typical sister.*

"You've never talked about a boy before. In fact, you've never talked about anyone the way you just talked about the prince." That realization causes her to start laughing outright. My face reddens as I pick up my pillow and chuck it at her face, hoping to get her to shut up.

"Oh, hush." I say right as I giggle with her. When Amelia falls off the bed from laughing, I bend over, laughing so hard I can't catch my breath. We continue on like that for a few minutes before I hear a knock on the wall. "Come in!" I shout over Amelia's laughing, throwing another pillow at her so she quiets down.

My mom steps over the threshold, a huge smile covering her face when she sees us laughing together. "Good morning, girls, breakfast is—"

She doesn't even have time to finish her sentence before Amelia and I are bounding out the door and towards the stairs, ravenous. As soon as we smell mom's cinnamon oats, smiles light up our faces. We enjoy the same favorite breakfast, and this is it. Maybe one day she'll tell us what she does to make them taste so good.

After breakfast, Amelia and I head outdoors, hoping to get some privacy away from our parents and to continue our discussion about alternate career options. We spend the day wandering the village trying to see which businesses need help. Other than the apothecary, no one has any openings. We set Amelia up to help at the apothecary when I can't to at least bring in some extra income. After we are done there, we head back towards home, sulking the whole way. When Amelia refuses dinner as soon as we walk in the door, I know that this defeat is hitting her the hardest. She has always wanted to protect me, so the truth that she can't this time is likely crushing her.

I attempt to eat dinner, not really tasting anything. Mom's stew just doesn't sit right in my stomach when I'm disappointed. Us not finding any work in town means I have to go through with this job, no matter what my heart is telling me. I've killed before, so why is this one so difficult? It might have something to do with knowing those nobles were dangerous, cruel men. But the prince isn't.

When I'm sick of not being able to eat properly, I bid mom and dad a goodnight, making an excuse that us girls just aren't feeling well. I make my way to my room, where I sit down on my bed, feeling hopeless. This plan has to be the one. I have to stick with it. *Get it together, Anna.*

Chapter Seven

Anna

I ARRIVE AT THE palace just before dark. Scaling the side of the castle without getting caught isn't easy, but a lifetime of climbing trees with Amelia and practicing rock climbing in a nearby quarry has prepared me for this aspect of my work. I had studied the map given to me along with the job letter extensively. After my blunder at the ball, I wanted to make certain I wouldn't waste time or energy on climbing walls that lead nowhere near the prince's quarters. Luckily, my map shows me exactly where the prince's quarters are located, so I will only have to do this once.

Once my hands find what I know to be his balcony railing, I hoist myself over and press myself against the castle walls, praying that no one has seen me.

I remove my grippy black gloves for a moment to flex my fingers after the climb before slipping them back on. I dressed in my usual outfit for stealth jobs—black trousers with enough give to allow for easy movement, but fitted enough that I don't need to worry about them catching on anything, a simple black tunic with long sleeves and a cowl that I am able to pull up to cover my face and hair, and a pair of worn black boots that have seen better days—hoping that it would help me blend into the dark stone and the shadows cast by the waning light. Once the sun sets, I will be nearly invisible to prying eyes.

I take a few moments to catch my breath before leaning over to peek into the prince's quarters, first verifying that no one is inside and then gathering details about the layout. His bed is positioned against the back wall with two bedside tables on either side. I tilt my head, planning how I'm going to reach the prince without making any noise.

The job letter mentioned that the guards do a full sweep of Charles' quarters for security breaches before he enters, so I need to be very strategic about this to avoid their notice. The balcony is scantily furnished and offers no concealment from view. I lean over the railing, searching for a hiding spot I can tuck into before the guards arrive. There is a set of stones that are sticking out from the castle, just below the balcony that would make perfect hand holds—*I wish that I had had time and funds to purchase new boots so that my feet could help me brace against the wall better.* The soles of my boots are so worn, and while I'm a strong climber, I'm worried about my feet slipping out from under me if I stay in one position for too long, especially on the smoother stones on this section of the castle wall. I must time this perfectly to conserve my strength.

I sit silently on the railing where it meets the wall, listening intently for the guards' approach. As I sit there in silence, it is almost impossible to quiet my mind. *He isn't cruel, but he must be a terrible person. Right? That's why the king wants him gone, especially now that he's sick. He must have an alternate ruler lined up. But...am I getting feelings for the prince? I can't be. This is my job. But Amy is right. I've never talked about someone the way I talk about him. And I've never felt like this about someone before. It must just be nerves. No parent would order the assassination of their own child if it wasn't for a good reason. Every other person I've ended deserved it. Prince Charles must...*

Finally, after what feels like ages, I finally hear the creak of a door, causing me to snap out of my thoughts and silently scurry over the railing and take my position on the handholds, just out of eyesight from the balcony. I grit my teeth as I carefully balance on the stones beneath my worn-out boots, keeping most of my weight on my hands. Did they file these rocks smooth before constructing this area or something?

It feels like I hold myself there for hours, but I hear no sounds from the balcony. The longer I hang, the more my arms feel like jelly and the more real the threats become. Finally, I have to decide which death I would rather face; plummeting to the ground from where I hang on the side of this damn castle or the castle guards catching me in the prince's quarters. I decide I would rather face the swords of the guards than face the indignity of being found bloody and broken on the cobblestones below by some unsuspecting courtier in the morning.

I cautiously put a little more weight on my feet and push my body upward, saying a silent prayer of thanks when my boots don't slip before pulling myself back up onto the balcony with the last of my waning upper body strength. Once my feet are firmly planted on the balcony, I glance around, shaking my arms out to get the feeling back into them. That's when I realize how dark the night has grown. No wonder my muscles felt so gelatinous. I really was hanging there for a while. Clouds cover the moon, and I blink my eyes rapidly to force them to adjust to the darkness.

I peek my head around the threshold once again to find the prince already asleep in his bed, no guard in sight. I silently let out a breath of relief and reach for the dagger in its scabbard at my waist. As I creep closer to the bed, all I can do is stare at the prince, his eyes closed and his breathing even. He almost looks...peaceful. Forcing myself to snap out of it, I step backward, barely avoiding the stones that are sticking up from the uneven floor. Catching my balance, I slink forward as silently as possible, flicking my gaze between the door and the prince. Being caught in the princes' bedchamber with a dagger in my hand would mean certain death.

The clouds shift, and moonlight softly bathes the prince's sleeping form. My breath catches. I hadn't thought that it was possible for him to look more beautiful than the moment I first saw him, but now, he was undoubtedly the most beautiful thing I had ever seen in my life.

Once you do this, there's no going back. This beautiful man will rot in the ground. You'll be a fugitive.

I stop abruptly once the thought slips into my head, almost dropping my dagger, but gripping it before it can slip from my grasp. So, I remind myself that the bounty I get for this job is enough that my family and I will not have to worry about finances for a long while. I resume my tiptoeing towards the bed—his chambers are larger than my family's entire home, and I feel so exposed making my way across the room. As I approach, I raise my blade, ready to complete this job once and for all...

Until I hear a guard talking, and freeze, listening to what they're saying.

Muffled voices come from the other side of the door. "I'm telling you we should just check on him. I have a bad feeling."

I'm out of time. Holding my breath, I silently flee back out the balcony and press myself against the castle wall. The prince's door opens with a low creek, and I risk peering cautiously into the room.

A serious-looking guard stands between the half-open door and its frame, surveying the prince's sleeping form. I war with myself about the risk versus reward of completing this job tonight. As the guard enters the room, my instinct for self-preservation wins out, and I decide that the risk does, in fact, outweigh the reward. I feel a strange sense of relief as I place my dagger back in its scabbard.

I take one last cautious glance towards the guard, now quietly checking a room that I can only assume is the prince's washroom, before looking over the edge of the balcony for a path down. Even with the moonlight, I cannot even see the ground. *This is going to take a while.*

I climb over the railing and begin my silent descent, keeping my eyes and ears alert for the sound of guards. Getting caught on the side of the castle would be nearly as incriminating as holding a dagger next to the prince's bedside. There are enough uneven and missing stones on the side of the castle that I fly down it. My descent is much quicker than my earlier climb since I remember where most of the handholds are. As soon as my feet hit the ground, I take off running toward my favorite cluster of trees—the same place I left Epona the night of the ball.

I swing myself over her back and head for home at a gallop. My heart doesn't slow until Epona's pace decreases to a trot a mile away from the castle. I want to go faster, but I know speed will lead to suspicion in the villages we will pass on the way home, and I cannot afford to attract notice while my contract is still open. My mind races with alternate plans to complete this task the whole way home. Each plan fills me with a deeper sense of dread.

I don't admit the truth to myself. But the relief of being foiled yet again doesn't lie.

A few days later, I'm back in the castle, dressed in my sharpest riding britches and cloak, ready to go horseback riding and pretending to be a princess. Princess Anna has officially become an extension of me while I wait for an opportunity to complete this job...at least, that's what I tell myself. I meet Charles at the stable, waiting for the stablehand to retrieve his horse, while he gives me a rundown of the day.

"Anna, I was hoping you would be willing to ride the property with me. I want you to see all my favorite places."

"I love that idea, Prince Charles," I respond to him with a genuine smile, knowing we'll have guards with us the entire time. This means I get to just enjoy my time with him without looking for an opportunity to execute my orders.

"Please call me Charlie. Prince Charles and Charles are insufferably formal."

"Charlie." The way it rolls off my tongue so easily brings a soft smile to my lips. I have the sudden thought that I wish we could stay like this forever, but I know it can't be that simple. The job that I have contracted to do looms overhead like a dark cloud.

When I look up at him, his face is lit up just like mine. He leans over, kissing me on the cheek, a blush spreading up my cheeks as he grabs my hand and leads me inside the barn where his horse is being washed. *I wish we could stay like this forever.* When we walk in, the stable hand grabs Epona's reins and begins cleaning her as well, causing the smile on my face to spread even further. "Thank you for cleaning her." I tell him, hoping he'll feel my appreciation in my words.

"You're welcome, princess. It's hot today, so I was hoping to cool her off. Prince Charles, your horse is ready to go."

Standing next to Epona is the most beautiful white stallion I've ever seen. The contrast between Epona's dark coat and

Charlie's white horse is striking. As he scratches his horse's nose, Charlie whispers to him quietly, giving me more insight into his personality—his very sweet, kind personality There isn't a cruel bone in his body, unless he's exceptionally good at pretending to have a heart of gold.

We mount our horses and head out of the barn, the guards not far behind us.

We ride along the edge of the castle grounds, which I realize is surrounded mostly by woods, for a few peaceful hours. Eventually, we come upon an open grass field meant for grazing on long rides, where Charlie had decided we would stop to relax.

As I dismount my horse, I look over at Charlie and see him digging in his saddlebags.

"What are you doing?" I ask, smiling his way as I watch him.

He pulls out a blanket as a guard walks over, carrying a picnic basket, and I don't think my smile can get any bigger than it is, but he just keeps shocking me. "A picnic?"

"Yes, I figured we could enjoy lunch." He walks a little way into the field, staying close to the edge while still giving us a sense of privacy, and puts the blanket down, setting the picnic basket on top of it. "Are you going to join me?"

I practically skip to the blanket and plop down onto it, excited to see what he packed for us. When he pulls out tiny sandwiches and a bottle of wine, I chuckle softly. *What is happening to me?*

I look around and spot Charlie's guard, just inside the tree line, eyes constantly scanning the area. As Charlie pours me a glass of wine, I gesture towards the ever-vigilant sentry. "Do you think he's hungry?" I ask, concerned, since he has been with us the entire time.

"Avery? No, I have offered to share meals with him during our rides around the property for years, and he has never accepted. He won't eat while on duty." *Hmm, strange. At least he's good at his job, I guess. Damn.* When I reach for the beverage from Charlie, our fingers brush, and an unexpected shock goes through my body, making my heart beat a little faster.

"Thank you, Charlie." I try to keep my voice even as I take a sip.

"You're welcome, Princess," he pours a glass of wine for himself, holding it up in a toast. "To us."

"To us." My heart never ceases to slow as I sit with him, sipping my wine and continuously glancing at the prince.

Time gets away from us as we lose ourselves in conversation. I force the job out of my mind, and I forget about Avery standing watch nearby...I forget about everything except this handsome prince who has chipped away at all my defenses with his easy conversation, kind heart, and molten chocolate eyes. Once we realize it is getting dark, we pack up the picnic basket and blanket, mount our horses, and begin making our way back to the palace.

The trip back to the castle from our spot near the field takes only a fraction of the time that it took us to arrive there earlier in the day—we had taken the scenic route there so Charlie could show me more of the grounds. The stablehand is already waiting for Charlie's horse by the time we ride to the front of the castle.. A severe-looking man I don't recognize stands beside the stall door too.

"Prince Charles, I was told you asked to see me before the princess departs?" the mystery man inquires after a brief bow. My heart drops into my stomach, and my palms grow sweaty. *What is going on?*

"Yes, thank you for coming." Charlie says with his amiable smile. "Anna, this is healer Adam. I requested for him to meet with you so you could share the symptoms of your father's ailment with him. He has helped many recover from their illnesses, and I have tasked him with finding a cure, or at the very least, relief for your father."

"Oh, umm," I begin.

"And please don't think I'm overstepping! We royals exchange information pretty frequently to help each other out. We currently have two experts from nearby kingdoms helping my father."

I swallow. They think my father is king and that I stay with dukes. And they haven't followed me to ensure that, which is quite concerning, but maybe I can get some information to help my father.

I clear my throat. "He has body aches, but only sometimes. He gets tired more quickly than he used to. And he's not eating properly." I continue to list my father's symptoms, wiping my palms on my trousers surreptitiously, hoping that my nerves don't show. I am thrilled that my father may receive help, but his symptoms are not common among the upper class and the wealthy with better resources. It is not lost on me that my father's ailment could expose me for the farce I am.

As I finish listing father's maladies, a beautifully dressed lady I don't recognize walks out the castle door and beelines toward us. Before I have a chance to inquire, the healer speaks again.

"I haven't heard of all of those symptoms presenting together before, but let me consult some of my more obscure texts and I will see what I can find."

Charlie offers him a nod of thanks, and Adam bows before turning around and walking away, right as this unknown noblewoman shows up.

"Charles, who is this?" she asks, looking me up and down with blatant disgust on her face.

"Hello stepmother, this is Princess Anna, the woman I told you I was courting," he says coldly, rolling his eyes.

Ice runs down my spine. So, he isn't always kind.

She doesn't pay much attention to him. My brain catches up.

Step Mother? Like...the Queen?! My already slick palms proceed to sweat more profusely, while I try to keep my rigid body calm as I encounter yet another royal. When the queen's leaf-green eyes gaze upon mine, twin senses, recognition and foreboding, run through me, but I can't place why.

"Hello, Your Majesty, it's an honor to meet you." I bow my head at her since I am still seated upon Epona and see no point in jumping down for a formal curtsey. My instincts scream at me to leave before she starts asking too many questions.

"Princess...Anna, was it? What kingdom do you represent?" she asks, her voice dripping with suspicion.

"I am so sorry, Your Majesty. The time has run away with the day, and I am already past due to return to my lodging. I would love to speak with you more another time," I say in a tone that I hope shows the respect a princess must give to a queen, but does not offer an opening to continue speaking now.

"Well, that just won't do," she grumbles before turning around and heading back into the castle, her haughty head held high.

I can't believe she accepted my feeble excuse, but relief makes my knees weak. Thankfully, I'm still on my mare.

Charlie watches his stepmother walk away, a frown shadowing his beautiful face that had spent so much of the day lit up in smiles. I swing Epona around toward the castle gates, and Charlie walks over to me, bidding me a goodnight.

I sit down at my vanity, dropping my head into my hands and replaying the events of the day. The prince...I can't. He's too good, even if he doesn't like his stepmother. There is only one decision my heart can survive, even if that means I lose the money my family desperately needs. I sniff and harshly rub the dampness from my eyes.

I have to decline the job.

If the king wants his heir dead, he needs to do it himself. I just hope I'm not signing my own death warrant, or my father's.

I push my chair out, scraping against the rocks on the dirt floor, and start digging through my vanity drawers to find my small supply of parchment. Sitting back down with my writing supplies, it finally dawns on me where I know those green eyes.

Chapter Eight

Anna

I WALK INTO THE *abandoned building, my senses on high alert. Even though I had circled the structure and ensured no one witnessed my dealings. I really hate arriving before a client because it gives me this feeling of being trapped, having them between myself and the door...Even as a skilled assassin, it's not wise to linger on the streets after dark.*

I hear a match strike and a sudden glow of light emanates from the tiny flame as my contact lights a small lantern. I'm shocked that they're already inside. They must have waited in the darkness for well over thirty minutes.

"You're smaller than I expected," the person says, their voice noticeably distorted, meaning this person doesn't want me to know who they are. Looking them over as well as I can between the slats, I glimpse a mask covering their face and mouth, which

must be muffling their voice. The hood on their cloak is pulled up over their head, and everything they're wearing is dark in color, giving me no hint at anything other than their build, which is similar to mine.

"My size doesn't impact my success rate. I've never failed to complete a job," I say, standing at my full height and staring into the shrewd green eyes looking back at me, the only thing about this person I can actually see.

"This will be the biggest job of your life," the person rasps, their voice low. "It will be difficult and dangerous. But it will change your life, and it will elevate you among all other assassins. Do you think you are up for the challenge?" The voice asks.

I watch them where they sit, unmoving, in total control, but my brain catches on one thought...it will change your life. I care less about being an esteemed assassin and more about earning enough to no longer have to be one.

"Yes," I whisper. "I am in."

Those fern-green eyes crinkle, as though this mysterious contact is smiling in triumph. "Your mark," the voice says with a dramatic pause, "is Prince Charles, the crown prince of Weide Saliba. Kill the prince before he finds a wife."

Questions swirl in my mind, but I don't get a chance to ask them.

"The prince's misdeeds must never see the light of day. Complete this termination, and you save your kingdom."

Then the light goes out and they disappear, leaving me stand-ing there, staring at the empty space where they had been. The only things left behind are a map, a job letter with instructions, information about a ball, and a bag of coins.

The biggest job of my life doesn't even begin to cover it.

Those green eyes...belong to the queen.

"No," I gasp, covering my lips in a feeble attempt to stay quiet so as not to worry my parents or Amelia. I jump out of my chair and run outside, concern coursing through my veins. "We're screwed. We're so screwed." I can't decline the job, or she is going to tell Charlie everything. But I can't complete it, because I am falling for this beautiful man.

His *misdeeds.* How could I have assumed the king wanted his son dead? No, the queen, the prince's stepmother, wants Charlie dead. I pace back and forth in front of my family's home, trying to separate my thoughts long enough to figure out what to do. I have to protect my family too.

"You're just going to have to pretend," I mumble to myself under my breath. My own thoughts don't make sense to me, but I latch on to the small bit of hope that blossoms with those words.

You can do this; you'll get out of this. Taking a deep breath to calm myself, I walk inside and go back to bed, hoping a good night of rest will prepare me for tomorrow. Tomorrow is the day I must end our relationship and disappear. If I do this right, he won't discover where I live and will just think a princess is snubbing him, and then I can find other work to support my family. Or I kill him, which isn't going to happen. Either way, I'll never see him again after tomorrow.

I fall into a restless sleep, nightmares plaguing me of choosing my family or him.

I dress in a haze of dread before beginning my journey to the castle. I watch the scenery roll by while Epona moves at a slow pace, sensing my stress. The closer we get to the palace, the faster my heart rate picks up. I try to calm myself, reminding myself that breaking the contract is for the best. I would rather deal with the heartbreak of never seeing the prince again than the devastation of ending his life. The image of him cold and lifeless by my hand makes me shudder.

I take down traitors to the crown, not heirs to the crown.

I have almost convinced myself that I can do this and nothing—not even my own heart—will stand in my way. That is until I see the one person who ruined everything...sitting on a horse...blocking my path. *How ironic*.

"Hello, 'Princess Anna,'" she sneers. Her expression twists cruelly.

"Queen Minerva." I bow my head at her, straightening my back at the same time trying to show both confidence and respect, although I feel neither. "I was just on my way to see the prince."

"Yes, the prince. Speaking of which, why isn't he dead yet?!" she asks, causing me to almost fall off my mare from shock.

"Keep your voice down," I whisper, my eyes darting left and right. I have not seen other travelers for some time, but I know you can never trust an empty room. Or in this case, an empty road. I wave at her to follow me somewhere a passerby would struggle to hear our conversation. Once we're inside the tree line, I raise my voice back to a normal volume, letting the disgust I feel drip through as much as possible. "Why do you even want the prince dead? Is he not your stepson? And why didn't you tell me who you were in the first place?"

"That is none of your business." The queen's quiet rasp is more unnerving than before, causing me to flinch. Birds in a nearby tree fly away. "The job should have been completed already, and yet he continues to breathe. If you don't do it without delay, you will regret it."

A chill runs down my spine. "Yes, *Your Majesty*," I say, self-preservation winning over anger.

"Soon, girl. This is your only warning." The queen hits me with a withering look before she expertly turns her horse around despite the density of the trees, and trots away once they reach the road. I watch them go, my stomach feeling leaden.

I take a deep breath, sorting through the conflict going through my head and my heart. I thought I had a solution, but the queen has demonstrated she is not a woman to be trifled with. She has known who I am the entire time, and she found me when I didn't expect her. I resume my trek to the castle, which comes into view much faster than I would've liked.

The same stablehand greets me once again, and I hand him Epona's reins with a forced smile and a word of gratitude.

All at once, understanding dawns on me, it's not just my family's well-being in the balance, this is my life or his. I don't even have a moment to sit with that realization, because Charlie walks out of the castle, stopping the stablehand from putting Epona in the stable.

"No need to put her away—we will need her again today. Please saddle Ryn as well." He walks over, kisses me softly on the cheek, and leads me back towards Epona as the stablehand goes to fetch his horse. "What's wrong, darling? You look as though you have seen a ghost."

Shaking my head, hoping it calms my thoughts, I take a deep breath. "Nothing, Charlie, everything is fine!" my voice comes out too high, and the smile I paste on my face feels comically large. He smiles at me tentatively before helping me mount Epona and turning around to grab the reins of his own horse. *Dang, that was fast.* I feel as though time is moving so quickly, and I'm almost out of it.

We go further than before on today's ride. We pass the field where we had our picnic and then keep going through the heavily wooded area beyond the field. It both surprises and pleases me that Charlie recognizes my riding competence and has faith that Epona and I can tackle the dense foliage. I hadn't realized the castle grounds were this massive, since the map from Queen Minerva certainly didn't show this area. When we get to the next clearing, I let out an audible gasp, shocked by the beauty in front of me.

"Charlie, it's beautiful." I am surprised to find tears filling my eyes, threatening to spill over as I take in the stunning private lake with awe. There is only one trail in and out of the clearing, where Avery stands, watching our surroundings.

Everything else in the vicinity is so tree-filled that it would be impossible for someone to sneak up on us without us hearing their approach. The land around the lake is covered in tiny yellow wildflowers with black centers that I've never seen before. Climbing gingerly down from Epona, I give my stiff back a stretch before I bend down, picking one of the flowers so I can admire it. The green stem, short but bright, draws my attention. I study it for a few seconds, noticing there is only one leaf on it, before moving onto the flower. I spin it around in my fingers until Charlie walks up behind me, touching me on the shoulder.

"Not as beautiful as you," Charlie says, causing my face to heat and my cheeks to redden. He raises his hand to my cheek before tenderly brushing a stray lock of hair behind my ear, his eyes burning an unasked question into mine the whole time. I feel my heart pick up once again. "I wanted to show my favorite place to my favorite woman."

I force a pained smile up at Charlie's beautiful face, but I sense the heat that had reddened my cheeks a moment ago cool to an icy chill as my brain decides to remind me that I have a deadly choice to make. The queen's confrontation has ruined everything, but I have no time to think of a way to save everyone.

I drop my gaze, feigning shyness before gently pushing Charlie's hand from my cheek and turning to walk towards the water, hoping that he won't notice how nervous I am or see the constant warring in my mind.

My family and I or the prince and the future of this kingdom? Of course...I have to choose myself. I have to kill the prince, and I cannot keep putting it off. But I also can't do it where all the guards can see me. My hands shake and my head swims so much that it feels like it's floating in that beautiful lake. I take a deep breath before leaning down and staring at my reflection in the water. I'm shocked at the image peering back at me—my skin is pale and my eyes are achingly hollow. My black hair falls forward and almost into the water, which causes me to lift my head up right as Charlie walks up behind me.

"Anna," he says, a question in his voice.

"Thank you for showing me this place," I whisper before turning around and walking back toward Epona without meeting his eyes. "I am very tired from riding so much these past days. I would like to head back and rest."

Disappointment crosses Charlie's face, but I know he will not push me for more. He walks towards the horses, a pace behind me. "Of course we can." He bends down to pick up another yellow flower and tucks it gently behind my ear as though I am the most precious thing he has ever beheld before whispering, "My flower."

Chapter Nine

Anna

LATER THAT EVENING, DRESSED in clothes that resemble the castle's servants, I once again ride toward the royal estate. I ride as fast as I can, hoping to make it to the castle before I stop myself. My mind runs through the plan I had devised to sneak in, and I desperately try to suppress the screaming in my head. I pat my jacket, double-checking that I have the poison and my dagger. As I near my destination, a gut feeling presses against my tangled thoughts. Something is wrong.

I push on, ignoring the apprehension until I get to my favorite little cluster of trees. Tying Epona up to a sturdy maple, I head toward the castle, avoiding the main entrance and crossing to the service door nearest to the palace kitchens, according to the map. It's late enough that no one should notice me sneaking in.

I know from our picnic conversation that Charlie often takes his evening meal alone in his room. I'm also aware that the kitchen staff will have his meal on a tray to be delivered. A sprinkle of the poison over his meat will appear like harmless seasoning, but will stop his heart within moments. Poison feels like the coward's way out, but I know that if I see his face I won't be able to go through with this job. My throat constricts at the mental image, and I blink back tears.

Don't think. Just do.

My fingers shake as I run them over my doublet. *I can't do this. I have to do this.*

Once I'm inside the service door, however, guards surround me. The prince's plate rested on the counter, far beyond my reach. A sick sort of relief hits my insides that my efforts are foiled, but panic claws up my spine.

They grab my arms and drag me away. I pull back as much as I can, trying to get a firm footing.

"What is going on?" I yell, struggling against their bruising grip. I don't get an answer. My mind screams.

They're going to kill me...and my family.

As soon as we're in the throne room, the guards holding my arms push me forward, causing me to fall painfully to my knees.

"What is going on?" I ask again before looking up, finding Charlie pacing back and forth, and the queen standing by the thrones with a bright red and puffy face. When she sees me looking at her, she smirks before plastering on a solemn expression, pretending that she's upset.

"Charlie, Queen Minerva, what is going on? The guards won't answer me," I ask, hoping someone will give me an answer. Not wanting to move from my place on the floor, I adjust myself so I am at least sitting up straight with a modicum of dignity.

"Anna. My stepmother here," Charlie pauses, gesturing towards the queen, who is wiping her eyes to keep up the appearance of the distraught and worried mother, "has been reaching out to the surrounding kingdoms to learn where you are from so we could offer them the information Healer Adam has found for your father. However, during that search, it has been brought to our attention that no one knows of a Princess Anna Marie." The look he shoots my way reduces me to nothing more than a speck of dirt on the ground.

My pride being the least important thing in this moment, I shrink into myself, trying to make myself smaller.

"Charlie, please. Let me explain," I plead. "I promise there is a perfectly good explanation. I just wanted to meet you, to know you, but I never thought you would decide to court me. I know I shouldn't have taken it this far, but I think I'm..." The breath is taken from my lungs as the guard that accompanied us on all of our outings, Avery, yanks me up from the ground and hands me off to another guard who starts patting me down. When they pull my dagger out of my jacket, I know I'm going to die. Especially when they pull the poison out right after.

"Your Highness," Avery says as he takes the items from his fellow guard and brings them to Charlie.

"She hired me to kill you," I scream, pointing at the queen. I know he won't believe me, but I have to try.

The queen gasps loudly and clutches her chest like I wounded her.

"She wants you dead. I don't know why. But Charlie, I swear I wasn't going to do it."

Because, despite the poison, the dagger, the sneaking into the kitchens...I couldn't do it. Had I not been interrupted, I still know I wouldn't have been able to do it.

"Guards," the queen shouts, suddenly not having any emotion on her face. "Take her to the dungeon for treason and crimes against the crown. Tomorrow she will be executed."

"No!" Charlie shouts, falling into the king's throne, defeat plastered across his face. "Take her off of castle grounds, and assign someone to escort her to the edge of the kingdom, just in case." Then he stops, turning to look at me as tears fill my eyes once again.

"Charlie, please," I all but whisper, hoping he won't do what I think he is about to do.

"Anna, if that really is your true name, you are now banished from Weide Saliba. Leave immediately. This is the only chance you will get. If you are ever discovered in this kingdom again, I cannot protect you from execution." Then, he stands up and walks out of the throne room before I can even say goodbye.

As the guards grab my arms and force me to stand, the queen walks up to me, leaning close to my face.

"I warned you," she spits at me venomously before walking out, following the same path Charlie did.

Then the guards drag me out of the throne room, to the front door of the castle, practically throwing me into the cool night air.

As soon as my feet hit the stairs, I run. I run as fast as I can with tears streaming down my face. I find Epona being walked up to the castle by a guard, who is already on horseback. Mounting her as quickly as possible, I flee as far away from the palace as possible, the guard not far behind. I ride until I physically cannot, only then pausing, passing out from exhaustion as soon as I lay down on the ground.

Chapter Ten

Anna

BANISHED.

I wake to the chirping birds with that one word in my mind. It's morning, and I don't know when I fell asleep or for how long. I stretch out, my body aching from sleeping on the ground and from the hard day of riding yesterday. I walk to Epona, rest my forehead on hers, and just breathe.

"I'm sorry, girl."

After putting her saddle and bridle back on her to continue our journey, we head toward the sounds of moving water, hoping it's a stream or lake so that we can both drink our fill and leave the guard who follows us. On the way, I scrounge for berries or any other plant that is safe for me to eat, knowing that I will need energy for the days to come.

Based on how long I rode through the night and the direction we have been traveling, I should be about a day from the border. A day from safety and freedom. I just hope there's a border village close to where I will cross so that I can regroup and figure out my next steps in relative safety.

When we find the stream, I drop Epona's reins and bend down, using my hands as a cup to sip some water while she drinks her fill next to me. When we're done drinking and I have filled my canteen, I lead Epona to a patch of thick grass to graze while I pack as many berries and edible plants as I can gather into my saddlebag. It is not enough to fill me, but if I ration it responsibly, it should be adequate to give me energy to travel. I mount Epona once again, needing to put distance between us and the castle...and my family. I must find a safe place to spend the night.

Despite knowing that I need to get out of the kingdom as quickly as possible, I proceed at a slower pace today. The constant riding of the last few weeks is catching up with her, and I cannot bear the thought of my beloved mare getting injured. I've seen no sign that we are being followed, aside from the guard ensuring my banishment, so I tell myself it is more important to move with care than to move with speed.

As the hours pass, I think about the past few weeks and how quickly everything changed. How everything went wrong. The worry for my family grows, eating at me more the farther

I get from home. I know Amelia can find employment, especially since we already discussed the possibility with Lyla at the apothecary, but who is going to take care of Father if Mom has to work? What are they going to do without the money from my jobs? How are they going to feel about me never coming home? What is Minerva going to do to them? She found me so easily—will it be just as easy for her to locate them?

Had you just completed the job the first night, you wouldn't be here.

"Had the queen given me a better description, I would have known to decline it," I respond aloud to the voice in my head, making me realize just how crazy this whole thing has made me feel. Maybe a fresh start will be nice. Maybe I won't have to be an assassin and a bounty hunter anymore. I'm going somewhere no one knows me, so I can claim that fresh start. Get a respectable job, make money from doing honest work, fall in love with a normal person, have kids...My heart feels heavy at the thought of falling in love with someone else.

I shake my head and drag my thoughts away from the memory of a pair of wounded chocolate brown eyes staring at me in anguish. I try to dash away the heartbreak I feel when I think of...him. I can be someone else. Someone that I'm not right now. Yeah, this is probably a good thing. I daydream of a life by a lake with a field of beautiful flowers to pass the time.

My growling stomach snaps me out of my daydreaming. I dig into my saddlebag for the food I scrounged for earlier and eat just enough to stave the hunger away.

The woods feel like they go on forever. I think I have seen more trees on this journey than in my entire lifetime. So when I finally reach the edge of the forest, I breathe a sigh of relief and decide this is a good place to stop for the night. Darkness will be upon us soon, so it couldn't have come at a better time. Once I dismount Epona, I set her saddle on the ground next to a thick oak before gathering more berries and plants for this evening's paltry dinner. *One more day*, I think to myself.

The guard is nowhere to be found, though I assume he's nearby. He has to observe me cross the border and report back to the prince and his stepmother that my banishment was enforced.

Climbing as far as I can up the tree, I settle against the trunk on a sturdy branch. I'm high enough that it would be difficult to sneak up on me and only another small person could reach me, but I'm close enough to Epona that I will hear her in a struggle. The food that I foraged does not fully satiate my hunger, but it fills my tummy enough for me to get some sleep tonight.

I settle against the rough bark, staring off at the new king-dom I'll be calling my home tomorrow. I scan the horizon, looking for a village or some kind of civilization, and when I don't see one, my heart drops. Just in case I can ever come back, I don't want to go too far. I keep scanning and scanning, hoping that something will pop out of thin air, and then it does. Closer than I was looking, but still far enough away that no sound reaches my ears, is a small settlement. It doesn't appear like it's anything special, which makes it perfect for me. I fall asleep thinking about that little village and the life I am going to make there.

I wake up before sunrise the next morning with stiff mus-cles, but am grateful to have my sleep schedule slightly back to normal. Carefully, I climb down the tree. Thanks to last night's search, I have a clear path of where to go. I saddle and mount Epona as quickly as possible before taking off towards the village.

Hoofbeats behind me verify my suspicion that the palace guard did indeed follow me. The moment I cross the invisible boundary, he stops and turns his horse around without saying a word.

It doesn't take long to get there, and the sun is barely up when I arrive, but the village center is already alive with people going to the market. I find a stable with an open stall to rent for Epona while I check out the area. The market stalls are magnificent—filled with clothes and food—we never had anything like this where I'm from. I'm so lost in my own thoughts and admiration for the place that I don't even notice when I bump into someone.

"Oh, I'm so sorry," I say.

They continue on, not even acknowledging me as they walk to their own stall filled with bread. My heart pangs, missing home and my village. *And my family.* Walking over, I give the lady a coin for a loaf of bread, immediately taking a bite when she hands it to me. *It's not as good as the loaves from the bakery at home.*

Out of the corner of my eye, I see a sign for a blacksmith, and I change direction, heading that way. I instinctively reach for my dagger, my breath stopping when I remember I don't have it. It's left in the Weide Saliba throne room along with my heart. As I recall Amelia giving me that blade, an ache radiates inside my chest. I don't know if I will ever see it again, but worse still...I don't know if I will ever see her again. In a futile attempt to soothe my spiraling thoughts about my sister, I remind myself *I don't need the dagger anymore...That's not my life now.*

As I reach for the door of the blacksmith, a big, burly man pushes it open, almost knocking me over. I catch my balance and grab the handle before it can close. The person standing at the counter glances up at me, likely assessing whether or not I'm there to buy, before going back to the ledger they were working on.

"Hi, I was wondering if you were looking for help around the smithy?" I ask once I'm standing directly in front of the counter.

"No," is all they say in response, their tone giving no leeway for discussion.

I don't bother with a farewell before I turn and walk out. *Fine, I didn't want to work with you anyway.*

I go back to wandering around town, taking in the array of market stalls, permanent shops, and flowers in planters. Next to every planter is a stall of some kind: next to the roses is a goldsmith, next to the peonies is a seamstress. I look for work at every single stall in the village, wishing for a little bit of dust in the air to remind me of home.

As the sun passes its peak in the sky, I am feeling a little defeated. I get to the end of the main road, and I hear a cheerful melody from a stringed instrument spilling out from the building next to me. The door groans loudly when I push it open, but the sound of the patrons inside is nearly deafening.

A tavern, of course.

From behind the bar, a giant of a man calls to me, "Howdy, little lady! Don't think I've seen you around before. What's your drink of choice?"

I step closer to him, not wanting to yell over the patrons, and climb up on the vacant stool as I glance around. "Uhhh, honestly, I'm not really sure. I'm new in town, and I'm not a big drinker. Just looking for somewhere to stay for the night."

He takes my measure for only a moment before all of a sudden, he's yelling again, "Ivy!"

The battered half-door to what I'm guessing is the kitchen swings open, and a flustered woman who looks to be around my age storms out. "What, Nick? I'm obviously busy, you see this place!" As she speaks, she swings her arm around the room, gesturing at the packed tavern.

"This lovely young woman is looking for a room. She's new in town." Grabbing another glass to polish, he walks away from where I sit at the counter, leaving Ivy to take over while he moves on to the next patron.

"New in town? How long are you looking to stay for?" Ivy's exasperation seems to melt away as she takes me in.

"Honestly, I'm not really sure, and I don't have a ton of money to spare."

"You don't need money today if you're willing to work for your keep. We need help around here if you want to stick around for a while." She offers me a small room at the neighboring inn—letting me know my wages will cover my stay and there should always be some left over. My face lights up and the first genuine smile I've had since I saw the yellow flowers at that beautiful lake crosses my face.

"That sounds perfect, actually." *This is the fresh start I need.*

Ivy passes me a glass of water and tells me she will get me settled in my bedroom once the supper rush dies down. I thank her and gulp my water down gratefully. I had emptied my canteen on my walk around town, and I am absolutely parched.

I pass the rest of the dinner rush listening to the fiddle and guitar duo while observing the tavern's patrons as they come and go. When business has drifted to a gentle lull, Ivy takes me across the street to the village inn and shows me to my new room. She gives me instructions for the next day and leaves me to get a good night of rest.

My room is small, but clean. It contains only a small bed, a washstand with a basin and a pitcher of water, and a mid-sized crate that serves the dual purpose of being a table and a place to store my belongings. I gratefully wash up for the first time in several days, unpack the pitiful contents of my saddlebag, and crawl into the small bed. For the first time in weeks, I sleep peacefully the entire night.

I wake to birds chirping outside the small window. Opening my eyes, I look around, and let out a deep breath. I allow myself a moment to feel at peace for the first time in as long as I can remember—certainly since before I started taking on illicit jobs—before throwing my legs over the bed and forcing myself out of it. It's funny how I can feel calm and safe, yet miss my family terribly at the same time.

I am ready for my first day of real, ethical employment. As I get dressed in the simple tunic and pants that Ivy had left for me yesterday, I can't help but let my mind wander. *What's going to happen to Charlie? Obviously the queen wants him dead, so I'm sure he'll end up that way...I wish I could save him. Why does she want him dead, though? What good does that do her?*

Shaking myself out of my thoughts, I head out of my room and back to the main tavern where Ivy had instructed that I meet her this morning. I find her at the front desk and join her behind it, ready to start learning. After showing me the basic tasks of running the inn for the morning, we walk across the road together so I can prepare for tonight at the tavern. I will work mornings at the inn and evenings in the tavern, with one day off per week. Nick greets us with a smile at the front door.

"Good afternoon, ladies. Anna, are you ready for tonight?"

"Honestly, I'm not really sure," I reply, fiddling with my tunic. "I'm kind of nervous. I have no experience working in a tavern...not much experience dining in one either."

"That's alright," he says, gently grabbing my shoulder and squeezing it in an attempt to reassure me. "You won't be alone. Plus, I'll deal with the rowdy ones, anyway."

Laughing under my breath, I wipe my palms off one last time before stepping inside. "Alright." I nod at them both. "Let's do this."

Walking around the bar, Ivy grabs a rag and immediately starts wiping off the counter. "We like to keep the place clean and the service good. Make sure you're wiping things down as soon as folks leave so new guests can take over their spot. We're going to stick with the basics for your first night, and we'll go over more tomorrow."

Trying to remember everything Ivy is saying, I take mental notes.

She adds, "Nick is good about stocking the beer so you don't have to worry about that."

"Was that a compliment, Ivy?" I hear from behind me and turn around to find Nick, in fact, stocking up the beer.

"Oh, be quiet. It won't happen again, don't you worry," Ivy mutters, winking at me before we move on. The laugh I let out at their easy back and forth is surprisingly loud and earnest, which just amuses me more. I fall into easy camaraderie with Nick and Ivy as we go about preparing for the onslaught of business when the tavern opens.

The closer we get to opening, the more my nerves grow. I run back through Ivy's instructions over and over again, *wipe things down as soon as people leave, refill beers when they ask, collect money with each new beer and place it in the till, keep customers happy...Easy enough.*

The afternoon goes by too quickly, and before I know it, the doors are open and people are piling in. I fall into a rhythm that I thought would take longer to find. I throw myself into the work with gusto thanks to my newfound confidence. The longer the night goes on, the easier it all gets, my hands moving through the tasks on their own.

And then it got harder.

The crude comments start as the clientele shifts from the supper crowd to the folks looking to lose coin and sense to Nick's brew. "Whatcha got under that apron, little lady?" A drunk behind me says as he reaches for me. "I've never seen you around here before, so why don't I take you for my private tour?"

Another one winks as I set his beer down in front of him. "I'd love to take you for a spin!" The one behind me shouts as he reaches out to touch me.

I gag a little as I avoid him and do my best to ignore them. I need this job, and I know I can put any of these men in the ground. Except that's not my life anymore. This is my fresh start. *Are these the rowdy ones Nick mentioned?* I am pulled from my thoughts in a white hot fury when someone grabs my rear. I whip around, prepared for a fight, but Nick has already stepped in with a protective roar before hauling the red-faced drunk out and tossing him in a heap on the street. The noise in the tavern dies down, but only for a moment before everyone goes back to their drinks and their conversations.

Comments keep coming, getting harder and harder to ignore, but I have to; quitting isn't an option. This is my fresh start. When Ivy finally comes out of the kitchen hollering for last call, I grit my teeth and push through the last stretch.

Once all the guests are gone, I breathe out a sigh of relief. Straight-faced and exhausted, I am relieved that the night is finally over and that I made it through. Ivy and Nick immediately shift into a seamless dance of deep cleaning the bar and putting the place back in order. It's clear that they have done this a thousand times. I wipe down all the surfaces, making sure they're sparkling clean for tomorrow. As I move from table to table, I listen to Nick mumble behind the bar about how much he hates drunk people while he restocks all the beer so we won't have to do it in the morning.

"Where'd Ivy go?"

"She's in the back, taking care of empties. She'll be back up in a few," Nick says as he finishes stocking. "Once she's done, we can head out and get some sleep. How was the first night?"

"Exhausting. It's gonna take a while for me to get used to the...comments. But the work is not terrible." When I glance up from the last table left to clean, I see Nick counting money. My heart rate picks up, wondering how much I made.

"Well, we made good money this evening." As he splits the coins into four piles, I see he's not wrong. Nick scoops the largest pile into the till and locks it before gesturing to one of the remaining piles of coins. "That's yours."

The kitchen door swings open, and Ivy and Nick both scoop their earnings into coin purses they tuck in at their belts. I rush to grab mine, almost dropping my coins in the process. Nick locks up before walking Ivy and I across the road to the inn, making sure we get in safely. Ivy and me offer tired smiles at the innkeeper as we enter. After saying goodnight to Ivy, I head up to my room, asleep before my head is even all the way to the pillow.

Chapter Eleven

Charlie

THE WEEKS FOLLOWING ANNA'S banishment are some of the worst times of my life. I keep thinking it will get easier, but it does not. The evening after I banished her, my father's illness took over his body and shut it down. So not only did I have to deal with being betrayed by the woman I wanted to marry, I lost the one person who'd always been there for me.

Seeing my stepmother heartbroken removed all the doubts I had about her. Anna had lied. The queen was devastated, and I could not fathom a reason why she'd want me gone. What would she do if she lost us both? She wouldn't be able to take it, which meant she had not hired an assassin to kill me.

I spend a lot of time in my chambers, avoiding the world, but finally, some days later, someone knocks on my bedroom door.

"Come in."

My best friend, Drake, strides into my room, more pissed off than I have ever seen him. "Charlie, we need to talk."

I jump out of bed, immediately assuming an unfortunate incident happened to my stepmother. We may not have been close in the past,, but I can't handle another death. Drake would only come in here like that if something was seriously wrong.

"What's going on?" I ask as I grab things from the end of my bed, making myself appear presentable enough to leave the room.

"Look, man, I know you're heartbroken; we all are. But our people require a king able to complete his duty. They need you. Please, Charlie, you must pull yourself together and rule."

I stop moving instantly, staring at him, jaw on the floor. My best friend is very open and honest with me, but he has never talked to me like that. "I..."

He cut me off almost immediately. "No. I'm serious, Charlie. Go to breakfast with Minerva. She needs your company anyway. And you should plan a new ball. It's time." Then he turns around and walks out, leaving me in disbelief that he said that to me. Knowing he's right, I get dressed and walk out of my chamber, my guard Avery following me the whole way.

Walking into the dining room, I find my stepmother sitting at the end of the long banquet table wearing all black, still in mourning.

"Good morning, Stepmother," I say. Considering I'd assumed she was with my father for the title alone for my entire life, I've never called her by her name, so it would be weird to start now. "I think we should host a new ball. It's time to restart the search for a suitable wife."

This causes her to perk up a little bit, but an expression of worry crosses her face. "Are you sure you're ready for that?"

"No, but it's necessary. Do you think you could plan it and send out invitations? Let me know when it is, and I will be there. The country needs a king."

"No!" she shouts, pushing her chair out quickly before resting her palms on the table and lowering her voice. "We should organize it together. We need to collaborate during this horrible time. Come to my room for tea this afternoon, and we both can plan it."

She's never invited me to spend time with her before, always being my stepmother in name alone. I barely even know anything about this woman since she sent me away every chance she got.

I run my fingers through my hair. "No, really, I trust your ability to arrange an appropriate party. My heart is still heavy, and I am not up for helping with the planning when I need to focus on the kingdom and our people. I'm behind on...everything."

"Please, just for a cup of tea. You won't have to help with anything." Her green stare turns pleading as she practically begs me to join her. Her eyes gleam with something I don't understand.

She is grieving too, and guilt rises in my chest. She just lost her husband, and I can't even take time out of my day to have tea with her. Have I always been this selfish? No wonder she pressured my father to send me away as a boy.

"Okay fine, one cup. For now, I will get some fresh air. Send a servant if you need me."

I wander around the castle grounds, not able to go to any of my favorite places anymore without seeing Anna. I never should've trusted someone who didn't even recognize me as the prince. All the princesses on the continent should know what I look like, especially since my portrait would have been included with the invitation to the ball. It's part of the arranged marriage process.

I don't understand how I could've ever been that foolish. That naïve. *Love makes you do crazy things, Charlie.* Unshed tears fill my eyes as my mother's voice fills my thoughts. I was just a child when she died, but she would always tell me that. She was hopelessly in love with my father until she got sick.

It was love that I felt toward Anna. *It is love.* But is she even real? Do I truly know her? She seemed to be filled with genuine anguish that day in the throne room, but even at the end she was changing her story, so how could I really be sure?

"Sir," Avery's voice snaps me out of memories. "Queen Minerva has called for you. It's time."

"Already?"

"Yes. But are you sure you're ready for this…ball? So soon?" Concern fills his voice. Avery might only be my guard in name, but he's been around since I was young, so he knows me better than most people. Through the years, he has become a trusted companion.

"I don't think I'll ever be ready, Avery. I was going to tell her I love her. While I don't know what it is about her…she is magnetic. Rulers sometimes have to make sacrifices for their kingdom, and this is one of mine," I confide in him as we head into the castle and up to my stepmother's quarters. "I must move on. And I need to get *this* over with."

As I raise my hand to knock on her door, Avery grabs my arm.

"Are you sure?" he asks quietly, his gaze flicking to her room. "She was acting strangely at breakfast. And if I'm honest, something has felt…not right with your stepmother for some time."

I smile weakly. "She is in mourning. I promise I'll be fine. Remain outside in the hall. If I need anything, I will call for you." As soon as Avery lets go of my elbow, I rap my knuckles against the door. I wait for the muffled invitation to enter before twisting the cool handle and entering the queen's sitting room.

"Hello, Stepmother, how are you feeling?"

"Hello, Charles, I am managing my grief as well as the circumstances allow. Please sit." Waving her arm at the chair across from her, I obey, walking over to it and sitting down. As she pours me a cup of tea, I look around the chambers that used to belong to my mother. I have not been in these rooms since I was a child, and the changes contrast starkly with my memories.

The space is covered with peculiar plants. One that resembles a fern but sports a unique leaf shape, a few unusual flowers in every color imaginable, and a variety of green flora that I have never seen before.

"I am eager to find you an *acceptable* wife," she says, reclaiming my attention. "I think it's a great plan to help us move on from this nonsense with that girl."

"Thank you, Minerva." I try to conceal the ice freezing my soul at her words, but her name feels foreign on my tongue. I take a sip of my tea, which is as unusual as the plants in the room. Trying to figure out what it tastes like, I forget my manners for a moment. "This tea is odd."

"Oh, I made it myself," she says, her eyes shining with a strange brightness. "I do so love to dabble with plants. I consider myself something of a botanist. If it is not to your taste, I could call for different tea?"

Another round of guilt tugs at my heart. "That isn't necessary. I like it!" I lie. "The flavor is just unique." I drink the rest of the scalding liquid in one gulp and pour some more. I don't want to distress her for trying to do something nice during our time of mourning.

"Okay, well, I have a list of princesses and noblewomen that I believe we should invite. All of them would make advantageous matches. Take a look at it and let me know what you think. We need to be picky this time. It is imperative that we find your wife soon. A third round of balls and courting would prompt people to question your intentions and weaken the kingdom in the eyes of our friends and enemies."

I lean over and peek at the list without really seeing it, my vision growing fuzzy and my mind feeling suddenly groggy. "This looks perfect. Please send out invitations," I tell her without taking a single name in. My stomach aches. "I'm not feeling well, so I'm going to head up to my room to rest before dinner." Finishing my cup of tea with the hope it settles my gut, I stand up, stumbling a little as my balance feels lost in dizziness.

Minerva jumps out of her chair and rushes to the door, waving for Avery. I think I hear voices, but I can't quite discern what they're talking about.

"Your Highness, are you okay?"

The words sound a hundred miles away.

"Yes, just fine," I rasp. "Ready for bed."

Avery leans down, wrapping my arm around his shoulders. He pulls me to a standing position and very carefully helps me to my quarters, concern etched all over his blurry face. When we reach my bedchamber, he tugs the blankets out before putting me on the mattress and taking my shoes off. As he covers me up and tucks me into bed, I hear something I can't decipher once again. "Avery, make sure you come and get me if I am needed," I say before falling into a dreamless sleep.

Chapter Twelve

Anna

THE WEEKS FOLLOWING MY banishment are more fulfilling than I could've ever imagined considering the circumstances. I spend my time wandering the village on my days off and working in the inn and tavern, which keeps my thoughts off home and Charlie. When my mind wanders there, I find something to distract myself, trying to keep up this happy act. I write letters home as often as possible, keeping things short and sweet and sending whatever coin I can spare. It's barely enough to cover the yarrow leaves, and certainly not sufficient for his other medicines, let alone enough to feed all three of them. *I wonder how Dad is doing. I hope he's okay...*

"Ivy, all the rooms are turned over and ready for new guests!" I shout down the stairs as I gather all the cleaning supplies to put them away. I run back to my room, hoping to get a few minutes with my book before I have my tavern shift. I've picked up reading since I got here. I always loved it, but in the fight-or-flight mode of my life before, perusing stories was a luxury that I could not afford. I love learning about the history of the village, and sometimes I read about the myths and local stories as well. It's nice to know information about the place I'm staying, especially if it is to be my home. Thankfully, I have a few minutes of a break before I have to go help Nick and Ivy open the tavern up.

"Anna, I'm heading over early. Make sure you aren't late today. I know how you get when you're reading."

I glance up from my book to find Ivy standing in the doorway.

"Yes, ma'am. I'm going to finish this chapter on the Continental War, then I'll head right over." I speed-read the rest of the chapter as she walks away. Once I get to the end, I redo my hair from this morning and head across the street to the tavern. As I push the door open, I overhear Ivy and Nick arguing.

"No, we can't ask her that. She's been nothing but respectful and helpful, but she's clearly very private. We can't dig into her past."

"I just want to know more about her."

"When she's ready, she'll tell us."

The door slams shut behind me, causing them both to jump and look at me with guilt etched into every line of their faces.

"I'm sorry I don't talk about it." Details swim in my brain, but I push all of them down. "I'm just trying to start over so I can help my family. I miss them so much," I whisper, water filling my eyes.

My mind wanders back to my family, not for the first time since I've been here. I wrote them a letter outlining what happened without telling them anything that could place them in danger, hoping that I'd be able to send them more money soon. I'm pulled back to reality when Nick wraps his arms around me, and I realize that the water did, in fact, turn to tears streaming down my face.

"I'm sorry, Anna. You don't have to talk about it. I just want to understand you better. But I won't ask anymore."

There is pity in his voice, but wiping my cheeks, I hug him back. "When I'm ready to talk about it, I promise I will." I tell him, my voice muffled by his chest.

After our touching moment, the air in the tavern seems subdued, but we still get ready for this evening's business as quickly as possible. Thankfully, since I've joined the team, we've been stocking the beer at night so it's less work for us in the mornings.

As the night goes on, like usual, the people get drunker. Walking by a set of customers, I listen to the patrons slurring their words, and saying something about the neighboring countries. As I lean over to grab an empty beer bottle from one of the tables, a man sitting close by reaches over and smacks my rear. I've finally had enough. Whipping around, I grab the man's hand, twisting it until his wrist feels about to snap.

"Do. Not. Touch. Me," I say, my eyes narrowed like daggers toward his shocked face.

I twist his limb just a little more, as far as I can without completely breaking it, before letting go. I turn and walk to the bar, ignoring the looks I'm getting from Nick and all the other patrons in the bar. A moment later, I return to the table with another beer and a smile on my face as if nothing happened. The man leans away, rubbing his injury with a grimace and a glint of fear in his gaze. I might not be an assassin anymore, but I won't let people take advantage of me.

No one else touches me.

As the night draws to a close and Nick gets everyone out of the tavern, I plop down on a stool as my anxiety rises, knowing I'm about to be questioned. Nick walks by me and starts stocking beers while Ivy wipes down tables. Neither look at me, both acting like nothing happened. "So...no one is going to ask?"

"Ask what?" Ivy tilts her head, confusion on her face.

"I almost broke that man's wrist, and we're all just going to pretend that nothing happened?" I ask, looking between the two of them.

"We told you earlier we won't pry into your past again until you're ready to tell us, and that includes you almost breaking a patron's wrist for touching you. If you had been unprovoked...we might need to have a few words." Nick chuckles a little as he shrugs his shoulders and returns to what he was doing before. "Besides, I didn't see anyone else mess with you the rest of the night. Obviously, you can hold your own."

Relief washes over me. I was certain I was going to get fired for hurting a patron. At least I know I'll still have a job at the end of the day. I go about my closing tasks while I mull over my story, my predicament, and the two friends I am lucky to have found.

"I guess I owe you some type of explanation." And I start talking. Starting from when I was a child climbing trees with Amelia with no care in the world, to my dad's sudden illness and needing to grow up fast...it's a long story and I don't think I have ever talked so much. I tell them about needing to become a bounty hunter and an assassin and the way the jobs weighed heavily on my heart. When I get to the part about the prince, the tears flow in earnest, and Nick hands me a beer. I take a giant swig of it, breathing as deep as I can to calm my nerves before I finish, "So yeah, that's the whole story. And now I'm here."

Nick and Ivy both stare at me, open-mouthed. They have long since stopped working and both lean against the bar, and have been enraptured with my story.

After a long moment, Nick takes a drink of his own beer. He is looking at me, but it feels like he's seeing through me. "That is... quite the ordeal. Sounds like you had a terrible time. We're glad to have you here, though."

"I agree with Nick. You're a hard worker and a great person; your past doesn't matter to us."

I close my eyes in relief, tears still flowing, when thin arms wrap around me. I lean my head onto Ivy's shoulder; her small frame matches mine. When giant arms wrap gently around us, I know Nick has come around from the other side of the bar to join our hug.

"I love you guys. Thank you for being amazing friends."

After a long, emotional night, Nick walks Ivy and me over to the inn like he does every night. "I'll see you both tomorrow." He waves as he walks away, towards his home.

My routine—*minus the nasty comments at the tavern each night*—continues as usual for the next few days. Nick and

Ivy seem satisfied with everything I shared and refrain from digging more into my past.

I start hearing comments that concern me.

"Did you hear about the prince of Weide Saliba?"

"I wonder who will rule the kingdom."

"Did he ever marry?"

"Maybe King and Queen Amoreli will take over the kingdom."

I try to ignore the comments and questions I overhear, hoping they aren't true. *The prince has to be okay. It hasn't been that long since I left, just a few weeks. I thought it would take longer for her to execute her plans. If they caught me, surely they'd have been on high alert to halt any other attempts.*

I prepare to clean my assigned rooms, and walk down the stairs to find out who checked out. However, when I walk into the lobby of the inn, a familiar voice calls my name.

"Lady Anna."

The words I hear from across the room stop me in my tracks. I shake my head, figuring I must be going crazy, and continue to the front desk again.

After a few more steps, the voice repeats, "Lady Anna, please."

Slowly spinning around, I make eye contact with a person I never thought I would see again.

Charlie's guard. Avery.

My throat tightens as panic makes my stomach clench. "What are you doing here? How did you know where I was?"

My words stop as I slowly put two and two together. The rumors are true. Something has gone terribly wrong in Weide Saliba.

"Prince Charles is dying." He glances down at his boots before clearing his throat. "He wants to see you before he...dies," he whispers the last part, sadness filling his face.

I gasp. Tears slowly start forming in my eyes. "No, it can't be."

"We need you to come back to Weide Saliba immediately. Please."

I can barely speak, but manage to rasp, "He banished me. The queen ordered my death. You were there. You know that if I go back, my life is forfeit." I can't meet his gaze.

"I know. But I wouldn't have come all this way and I wouldn't be asking if it wasn't important. I'm begging you. He needs to be able to say goodbye."

In Avery's hand is my dagger. The one Amelia gave me. He holds it out like an olive branch, as though he is planning on using this tool of death as a symbol of peace between the two of us.

Finally, I have the courage to lift my chin and meet Avery's eyes. They're shiny with unshed tears. He is going to cry, too.

"Okay." I nod as the pit in my stomach grows. There really was no other choice. I take my dagger from him, the weight feeling foreign in my hands. "Wait here. I need to pack some things for the journey."

I head for the stairs only to run right into Ivy. Realization courses through me. I can't just leave—I have a job, responsibilities, friends...

"Ivy, I need to take some time off...I don't know how long I will be, but it's important. Please?" I practically beg, fearing that she will tell me to get lost and not come back. Ivy peers around me, and seeing the royal guard standing behind me, nods her head.

"Whatever you need, Anna, just please come *home*." Taking my hand, she squeezes it reassuringly.

Home. I feel the truth and the relief of the word.

"Thank you. Please tell Nick goodbye...I'll try to come back as soon as I can," I whisper, pulling her into a hug before bounding up the stairs to pack a bag.

I take one last look around the room, my home. I had not expected this place to become my second home so quickly, but it has been my safe haven for the last month. I appreciate Ivy and Nick for everything that they've done for me and for being true friends. I just hope I will see them again.

Knowing there is a chance of death as soon as I cross the border. I say a silent prayer, *Please let me survive this. I want to come back home.*

Chapter Thirteen

Anna

AFTER RUSHING TO THE stable to saddle Epona, we start the arduous ride back to the castle. The two-day journey to the palace feels like it lasts weeks. The closer we get, the more nauseated I become. *What if the queen has me executed before I even get the chance to see him?*

"Anna."

My name causes me to jump, looking around for who called it.

"Anna, it's just me."

"Oh, Avery, sorry. I'm a little spooked," I mumble, holding my chest as I take calming breaths, hoping to slow my heart rate.

"It's okay, I understand. I'm not going to let anything happen to you. Prince Charles asked for you himself, and coronation or not, he holds more power than the queen. She can't do anything about your presence. I'll make sure of that."

It's like he read my thoughts. How did he guess that's what I was worried about?

"What if we don't make it back before the prince dies? I'm hoping I can say this to you in confidence, but I believe the queen is responsible for this."

"I agree with you. But without proof, we can do nothing about it. Let the healers do their job."

I return to staring directly in front of me, worrying about Charlie and what might happen. When we exit the woods that seem like they go on forever and I view the looming castle, my stomach drops to the ground.

Avery rides right up to the door, with me not far behind him. *I can't do this.* He dismounts and approaches the front entrance while I sit there on Epona.

I can't do this. He doesn't want to see me.

Then, as Avery pulls the door open, he stops, turning to check on me. The pleading look in his expression is all the confidence I need. I dismount Epona, handing her reins to the closest servant, before running up the stairs to catch up. As we walk into the palace, Avery leads me right up to the prince's chamber. My heart beats out of my chest, harder the closer we get to the room. As Avery creaks the door open, it just stops altogether. From the doorway, I see the prince lying in his bed, paler than normal. His chest barely moves. I can hear him gasping for breath from across the room, like he can't get enough air. His eyes are closed, so I walk up quietly, and noticing multiple chairs surrounding the bed, I pick one. The chair creaks as I sit down, causing the prince to open his eyelids.

"Anna, you came," he croaks. As he attempts to sit up, I reach my hand out to him. I don't know if I should help him or urge him to lay back down, but he collapses back onto the bed even as he reaches out for me.

"I wasn't going to, but I couldn't live with myself if I didn't see you again. What happened to you?" The pain leaks through without even realizing it. He shouldn't be in this position.

Guilt gnaws at me. I did this to him. I never should've taken the job; it wouldn't have happened if I hadn't. *Yes, it would, Anna. The queen would have gotten her way either way.*

"I don't know." A coughing fit starts, lasting several minutes.

I help him with the glass sitting on the bedside table, hoping some water will soothe his throat. "The healers will figure it out," he rasps.

"You need rest, Charlie. Get some sleep. I'll be here when you wake."

He slowly drifts off, rubbing small circles on the back of my hand as if he's trying to soothe me when it should be the other way around. When the rubbing slows, and his eyes are closed, I gently pull my hand away. Needing space to think, to try to come up with a solution, I wander out of the room. I pace up and down the hallway until finally an idea comes to me.

"Take me to the healer, please."

After glancing at one another, one of the guards outside Charlie's room finally waves at me to follow, putting the start of a plan into motion.

Walking into a bright space with white walls and beds lining the entire area, I assume we've arrived at an infirmary. The guard leads me right to a group of people in long robes, one of whom I recognize.

"Anna, it's nice to officially meet you finally and not just from the prince giving me a list of symptoms to research." As he holds his hand out to me, I laugh nervously. Healer Adam.

"Hi Adam, I apologize about that, by the way. I understand he was just trying to help, but my father's disease is incurable according to every physician and healer we've talked to."

"Well, it wasn't the right ones then. Nothing is incurable; you just have to take the time to find the cure. But we'll talk about that another time. Let's head to my office."

The hallway leading to Adam's office is long and white. The whole place smells clean, almost too clean. There is nothing on the walls, the lights are too blinding, and when I say white, I mean everything. The floor, the walls, and the ceiling are all a bright shade of white I don't think I could compare to anything. But as Adam opens a creaky door leading to a small study, no bigger than the prince's water closet, I notice the contrast. Adam's desk is tiny, but it is a mess of paperwork and books. There are three chairs, two opposite the other one, I'm guessing for other healers when they're doing research. There is a small window towards the ceiling in which one can barely make out the sky and the trees outside. It feels like a dungeon in here. Adam's chair scraping on the floor pulls me out of my daydream. I sit down across from him and lean back in the chair.

"Obviously, you're aware that I am banished; everyone is. But there is more to the story. I need confirmation you're not going to have me thrown in the dungeon until the prince is better." My voice comes out stronger than I expected, and I give myself a mental pat on the back.

"Okay?" There is confusion clear in Adam's voice, like he doesn't understand why I would ask him for a favor like that.

"The queen hired me to kill Charlie, but no one believes me."

His eyes gloss over, like he's disappeared into his own head. Hopefully, he's putting more information together that I'm not aware of. When he snaps back to me, there is something in his gaze I don't recognize.

"We can't do anything without proof, but this is helpful information. Thank you for trusting me. I will inform you if we find anything." His chair scrapes the floor once again as he stands up and waves me toward the exit. "Feel free to return to his chamber, and I promise we will keep you updated. I will have food sent up shortly."

I nod my head at him before turning towards the door and heading back to the guard that brought me down here. Tears fill my eyes once again, and by the time we're back in the prince's room, they're rolling down my face.

Chapter Fourteen

Anna

DAYS GO BY WITH no answers, as the prince's health only further deteriorates. Different people filter through to check on him, and me, I suppose, but the only one I recognize is Avery. Thankfully, the queen doesn't come in once. He gets worse by the day with nothing I can do until one day the door bursts open, slamming hard against the wall.

"Anna!"

I whip around as Avery comes barreling in with Adam not far behind him. Two guards follow, holding a shackled individual between them. I do a double take as I realize that the prisoner is none other than the queen herself. I survey each face as concern and confusion run through me in equal measure.

"What's going on?"

"One of the castle staff overheard Minerva talking to her guard in her quarters. She confessed to poisoning the prince during their tea time, with the goal of gaining control of the throne." Avery glares at the disgraced royal, disgust written all over his face.

My eyes widen. "Poison? There must be an antidote. What do we need to do to treat him?" I ask, hope starting to fill my soul for the first time since Avery found me at the inn.

Adam answers, "We don't know; she won't tell us what she used."

My thoughts wander, trying to think of what I can do to help.

The queen interjects with a snarl, "You'll never—"

A guard yanks her backward, not allowing her to finish the sentence.

"I'm trained in herbs and poisons from the apothecary." The words come out as nothing more than a whisper before I glance back up at Adam. Realization dawns on his features just as quickly as it did mine. "I'm trained in herbs and poisons from the apothecary!" I say a little louder, excited that I can actually help. "I'll search her rooms and try to figure out what we're working with. I just need someone to tell me where it is."

Avery takes off running, and I follow, doing my best to keep up. When he gets there, he busts the door down after finding the handle locked. I start the search, and to my horror, it takes days. Sadly, I discover nothing dubious. In fact, the *only* suspicious thing I find is a strange collection of hundreds of plants in her sitting room and bedchamber. I tear the castle apart, brick by brick, only to find more flora I've never seen before, or ones I know are not poisonous.

What are we going to do? We'll never be able to heal the prince.

Chapter Fifteen

Anna

I WAKE TO SCREAMING.

My eyes dart around the room, only for me to discover that it was my own screaming that woke me. The moment I sit up, I find, to my shock and horror, that I'm back in my bed at the inn.

What is going on? Getting up and running to the window, where I observe the tavern across the street, I accept the only possible explanation: *this has to be a dream! There is no way it's anything else.*

Still in my sleep clothes, I run outside and over the road to the tavern. As the door creaks open, causing the bell to ring, Ivy looks up from the glasses she's cleaning.

"Anna, are you alright?" Her brow furrows with concern as she takes me in.

"Ivy, what is going on?! When I fell asleep, I was at the castle, and now I'm here? When did I get back?"

Ivy puts the glass down with a clink on the bar and walks over to me, staring at me like I've grown a second head. As she reaches up to touch my forehead, as if to check my temperature, I take a step backward. "Anna, you never left. What are you talking about?"

"No, Ivy, I've been at the castle for a week." I stumble another step back as realization hits me. *It was all a dream.*

"Nick, can you come out here, please? I think something is wrong," Ivy yells to the back, where I'm guessing Nick is prepping dinner.

Nick walks out of the kitchen, and my heartbeat picks up the longer I stand here. "Anna, are you feeling okay? You're really pale."

"No," I say between wheezing breaths. "I've been at the castle for a week. I've been helping find a cure for the prince. How am I here?" I keep repeating it, waiting for them to remember, or to wake up from this nightmare.

"Anna, you just worked yesterday," Nick says, walking over to me and putting his warm hand on my back.

"You've been here every day since you got here months ago. Maybe you should go see the physician." Ivy takes my hand, pulling me towards the door.

"No!" I yank my arm away from her, refusing to accept these lies. "The queen paid you guys off. You're lying to me!"

I storm out of the tavern, shaking my head. There's no way it was a dream. I was there! But if it was a dream, that means the prince is safe. At least for now. Maybe the queen won't poison him and will leave him alone. I slowly walk back toward the tavern to let Ivy and Nick know I'm alright. As I walk back in, making the bell go off once more, they're sitting at the bar, concern all over their faces as they whip around to look at me.

"I'm so sorry. Perhaps it was a really vivid dream. I didn't mean to worry you both. So, I'm gonna go get to work," I nod my head towards the door, indicating that I was going to go back to the inn. Hopefully, work will shake me out of this trance.

I walk back to the inn, a sinking feeling in my gut at the thought that my return to the castle never happened. It all felt so real, like it was actually happening. There's no way it was all just a dream. There has to be something else going on that I don't understand.

I spend the day cleaning up the rooms and failing to not worry about the prince. Shaking off the sense of doom as much as I can, the churning in my gut makes me more anxious than ever. If I'm not working, I obsess about the prince, the castle, the poison. It's like my mind knows I need to be there instead of here. As long days pass, I try to pick my hobbies back up: baking, sewing, anything I can find.

The more I stay busy the less I think about the castle, and thankfully, the dream never comes back.

After one rather exhausting day, I climb into bed, falling asleep before my head even hits the pillow. Early the next morning, I'm awakened by doors slamming against the wall behind. I startle awake only to find myself next to the prince's bedside surrounded by healers. I jump once again, confusion hitting me.

"What?" I gasp. "No. This is another dream. Just another dream." I repeat these words to myself, not wanting to be tricked again.

Healer Adam steps up next to me, putting his hand on my shoulder. "Anna, are you feeling well? Did you find the poison?" The hope in his eyes makes this dream feel more real than it should.

I shrink away from him. "I know you're not real. There is no poison. When I wake up, I'll be back at the inn. In my own bedroom, banished."

"No, Anna, this isn't..." His voice trails off before his head tilts. "Did you find the poison?"

"No, I didn't find anything," I say with more attitude than I intended, sick of repeating myself. "And everything that seemed off obviously wasn't poison since I tasted it and I'm not—"

Adam didn't even let me finish my sentence before he took off running. I have no clue where he is going. I roll my eyes and return my attention to the prince. Who knows when I'll have to go back to reality?

Chapter Sixteen

Anna

MY EYELIDS, HEAVY AS bricks, drift closed for the fourth time. I shake my head, compelling my aching body to stand up and pace once again as a way to force myself to stay awake. I'm not quite ready to wake up from this dream.

Wanting answers as to what the healer *thinks* is going on in this dream world also has me forcing my eyes to stay open. *If I know, maybe I can prevent this from happening to the prince in reality.* Finally, I get to the point of exhaustion that I'm falling asleep standing up and decide it's time to face real life. My eyes close and I drift off, only waking when a loud bang sounds behind me. I jump up, wide awake, and more alert than before. I whip toward the sound, ready to fight whoever is breaking into the room.

When Adam meets my gaze, I take a few deep breaths, calming my heart rate. I look around, grateful to still be in the castle, in my dream world. With a sigh of relief, I finally glance back at Adam.

"What's going on?"

"Anna, we figured it out! Not a cure, but we at least know what he was poisoned with," Adam says, out of breath, possibly from running upstairs?

A smile spreads across my face as my heart rate picks up. "You're going to be able to heal him?!" I ask, excited that he's making progress.

He walks over, taking a seat next to the bed, multiple healers following behind him with stacks of books. Their stoic expression...that must mean...

Sitting down next to him I prepare myself for the inevitable.

"Anna," he grabs my hand, trying to make the news less heartbreaking, I'm sure.

"Have you ever heard of time lace?" As he asks, a healer behind him steps forward and hands me a book, open to a page that has **Time Lace** written in big bold letters across the top, and a plant drawn on the page.

I shake my head. "No, but that's a plant from the queen's room. It's not poison, or I would be dead," I say matter-of-factly because I'm *definitely* not immune to poison.

"That's one of the plants I thought was strange, so I tasted a leaf of it."

"Well, in large doses, especially when mixed into food or water, it is lethal. It slowly shuts down someone's body from the inside out, starting by putting them into a deep sleep. It takes years to kill them because it works so slowly; no one knows why. Everyone considers it to be a myth, though, because of what it does to someone in small doses."

"Well, what does it do in small doses?" I ask, curiosity filling my voice since I had it in a very small dose.

"Anna, you're familiar with the idea of multiple realities, correct? The idea that there are other timelines happening at the same time as this one, just on different planes?" The question causes me to flinch. I've definitely heard of them; my sister is obsessed with the idea of alternate realities and timelines. *What does that have to do with the time lace?*

"Well, yeah, everyone has. But no one has ever proved it since you cannot live in two realities."

"That's the thing. After you freaked out this morning, I remembered something I read once, and I don't think it's a myth. I believe you are living in two different realities. That's what time lace does; it takes a person's soul and splits it in half. Separates it into two distinct realities."

I don't feel my jaw fall, only noticing it when I sense my tongue is getting dry. Adam watches me like I'm going to panic any minute, which I might. "We don't know how to heal him, but whatever heals you should work on him."

"So you want to use me to figure out a cure for the prince?"

"Yes."

I guess it's better than sitting here moping around. "What about when I..." I trail off, not being able to comprehend the fact that I'll just switch realities at any point? And no one but me will know? "What happens inside the other reality when my soul focuses on the other one?"

"No one knows. But when you switch, you should still be here, so we'll figure it out as we go, I guess."

"Okay, let's do it."

The healers stack books on the prince's side table. All of them with covers just different enough to tell the books apart, but obviously on the same subject, *Time Lace.* I don't know when, or if, they're going to start running tests on me, but I need to be prepared. But I'm still exhausted from not sleeping, so I decide it's best to get some sleep before I start reading the new volumes. I doze off, head on the prince's bed, holding his hand. Hopefully, the healers can find answers. *They'll find a way. They have to.*

Chapter Seventeen

Anna

I WAKE WITH A jolt, back in my room at the inn.

I scream in frustration, throwing my pillow across the bed-chamber. "How long am I going to be here *this* time!"

Huffing, I force myself up and get ready for the day, hoping it's just a quick visit this time. I brainstorm ways to get home quicker, back to MY timeline.

I should check the library before I go to the tavern for the night.

As I mope down the stairs and grab the list from the front counter, I say a little prayer to whatever higher being decided to let this happen. It doesn't take me very long to get through the rooms since so few people left today, and I head over to the tavern earlier than normal hoping Ivy can help me.

"Good afternoon, Anna," Ivy's sing-songy voice greets me before the door even opens all the way.

"How'd you know it was me?" I ask, peeking around the door to glimpse both Ivy and Nick cleaning glasses, getting ready to serve beer tonight.

"No one else would be here this early, silly."

"Oh, right."

"What's got you in such a mood?" Ivy asks

"Nothing, I'm fine," I murmur, contemplating what is safe to tell them. "Actually, what do you guys know about time lace?"

Ivy glances up at me, answering a little too promptly. "Nope, never. Maybe check the library."

The way she says it just seems weird.

"You have time before your shift," she continues. "Why don't you go take a look and see what you can find?"

I turn around, the doorknob still in my hand. "Thanks, Ivy, I won't be long." I hurry to the library, striving to find information as quickly as possible.

My lungs are gasping for breath by the time I reach the library, even though it's not far. I yank the giant, heavy door open. After slowing my breathing down, I start searching the books. Thankfully, the books are easy to search through since it seems they're in alphabetical order. As I get to the T's section, I bump into a small cart laden with volumes. A little old lady stares at me with raised eyebrows from the other side as she takes care of books.

"Hi honey, can I help you find something?" she asks, her voice a little croaky.

"Yes, please. I've been wanting to study some old myths. Do you have any stories with time lace?"

"Um, I'm not sure. If you want to follow me, we can take a look." She stands on tiptoes to read the top shelf of the *T* section, whispering the titles to herself. "Sorry, honey, I don't see anything for time lace. We could look for something broader, maybe?" The hope in the librarian's voice makes it obvious that she doesn't want to disappoint me.

"Okay, I actually need to go to work, but maybe tomorrow! Thank you, anyway!" I wander outside and slowly return to the tavern. *How am I going to get back now?*

I walk into the tavern and grab my apron, not speaking to anyone. I'm guessing Ivy can see the disappointment on my face because she doesn't ask any questions. The whole evening I wrack my brain, hoping to come up with an idea to help me switch back to my correct timeline.

Chapter Eighteen

Anna

I WAKE UP WITH a start. Someone is touching my shoulder, shaking gently. I glance around, trying to discern which reality I am in. When my gaze connects with Adam's, a sigh of relief releases from me. "Thank God, I'm back."

"Did you get a chance to read anything last night?" Adam smiles when he asks.

At least we have an answer to one question.

"Sadly I did not. I was so exhausted that I fell asleep rather quickly, but I will get some done today. However, I did switch realities again. I think the other one just...pauses...when I'm not in it. I was stuck for a whole day in the other reality, but apparently, only the night in this one?"

Desperate to fix these time-reality switches before something bad happens, I explain the entire experience to Adam.

"Hmm, strange," he muses, rubbing his chin thoughtfully. "I'll make a note of that and see if I can find any information. Did you do anything to cause you to switch back? We haven't made much progress finding a cure but we are going to continue to try."

I shake my head. "I don't think so? All I did was visit the library before work then fall asleep after my shift, and here I am." With a stretch, I brush a finger against one of the leather-bound volumes. "I'm going to start on these books, but please let me know what you find."

With that, Adam leaves and I grasp for the thick tome, needing to dive in as soon as possible. I read all day, forcing myself to scan the pages as fast as possible until I've finished all the books. The only thing I learn is that speed reading all day will leave a person with a splitting headache, and that I will also die eventually. Several texts mention how exposure to time lace will cause my body to crash out and burn up, leading to my death. We already know that Charlie's organs are shutting down, slowly. As of right now, there is nothing we can do.

I pick up the books that I discarded all over the floor and head down to the infirmary, hoping they have more options down there, or that they've found something. As I walk in, I'm greeted by a healer whom I don't recognize. The treatment team must have called in back up from other kingdoms. "Good evening, Lady Anna."

"Oh, hello. Um, is Healer Adam available? I've finished all the books."

"Yes, if you head down the hallway, his office is the second on the left." He extends his arms for the stack of books, and I hand them over before we both head in opposite directions.

I approach Adam's office, hoping he has found something useful. As I stop at the entrance, I can tell by the exhaustion on his features that his answer is no.

"Adam," I call softly as I knock on the open door to get his attention.

"Anna, please come sit." He waves his hand toward the two chairs in front of his desk.

I walk in, plopping down across from him. "Did you find anything?"

"No, I didn't. Did you?"

"Sadly, not yet. There is nothing written about an antidote for this poison."

His head drops into his hands, looking exactly how I'm feeling—defeated.

"It can't be possible. There has to be something." I stand up, storming off to the prince's room. This cannot be it for us. As I get to the prince's room, tears are already welling in my eyes.

Breathe, Anna, he'll be okay. You can do this.

I sit down in the comfortable chair next to his bed, urging the tears to go away. He's in a coma now, and I don't know how to fix it. Picking up Charlie's hands, I lay my head down on his chest, the tears finally falling.

"We will get a chance to be together for real. No pretending. No lies. Our time is not over," I promise in a whisper. As I pick my head back up, several tears drop onto his face and soak into his skin. But it's odd how quickly they absorb. I have never seen that happen to anyone before.

The days to come are the hardest. I don't leave the castle, however. While I miss the village that became home and my new friends, I am grateful to have some time with the prince. Once he's better, I'll probably go back to my quiet life. He'll learn the truth about the queen when he wakes up, but that doesn't mean he'll forgive me. Maybe he'll let me see my family one more time before I leave for good. What if he moves on and is happy without me? I'll have to move on and be the best person I can be without him. It'll be fine. I continue to lie to myself, over and over again, until I think I might be starting to believe it. That is, until...

The crash of the bedroom door banging open and into the wall startles me into alert mode. I jump out of my chair, ready to fight.

"Anna." Avery is out of breath as he stands in the doorway. Hands on his knees, taking deep breaths in an attempt to slow his breathing.

"What's wrong?" I ask.

"The queen," gasp, "isn't," gasp, "in her cell." As he rushes out the last part, my stomach drops.

My heart and breathing speed up, sending me into a panic. "What do you mean she's not in her cell?" I ask, trying to stay calm and not show the fear I feel.

"She slipped out somehow during the guard's shift change. She escaped. We locked the castle down, so we will find her. But you have to stay in this room, just in case," He tells me, knowing I was going to insist on helping like I usually do.

I open my mouth to protest, but movement behind me catches my attention, temporarily making me speechless.

I turn around. Charlie's eyes open.

Chapter Nineteen

Charlie

THE FIRST THING I see is Anna standing in my room.

What is she doing here? Then, as my eyes continue to wander, I notice Avery standing in the doorway. *Why is he in here? I ordered him to stay outside the door. Anna must have sneaked back into my room to assassinate me.*

The shocked looks on their faces confuse me. They're in my bedchamber, what are they confused about?

When I attempt to talk, my rough voice sounds like I haven't spoken in weeks. "Anna, you're still here?"

She rushes over, grabbing the water off my side table.

"Go find Adam," she says, whipping toward Avery as she helps me drink the water. *Why do I feel so weak?*

She turns to me as soon as Avery leaves. "Hi, I missed you." She puts the water down, and lays her head on my chest. "I'm so glad you're okay."

"What are you talking about, 'okay'? You missed me? What is going on? Why are you here when you're banished?" The words spill out of my mouth with one breath. I don't understand what's happening.

Adam walks into the room, only to make me even more confused.

"Prince Charles, how are you feeling? We're all so glad to see you awake."

The worried look Anna gives Adam concerns me.

"What are you talking about? I just felt a little sick, so I took a nap."

Adam glances at Anna, and they seem to have a silent conversation between them.

The healer steps closer, touches my forehead and then neck, checking my pulse. His nostrils flare as he leans forward to examine my eyes. "You're better," he finally says.

When Adam nods his head to the door, Anna gets up and follows him. *This is so weird.*

I'm out of bed in no time and eating in the dining room—I'm so hungry for some reason—with all my friends while they explain what happened. "Yeah, so basically, when you were dying, you asked for Anna, so she dropped everything to come. Witnesses proved that Minerva was trying to kill you—she poisoned you, by the way—and detained her. And apparently, they discovered a cure, but no one has told me about it yet. So, really, if it wasn't for Anna, Adam and Avery, you'd probably still be in a coma...and dying." Drake finishes the story and takes a gulp of whiskey, wincing as it goes down, because apparently, they've been through a lot the past few weeks.

"Wow, how did she even poison me? I don't understand?" I ask, trying to put a timeline together.

Drake sets his empty glass on the table. "When you had tea with her. She confessed to dumping time lace into the tea, and since you ingested so much of it, it was killing you."

"Oh. Well, Adam gave me a clean bill of health, so I guess I'm okay now." I rub my forehead. "This is a lot to process."

"I get that, Charlie. Just remember that Anna had a big part in saving you, so maybe you should give her a chance. You know, not the whole 'life will be forfeit' thing. And at least let her see her family."

"Yeah...I'll think about it." I finish my whiskey before getting up and heading outside. I need some fresh air and a walk.

Chapter Twenty

Anna

"WHAT IS GOING ON?" I stumble after Adam through the halls. "He was almost dead and now he has no memory? I don't understand," I ask, feeling overwhelmed and confused.

"We aren't sure, but I assume the poison must have affected his memory. What did you give him to wake him up?"

"Nothing, I thought *you* did something. I talked to him and cried, then accidentally fell asleep on his chest. Avery came in and startled me awake. Charlie opened his eyes not long after that."

The healer glanced over his shoulder, his forehead creased in thought. "I wonder if..."He blinked before stopping and turning to face me fully. "I hate to ask, Anna, but can we get a sample of your tears? Before you leave."

I'm leaving?

I cross my arms to stop myself from showing any more emotion in front of him. "Um, yeah, sure, and then I'll be free to go back to town? Since he doesn't want me here anymore? Or will you be arresting me?" I ask sadly. Tears slowly spill down my cheeks.

"Yes of course, you'll be free to go. Thank you for all your help."

So I follow him to the infirmary, where he collects the tears already streaming down my face. I finally accepted that I cared about him and wanted to try to get to know him for real, but now I'm losing him again. Once I the healer fills a vial with my tears, I leave the castle to return to banishment, and back to my little town. *I knew I shouldn't have left. Except Charlie would be dead if I hadn't.*

After two days on the road, I finally made it back to the inn. Ivy is sitting at the counter for me and while her face brightens at first, she slumps back in her seat with a sad look. She knows me well enough to understand something happened, but I'm not ready to talk about it.

I go through the motions of my new life. Cleaning rooms, working the tavern, reading, bathing, and sleeping. Every day for who knows how long. Just going through the motions. Until one day...

Trumpets blast outside the window of the room I'm cleaning. I clutch my chest from the surprise, then hurry to the window. A bunch of horses and a crowd is gathered by the inn. Confused, I run down the stairs, skidding to a stop when I reach the lobby and see Ivy, just standing there, staring at me. Tears are running down her face but she has the biggest smile I've ever seen on her before.

"What is going on outside?" I ask her in a panic.

"Well, Anna, before I tell you, I want you to know that you will *always* have a home here because you are family. We have been so blessed to have you here in our little town and I hope you never forget about us. However, the prince is here to take you home. Again. As long as you want to leave."

My jaw drops. "What do you mean—"

She interrupts me with a soft laugh and points at the door. I whip around and see the big brown eyes I've been dreaming about.

"Hello, Princess Anna," he says, his beautiful voice pulling me from my trance.

My heart nearly explodes, but I keep it in. "I'm not a princess, remember?" I say, with a smirk.

"I do remember." Now he grins. "However, I'm here to ask you if you will do me the honor of marrying me?"

I stare at him. He did not...he actually...

Noticing my confusion, he continues, "The healers told me everything. The fact that you were willing to risk everything to be there for my dying breath reminded me why I fell in love with you. You are kind, beautiful, and thoughtful, and care about others more than yourself. You willingly risked being locked in a dungeon or executed for returning, and you still did it because I asked for you." He chuckles. "Not very assassin-like of you, was it? You are everything I am looking for in a wife and queen and then some. So, if you would do me the honor, come home with me?" He holds his hand out for me to take.

I cover my mouth, shock, joy, confusion, and elation all running through me at once. Tears gather then start running down my face.

Concerned, Charlie asks, "Why are you crying? I didn't mean to make you cry, my princess."

I suck in a breath and find my voice. "Of course, I will Charlie. I will marry you. Yes! Thank you for making me the happiest girl in the world!"

I wipe tears on my sleeve before rushing to pack the few things I've gathered since I've been here.

Chapter Twenty-One

Anna

WE PROCEED AT A slow and steady pace for the return trip to the castle. Charlie wishes to explore the villages nearby, and experience the parts of the kingdom his father and stepmother kept from him. Every settlement we encounter has varying levels of poverty, and Charlie did not realize the extent of what occurred in the castle affected the people outside of it.

The queen still being at large makes me nervous to reenter the palace, and it angers Charlie. I've noticed his nightly meetings with his scouts brings out his aggression.

But during the day, we get to know each other better. We ask silly little questions while we ride our horses

"What's your favorite color?" I ask him, realizing how little I know about him, really.

"Blue, just like the color of your eyes," Charlie says, red creeping up his neck as he finishes the sentence.

"My eyes aren't anything special." My cheeks heat, and I'm sure they match his neck.

"They're the color of lakes, not like dirty ones but the ones that you can see the bottom of because they're so clear blue. Like the one I took you to on one of our first outings."

I don't think my cheeks can get any redder after that compliment. I glance down at Epona's neck, too embarrassed to respond.

He turns away, smirking up at the sky before he turns back towards me. "What's yours?"

"Yellow," I say. "It's been my favorite color since I was a child. I saw a yellow dress in the seamstress' window and fell in love, and it's been my favorite color ever since."

As we come to a river I pull Epona to a halt. "Can we go swimming?" I ask, eyes lighting up. I haven't been able to swim for fun in longer than I can remember.

Charlie appears apprehensive, like he's concerned something bad will happen. But he nods his head anyway when his gaze meets mine. I jump off Epona and run to the water, pulling off my boots as I go. When I reach the water's edge, I stop, turning to glance at Charlie who is slowly sliding off his horse, watching me. I roll up my trousers before jumping into the river. The water is only up to my knees, but it's the perfect temperature for cooling off, which Charlie quickly discovers when I splash him as he gets closer to the riverbed. Whipping his arms up to cover his face, he looks at me in shock before taking his jacket off and rolling up his trousers like I did before wading into the water with me. Eventually, we climb out of the river, plopping onto the forest floor to stare up at the trees.

"Charles?" I ask, treading lightly at the idea that pops into my head.

"Anna, we're engaged. You don't have to use my full name."

"Well, since we're engaged, can we go back to my village? I can't get married without my family there."

His face drops and I can't tell if it's because he doesn't want to meet them or because of nerves. He debates my question for a few minutes before he waves a guard over.

"Tell them where to go. Let's go see your family," he says. The excitement in his voice fills my heart.

It's about a two-day ride to the village from our current location, so we leave immediately. On the way, Charlie tries to teach me about being a royal, at least what he can explain while traveling. In public, I have to wear dresses and always have my hair done. They typically have some kind of powder on their faces to help make their complexion look more even, but I'm already experienced with cosmetics. I am expected to act in a specific way, and if I don't, it reflects poorly on the whole kingdom.

There are a lot of rules to being a royal. I had no idea becoming a queen would require changing myself so completely.

The closer we get to the village over the next two days, the more anxious I get. *Is Dad still alive? I know I've been sending letters, but what if something happened more recently, like while I recovered from the time lace poison? Did they miss me at all? I'm sure they did.*

When I can see my village in the distance, I urge Epona faster, as do the guards and Charlie as they follow close behind me. By the time we get to the shack, tears run down my face. I see my parents standing outside in the garden, perhaps picking vegetables for dinner. When I realize my dad is not only out-side, but also standing up out of bed, the tears fall faster.

"Mom! Dad!" I yell, wiping my eyes with the back of my hand.

"Annabelle?" My mom twists toward the sound of my voice, and even from this distance, I make out the surprised expression on her face. "Annabelle!" she yells, running toward us.

I jump off Epona, and run into my mom's arms, squeezing her as hard as I can.

"Oh Ananbelle, we're so happy to see you." My dad says once he catches up. He wraps his arms around my mom and me, embracing us warmly.

"I'm so excited to see you too! Where's Amelia?" I ask, looking around for my sister and not finding her.

"She's at work, sweetie, but she should be back soon." As she says that I realize she's staring over my shoulder.

I glance behind me, finding Charlie off his horse and standing there awkwardly. I step to the side and hold my hand out, waiting for Charlie to reach out and grab it.

"Mom, Dad, this is my fiancé, Prince Charles Greystone." I speak slowly, giving them time to process what I'm saying.

My mom and dad stare at me, grinning from ear to ear. Then I hear a voice from behind me.

"Mom, Dad, what's going on? Why are there so many people around?" My sister abruptly ends her sentence when I make eye contact with her.

"Hey sis, I missed you." I say softly.

She *sprints* and nearly crushes me in her embrace.

"Annabelle, I missed you!" The crack in her voice has me tearing up again.

Mom ushers all of us into the dilapidated shack home, wanting to hear the stories about what happened when I was gone. Most of the guards wait outside, except for the two who remove their helmets so they don't bash them against the doorframe.

It doesn't take long after we get inside for Amelia to tell me that she is also engaged, which makes me cry yet again, because this is our dream. Mom brews some tea, shoving the kettle next to a covered pot already steaming slightly, and slices a few fruits after ensuring Charlie and I sit down at the table. I notice freshly dug up potatoes and carrots on the small counter by the fire. After we all hold our own mug of tea, everyone just stares at us, like they're waiting for one of us to start talking, so I do.

The story is long, and I fear she feels a little betrayed when she frowns because I confess my old profession, and admit the prince was my mark. I describe how Charlie banished me, since he found out I was supposed to kill him, and then explain that the queen was the one who hired me. When I get to the part about the time lace and how Charlie and I were poisoned, she cries, realizing how close she was to never seeing me again. Then I tell her about Ivy and Nick, only for a pang in my chest to knock the breath out of me at the thought of them. *Will I ever see them again?*

Lastly, I describe the days Charlie and I have spent together traveling, because I want her to know everything.

Except that the queen is missing. I leave that part out.

"Yeah, so that's it. Now we're engaged," I finish, glancing over at Charlie. The look in his eyes reminds me how much he loves me.

"We would love for you to join us, at least for the wedding. But you also have an invite to come live with us if you would like."

My jaw drops and I whip around to stare at Charlie, shocked with his kind offer to my family.

He smiles softly at me before continuing, "I can see how much you love each other and how close you all are, and I don't want to ruin that."

My mother and father look at each other, then my sister, having a silent conversation. I'm sure they're going to say no because we've lived here my whole life, but I hope they say yes. A new start for them right along with me.

"Give us some time to think about it," my mom says, grabbing my hand. "We'll have an answer for you by this evening. Stay for dinner, and we can discuss it."

"Okay, Mom," I say, tears stinging my puffy eyes at the thought of them saying no. I just want my whole family together again. "While you, dad, and Amelia talk about it, I'm going to show Charlie around the village."

I grab Charlie's hand, yanking out of the chair and dragging him behind me, the guards following close behind. Once outside I face Charlie, causing him to stop walking. "Did you really mean what you said inside? You want them to live with us?"

"Anna, I want you to be happy, and you're happy with your family, with your sister. You need them, and they need you. And I also need you, so selfishly, yes, I want them to come to the castle, so I have you. Plus, this is way too long of a trip to bring our kids on to see their grandparents," he says with a smirk. The look of horror on my face makes him laugh.

"We aren't even married yet!" I respond in a shrill squeak. I've never even thought about children. My job was so dangerous that it seemed impossible to find love.

As Charlie gasps, trying to catch his breath from laughing so hard, he finally responds. "I'm only kidding! Well, kind of. There's no rush on the kids aspect, but I really would like some, someday. Plus, we'll need an heir."

Letting that be the end of the conversation, I turn and start heading into the village, Charlie close behind. We wander around the shops, while the guards not directly watching us scatter throughout the village to not draw too much attention to themselves.. No one here recognizes him since we're still a ways from the castle, but his rich clothing and entourage reveal he's someone important. When it's been about an hour, Charlie and I return to my home, since that's usually how long it takes mom to make dinner.

Walking into the shack, I'm met with the delicious smell of my mom's beef stew. My favorite meal she makes next to her oats. She must have already had it simmering when we arrived and added all the savory spices and root vegetables while we were gone. I immediately grab bowls and start dishing stew into them, sending mom to rest at the table since she already did all the hard work.

Once everyone has dinner we sit down. Mom and Amelia catch up on what's been going on in town. Apparently, the baker's daughter and Lyla's son are engaged. Amelia is engaged to a hunter from the neighboring village whom I've never met before, which is weird. As happy as I am for her, I'm a little sad she never told me about him before.

It seems everyone has been waiting for updates on the prince, as well, since news takes a while to arrive here. Clearing the table, I hear Amelia clear her throat behind me.

"Who wants desert? I got carrot cake from the baker."

My mouth instantly starts watering at the thought of her carrot cake.

"Yes please! I've missed her carrot cake."

Amelia gets up and follows me to the kitchen to help plate it. I notice Charlie ate his portion, and I smile. He likes my mother's cooking, too.

"So, a hunter? How's that going?" I ask her, handing her plates as she cuts out pieces of the cake.

"It's going well. He's gone a lot, obviously, but he's already helped the family so much."

"So I'm guessing you're staying here? If he makes you happy then you deserve it."

"If mom and dad go, then I'm going too. If he loves me, he'll understand."

The smile that spreads across my face is huge. My cheeks actually ache. I'm beyond proud of my sister for knowing her worth, and I cannot wait to meet her fiancé. We walk back out to the table and set everyone's plates down before joining them.

My sister starts the conversation back up. "What would going to the castle entail? "

"Nothing! We'd have to get a carriage of course to safely transport you and your things. But other than that, you'd just come and live there. You'd be free to do whatever you wish whenever you'd like. I just don't want to separate this family again." Charlie glances at me and then back to my family before continuing. "I can see how much Anna loves and needs you. But I also love and need her. So, I want her to be happy and she is happiest near you all. None of us would be happy without the other, so admittedly, asking you guys to move is slightly selfish on my part, but it is because I love your daughter."

I know when I look up from the crumbs of carrot cake on my plate that he won them over. Mom and Amelia have tears forming in their eyes while my dad has them running down his face already.

"So, no one will be trapped in the castle?" My dad asks, drying his face with the back of his hand.

"No, sir, I would never do that to anyone. If you guys decide living in the castle is too much, I can always get you a place to stay in the nearby village so you're still close by." My mom and dad look at each other before nodding their heads.

"Okay, we want you both to be happy, but we also want our daughter back. So we'll come."

I knock my chair over jumping out of it so hard. I run around the table, wrapping them up in a hug.

"You guys will love it there!" I tell them, more excited than I've ever been. Charlie and my father, cane in hand, head into town, needing to find a carriage to get them to the castle, while my mother, sister and I start packing up the house. Guilt gnaws at me while we work because I never told them about the queen escaping. "I need to tell you guys something," I whisper, barely loud enough for them to hear.

"What's wrong, dear?" My mother asks.

"The queen got arrested, but she escaped the dungeon, and we haven't been able to find her yet. Please stay with a guard as much as possible just in case," I basically beg, wanting to keep them safe. They both glance at each other, concern written on their faces, before turning their heads back to me and nodding. A sigh of relief escapes me, because I know the guards at the castle will keep them safe.

Chapter Twenty-Two

Anna

EARLY THE NEXT MORNING we load the carriage with everything from the shack, not wanting to leave anything behind. We head out, keeping a steady pace since we aren't in too much of a rush. *Plus, Charlie and I want time to come up with a plan for the queen.* Every once in a while I turn around, checking on my parents. Eventually, Charlie notices the worry etched across my face.

"So, Annabelle is your full name, huh?" he asks, drawing my attention to him.

I chuckle. "Yeah, I guess I never told you that. It seemed so unimportant, I didn't think about it. The only one who uses my full name is my mom."

"Yeah, I guess not. Are there any other surprises I should know?" When he asks that, I think really hard about the things I've told him and if I missed anything important.

"No, I don't think so."

"Good, when we get back to the castle, I really want to get to know your family better, since they're going to be my family too."

"I'd love that, Charlie." I glance over my shoulder one more time, concern flooding my body.

"My flower, what's wrong?" As he asks, he glances back towards the carriage, just like I have been.

"I'm just scared. I finally have them back, and I don't want to lose them again. Plus, what if being queen is too much for me? What if I can't handle it? Up until now I've been a villager, not even a noble." I tell him, finally confessing the thing that's been bothering me during our time on the road.

"I won't let you lose your family again. I will do everything in my power to prevent it. You are going to be an amazing queen because we have each other, and that's more powerful than any royal could ever be."

Tears sting my eyes as he says it, filling my heart with love.

"Now let's make a plan to find my stepmother." He waves the guards over, telling them that we're going to stop early and set up camp for a lunch break. Once we're set up, and a few guards multitask with food preparations, I ensure my family is comfortable while Charlie and his remaining guards go to a quickly constructed tent to start planning. Once my family members seem content, I walk into the tent and find a map of the whole continent spread out. Looking at the map, I realize how big the continent of Ithas truly is. With Weide Saliba being the farthest northeastern kingdom, we are surrounded by three other kingdoms that are our allies. We are the second biggest kingdom on the continent, with Veirda Shadow, the kingdom in the southwest corner, being the largest. Veirda Shadow is also known as the "Shadow State," because the whole kingdom is dark and gloomy, all year long. They have no allies, because they don't need them. Everyone is too scared to start a war against them—that is until now.

I drop my finger onto the map, right on the shadow state. "She's there," is all I say before turning and looking at Charlie, who is peering at me like I've grown a second head.

"Even she wouldn't be dumb enough to go there," a guard interjects, looking at me like I'm just a stupid girl, before he goes back to looking at the map.

"No, I think she's right," Charlie says, staring at where my finger still rests. "Everyone else would inform us, especially since there is a reward. They are the only people who wouldn't."

We spend the next hour finishing our planning before return to the castle. My family is confused as to why we stopped for so long, but Charlie explained it was easier to brainstorm in the fresh air. When we arrive, we unpack and show my family to their new rooms.

"We eat lunch and dinner together, if you all want to, of course. A maid will be around to help you get settled and to assist with anything you need. Charlie and I will be in the sitting room if you need us. Feel free to wander about and do whatever you would like."

While I want to spend more time with them, I promise myself I will get to see them all the time now. I hurry off to meet Charlie so we can set the plan into motion, and get the help we need.

Chapter Twenty-Three

Anna

WALKING INTO THE SITTING room, I find Charlie standing by the fireplace, surrounded by people, some faces I've seen before, and some new. I clear my throat when I walk in, causing all of them to turn and look at me, kindness in their eyes but worry on their faces.

"You must be Annabelle," the girl with gorgeous long brown hair and violet eyes says to me. "It's nice to finally meet you, I'm Diane."

"Hi Diane, it's nice to meet you! Yes, I'm Annabelle, but you can call me Anna. I assume Charlie has caught everyone up to speed?"

"Not yet, dear, I was waiting for you," Charlie says, causing a smile to spread across my face. "Let's get started. We think Minerva is in the Shadow State, we have a plan to find her, but we need your help. We're going to organize a ball for mine and Lady Anna's engagement, and make it a point to invite the king and queen. They won't be able to refuse. When they come, we will send guards into the state to search for her."

"At that point," I continue, "we will let the king know what is going on, so that our guards don't get attacked, and we can find Minerva faster. We are hoping they will help us, but if they don't we will have to keep them distracted as long as possible. That's where we need your help."

When a round of "got it" comes from everyone in the room, we separate and get to work. Guards get called in so that we can debrief them, and figure out who to assign where. We also have a ball to plan and invitations to send out. Hopefully, with enough notice, everyone will come.

When planning is done, and Charlie's friends start putting the first steps into action, I decide to wander the castle, since I need to learn the layout a little better. Leaving the sitting room, I see the formal dining right across the hallway with the front door to my right. I take a left and head around the grand staircase, hoping to find the kitchen first. As I head down the hallway, I smell some delicious stew, leading me right to the kitchen. When I walk in, everyone stops, making uncomfortable eye contact.

"My lady, how can we help you today?" the head chef asks with a bow. I'll never get used to that.

"Oh, I'm just trying to learn my way around the castle, and please, that's not necessary. Anna is fine," I tell them. That's going to take some getting used to.

That causes them all to go back to cooking, leaving me to head back out the doors and attempt to find the next thing. Deciding I should get ready for dinner, I walk toward the grand staircase and wander up it. Finding a maid in the hallway and taking the opportunity to ask for directions, she points me towards my chambers. I open the door, expecting the room to be empty, and instead I find my fiancé, shirtless. I stop in the doorway, staring at him, both in awe and in shock that he's standing in my chambers with no shirt on.

"Anna, my love," Charlie says as he pulls a fresh shirt over his head, snapping me out of my daydream.

"I didn't mean to barge in. The maid told me this was my bedroom," I tell him, spinning around so he doesn't see the embarrassment spread across my face.

"I mean, if you would like me to prepare separate quarters for you, I can. I just assumed it would be easier to move you into mine since we're already engaged."

"Oh! That's totally fine. I just assumed it was customary to have different sleeping arrangements until we're married."

"Well, it usually is. But when you're in charge, you can break some rules. Plus, it didn't make sense to get another room around if we didn't need it."

"Okay, I'll get ready for dinner then," I say, walking towards the closet, hoping Charlie got a dress or two for me before we got back. Instead, I'm met with a closet full of clothes in different styles.

There's no way these are for me.

"Charlie?" I yell, causing him to step into the doorway of the closet.

"Yes?" he asks, a smirk already plastered on his face.

"Are they all mine?" I ask, jaw on the floor.

"Who else would they belong to?"

"How did you manage to do this?"

"Well, I had the seamstress make them for you, of course. They're all custom-made just for you. Now pick your favorite, and I'll send a servant in. I'll get you set up with your own handmaid soon." Then he turns around, leaving me with a very difficult decision to make.

Chapter Twenty-Four

Anna

DRESSED IN A SUNSHINE yellow, knee-length gown, I head down to the informal dining hall. I'm the last person to arrive, and sit at the large wooden table as the butlers set down the last of the plates. "We have important information to tell you all, so please feel free to make your plates now," Charlie says, looking toward me with a nod.

"We are going to be hosting a ball to announce mine and Charlie's engagement! Everyone had to attend, so we will make sure you all have proper attire." I look at my mom and sister specifically when I say that, since I don't want them to feel out of place. "All of the surrounding kingdoms are invited."

The shocked expressions on my parents' faces concerns me until they start chatting with everyone about it like it's totally normal for them. A smile spreads across my face at the sight of them all talking and smiling, knowing that this is the life I wanted, just maybe without the title. Taking care of my family is why I became an assassin, and now I don't have to. They are safe and cared for here. Now, we finally have the life we only dreamed of.

After dinner, my mother, sister and I go into town, stopping at the seamstress' shop to get dresses before it closes. They need ballgowns and some new dresses that aren't stained from hard work and gardening. As I open the door, wanting to get them measured, a little bell dings, signaling that we arrived.

"Helloooo," a lady sings as a petite blonde woman walks out of the back room. "Oh, my lady, welcome in," she says with a curtsy. *Damn, word travelled fast.*

"Oh dear, that's not necessary. It's Anna. I'm here to get my sister and mother fitted for some dresses. I would love them to have custom gowns for our engagement ball," I explain.

"Dresses for the ball? I can do that!" she says excitedly, while running around and grabbing a tape measure, pins, parchment and a pen. "If you both would just stand in front of the mirrors, I will be over to get you measured in a moment."

I sit down in the armchair next to the mirror, allowing the seamstress to do her job. As she measures, wraps, and checks skin tones, she moves so fluidly it's like she was born to do this. It takes an hour, but when she's done; she seems to be glowing with pride and anticipation.

"You all are free to go. I'll sew these dresses and gowns and have them delivered to the castle as soon as they're finished!"

"Perfect, thank you so much," I say before turning towards the door. The bell jingles once again when we leave and our carriage is already waiting for us.

As soon as we are seated and the carriage is moving my mother says, "You seem to be adjusting well to royal life." I can't tell if she's happy or upset about it.

"I'm just trying to play the part," I say with a sigh. "I don't know what I'm doing, but I can trust and rely on Charlie to help me, so I'm trying my best. It's hard to not get overwhelmed with everything."

"I know, dear. I just want to make sure you are confident that you're doing a great job. It's a stressful time, but we'll get you through it, all of us." Reaching over to grab my hand in a comforting motion, a weight lifts off my shoulders. I don't want anyone to be uncomfortable here.

"Thank you, Mom." I lean over, squeezing as hard as I can. Knowing that people can see that I'm trying loosens the knots in my stomach. Royal life is hard, but missing someone is harder. *I can do this. It'll take time, but I know I can.*

Chapter Twenty-Five

Anna

WHEN WE ARRIVE BACK at the castle, my mom and Amelia wander back to their rooms to check on dad and rest after our long day. I head right into the sitting room, assuming that Charlie will be there. When I walk in and find it empty, I plop down onto the loveseat and pick up the closest book I can find. Thankfully, it's about the history of Weide Saliba, so I can learn more about the kingdom. I don't know how long I spend reading, but I only stop when I hear someone clearing their throat. Looking up, I find Avery standing in the doorway staring at me.

"Lady Anna, I was sent to find you. Prince Charles has requested your presence in his study." He bows at me as he extends his arm in the direction we need to go.

"Oh, thank you, Avery. Lead the way." I set the book down on the table and stand up, following right behind him as we walk down hallway after hallway. The twists and turns are more than enough to confuse me, especially considering the distance. Walking to the farthest wing of the castle is not something I want to do everyday. When we finally stop, Avery raises his fist, knocking on the door rather loudly.

"Come in," Charlie's voice calls from the other side of the door. Turning towards Avery I nod my head, stepping in front of him to open the door myself.

"You needed me?" I ask as I step in, closing the heavy door behind me with a bang.

"Yes, my flower, everyone is on their way in. I want to introduce you properly and give you the opportunity to listen in and help with getting guards to the shadowlands. Obviously, it is up to you if you stay."

"I'd love to stay. Thank you for including me."

"No thanks needed, my love. You are going to be queen, so you are welcome in all the meetings." As Charlie finishes that sentence, all his friends enter. Looking around, I realize that these five people are going to be the people I love and trust the most, outside of my family.

"Anna, I want you to officially meet Alex, Melanie, Lucas, Stephanie, and Drake." I observe each individual, trying to commit to memory who is who. When I meet the bright blue eyes of a man who is only slightly taller than me, he winks. I realize after a second that he is Alex. Continuing my scan I meet Melanie's gaze next. She smiles as I take her in, noticing how long her hair is as it reaches her lower back. A swish of bright blonde hair distracts me, causing me to turn and make eye contact with Stephanie, her friendly brown eyes causing me to soften. As I step closer to Charlie, Drake reaches for me to shake my hand, and I study his pale complexion. The man next to him looks very similar but much tanner, Lucas, I'm assuming.

"It's nice to officially meet you all. Are we ready to continue planning?" I ask everyone, causing us to buckle down and get to work.

It takes hours, but by the time we all retire for the night, we have a solid plan. Invitations are scheduled to be sent out in the morning, officially inviting all the kingdoms' royal families, including the Shadow Land rulers, and we have guards picked out to send. We decided to deploy ten guards in teams of two to cross the border in the most inconspicuous way possible. By the time we head to bed, I realize how draining being in charge of a whole kingdom can be.

"I don't know how you do it," I mumble to Charlie while collapsing into bed, still in my day dress.

"It's exhausting at first, but you adjust. Why don't you go take a bath to relax, and I'll have the handmaiden get you a

nightshirt," he suggests, helping me stand back up and pushing me gently towards the bath chamber.

"If that's your polite way of telling me I stink, it didn't
work," I tease, smiling at his deep chuckle as I close the door.
There is already steam rolling out of the bath, telling me that
the maids already filled it for me. I find the scented oils on the
edge of the tub, and start dumping a mix of lavender and citrus
in before undressing and climbing in. As I sink into the tub
I realize how much I need the heat to relax my body. I close
my eyes and lay my head back, letting the last few days sink
in. A week ago I was banished and working in a tavern and
now I'm helping run a country. I miss Ivy and Nick and I miss
the simplicity of that life, but I am so happy with how far I've
come.

After a while, my fingers prune and the water cools, so I
decide it's time to get out. When I get up, my handmaiden
comes in with a towel and a fresh nightshirt. After tying my
hair into a braid, I walk back into the room to find Charlie
already almost asleep in our bed. I climb into bed and lay my
head on his chest, exhaustion hitting me faster than I expected.

"Charlie, I love you," I whisper to him, my eyes drifting
closed.

"I love you too, my flower."

Chapter Twenty-Six

Anna

I WAKE UP TO Charlie climbing out of bed. It's well before daylight, so I roll over, burying my head into the pillow hoping I'll fall back asleep. Tossing and turning, I finally give up, sitting up just as my prince walks out of the bathroom, hair still wet.

"Sorry, love, I didn't mean to wake you," he says, looking surprised that I'm awake.

"No you didn't, love. I'm an early riser. What are you planning on doing today?"

"Just finalizing strategies for crossing into the Shadowlands with the guards. I'd love it if you could meet with Melanie and Stephanie to continue organizing the ball. Maybe ask your mother and your sister to join you so they feel included?"

My face lights up at the idea of letting my mother and sister help. "Yes, I think that's a great idea," I say, jumping out of bed to get ready. As I enter the closet to pick clothes for the day, a knock sounds on the door.

"Your Majesty, breakfast is served."

The door opens and shuts while I decide what to wear—a long flowy green dress with lots of detail. I change in the closet and walk out to eat breakfast. But when I get out, my hand-maid is there to get me ready with no Charlie in sight.

"Good morning, my lady. I see you're dressed. Why don't I help with your hair while you eat?"

"Okay," I say. At least I get to eat. "Can we do something simple today? I'm just finalizing ball plans."

"Absolutely. Let's just make this braid look a little more royal shall we?" And with that, she gets to work.

I find Melanie and Stephanie already on the plush, royal couch when I enter the sitting room. Papers, books, and writing utensils are spread out across the table, and the girls shuffle the items when they need to look at the other ones.

"Good morning, ladies," I say with a smile spread across my face, which they both warmly return.

"Good morning, Anna," Melanie says. "We are so excited for the ball, if you can't tell." She swings her arm over the papers they have everywhere.

"I am as well! My mother and sister are on their way, and I'm hoping they're just as excited." As I finish the sentence, they walk through the door.

"We are excited, Anna," my sister says, jabbing me with her elbow as she walks by.

"Ready to work?" my mother asks, taking a seat next to the young women.

"Ready!" the rest of us reply, nodding dramatically.

We pick flowers, theme colors, and paper for the invitations after flipping through as many books with ball information and ideas as we can find. I realize how clueless I am about color shades and flower types that aren't related to apothecary work, and pretty much anything when it comes to balls and royal stuff. However I do get a rough idea of what kind of dress I want, and we get close to everything being finalized.

After hours of planning and getting things finalized, the ball is ready. We have all the invitations done—poor Melanie got a cramp in her hand from all the calligraphy—and sent messengers out to deliver them to the surrounding kingdoms. This plan relies on the shadow kingdom traveling here so we can find Minerva there. I can't help but worry about that part of the strategy. As I walk toward my chamber, someone calls my name, causing me to jump. It's Melanie and Stephanie trying to catch up to me.

"Anna, we are getting drinks later at the tavern in the city, and we wanted to know if you wanted to join us?"

"Is it appropriate for me to be seen out drinking?" I ask cautiously, I'd love for them to be my friends, but I don't want to do anything that is frowned upon.

"We already talked to Charlie and told him what tavern we were going to, and he approved. We'd love for you to join us."

"Then yes, absolutely! I will meet you down here after dinner!" I tell them as they turn to head toward their chambers. After they're out of sight, I skip to my bedroom, excited about the possibility of them being my actual friends.

My door creaks open as I walk up. *Weird. Why is it open like that?* I step in as quietly as possible, only to find my handmaiden already in there, I guess waiting for me. I clear my throat, startling her.

"Hello Lady Anna, I'm here to get you ready for dinner."

"Oh, no need for the formalities. I am going to a tavern in the city with the girls after dinner, so I'd like to be in something comfortable!"

"You got it!" she says as she disappears into the closet looking for an outfit appropriate for dinner and the tavern. When she emerges with a pair of dark gray leather trousers and a long-sleeve light blue top, my face lights up. It's exactly what

I used to wear. "I have a corset for it, too. Hold on," she says, grabbing it from a drawer.

"It's...perfect," I say, shocked that she picked something so amazing out of my closet. "It's just like what I used to wear, before everything happened with Charlie" I explain. I strip and put on the outfit, the dark gray corset pulling in the pants, and grab some black high-laced boots out of the closet. After we fix my braid and add some accessories to the look, I stare at myself in the mirror with a huge smile. When Charlie walks in to get ready for dinner, he is stunned speechless.

"You're beautiful," he says. "If this is the woman I would've met at the ball, I don't think I would have been able to deny my feelings for so long. You look...happy"

"This just feels more like me." I say. "I've never been one for fancy dresses, but I am trying to get used to it. But since I'm going to the tavern tonight, I figured I should look the part."

He continues to stare at me like I'm the only thing in the world.

"You look perfect, please don't change yourself for me, you only need to wear the fancy dresses in the public eye." That sentence makes me feel more at home and accepted than anything else he could have ever said to me. Amelia was the dress girl, I was the trousers girl, and I'm ready to be me again.

Chapter Twenty-Seven

Anna

As someone who has only ever been close to her sister, heading towards a tavern with two girls I barely know is insanely out of my comfort zone. Thankfully, they bring me out of my shell with their fun chatter. The fact that they are willing to gossip with me and talk about boys makes me feel comfortable enough to interact, instead of retreating into myself, which is a big step in the right direction. By the time we arrive at the tavern, we're laughing so hard I don't even realize it. Thankfully, they aren't too busy, so it's easy for us to find a table.

Getting to know Melanie and Stephanie is easier than I expected. Even though they grew up in the palace, we still have a lot in common. They love reading and history, which leads us to talk about the history of Weide Saliba. All the magic users that used to live here are extinct because Charlie's great, great, great grandfather didn't trust them. He started a war against them, which they lost, pushing them off the continent. When the ones that did survive left, no one saw them again. Melanie and Stephanie weren't alive for that, but they did grow up around arguments about whether it was right or wrong when people would talk about it. Most people now lean towards it being wrong, but way back then, people loved the idea. They thought it wasn't fair that only some people were blessed with the gift of magic.

The conversation leads to a question I've been dreading. I didn't want to upset Charlie by asking him about his mother, but the girls have been in the palace their whole lives, so they're willing to tell me all about her.

"She was such a lovely person. And queen. She treated all of us kids like we were her own until the day she passed away. She got really sick, but never let us kids see her when it became bad." Stephanie blinks back tears, and she grabs a napkin to wipe her eyes.

"I wish I could've met her," I admit softly, "Her portraits show a kindness in her eyes I would've loved to have known."

The fact that Charlie has had to suffer without his mother for so long makes my chest ache.

"She would've loved you," Melanie says, a slight smile forming on her face. "And she would be so proud to have you as a daughter. And Charlie, he's going to be an amazing king."

Looking at my new friends, my heart fills with more warmth and gratitude than I've ever felt in my life. It lights something inside of me that I can't put words to. But I am going to be the best queen I can be for my friends, for my people, and for my king.

I smile at Melanie and Stephanie. "Thank you both for bringing me here and sharing part of your lives with me. But now it's time to drink!" I raise my hand, signaling the barkeep for another round, causing cheers to ring out from my companions.

After a few more drinks, we decide it's finally time to head home. The barkeep knows that the girls are part of the prince's household, so we don't have to pay anything when we leave, but I leave a few silver coins anyway as extra. We decide to walk home, our guards staying out of sight, so the girls can show me around a little bit. Even though most of the shops are closed, I learn about a bakery that, apparently, has delicious bread I must try. I also discover that the blacksmith sells already made daggers, which means I'll be visiting soon to purchase one, just in case. Making a mental note of the florist, so I can send my sister's fiancé there when he arrives to get her something, we round the final corner to go back to the castle.

In the shadows, something lurks. My stomach sinks. *Who is watching us?* I freeze, staring at the now still shadows, not being able to make out who is there. A chill creeps down my spine when my fingers discover none of my weapons are on my belt, or in my boot.

"Hey are you okay?" Stephanie asks. I glance over my shoulder at her, but when I turn back to the darkness, the figure is gone. "Uh, yeah. I thought I saw something, but it must just be the ale!" I say with a shrug, attempting to hide how my assassin senses are on high alert. Yes, I definitely will visit the blacksmith soon. "Let's get home. I'm exhausted." Linking my arms in theirs, I pull them towards the castle at a little quicker pace, the unease in my gut never fading.

As we walk in the door of the castle, I say goodnight and immediately head up to my chambers. I bathe and change into my nightdress, all senses heightened. If I could climb the castle wall, so could someone else. It's too dark to search for my weapons without a candle.

I ensure the bedroom window is bolted and the guards are on duty outside the door before crawling into bed. Charlie stirs, rolling over to pull me into him.

"Hi beautiful," he mumbles sleepily. "How was your night?

"I'll tell you all about it tomorrow," I whisper, snuggling into him his soothing warmth and hoping his scent will help me forget about the shadowy figure. But as he drifts back to sleep, all I can think about is Minerva and if she's hired someone else to kill him, or us. Restless sleep is all that finds me.

Chapter Twenty-Eight

Anna

I GIVE UP ON sleep before the sun rises. A run should clear my mind, so I silently slip out of bed, leaving Charlie fast asleep. With dexterous fingers, I braid my hair as I step into the closet, and pick out a flowy yellow top and trousers to wear. Hair done and clothing on, I shove my feet into my boots, and am about ready to leave when..."You're up early," Charlie says, awake with the blankets half removed and raising an eyebrow at me.

"I couldn't sleep, so I figured I'd go for a run and maybe brush up on my dagger practice since I haven't done anything in awhile." I start digging through the drawers in the room but find nothing. "Where are my daggers?"

"They are in the armory, in a special cabinet for only you. Let me get dressed and I'll take you!"

I plop onto the bed until Charlie is ready. He leads me down the halls, pointing toward different rooms I haven't seen before. I try to remember everything he's telling me, but there's so many I can't keep track. Charlie pulls out a keychain with more keys on it than I've ever seen in my life, then stops at our destination and unlocks the old door.

Machetes, daggers, swords, and who knows what else line the walls and counters. On the far wall is a locked cabinet that Charlie walks to. As he opens it, there are all my daggers, waiting for me. I run over, reaching for them, until Charlie grabs my arm to stop me.

"You can have them back, on one condition," he says looking at me with a straight face that concerns me.

"Okay?" I question, not knowing what he's going to say.

"You tell me what was bothering you so much you didn't sleep a wink."

My face drops. I was hoping he wouldn't notice. I feel crazy, because no one was there, so it shouldn't be bothering me.

"If I tell you, you're going to think I'm crazy. It's nothing."

"Please tell me. I can't help if I don't know."

"When we were on our way back to the palace last night, I thought I saw someone watching us, behind a building. It's the reason I wanna get some practice with the daggers, just in case."

Charlie frowns.

"Did you tell Melanie and Stephanie?" He asks, handing me my daggers.

"No, I didn't want to worry them if it's nothing," I say, accepting them. "It's probably nothing, but I just want to be safe. I've always been able to defend myself, and I don't want to stop now."

I've never felt defenseless like I did last night not having my daggers, and I don't want to feel like that again. Yes, I can defend myself in hand to hand combat, but I'm still a small woman and feel safer with my daggers. "I'd like to carry them again," I explain, flipping my daggers in my hands. "Just until Minerva is found, please. I'll make sure it's discreet."

"Of course you can have them again. We'll figure out a way to discreetly carry them when we're in public, and when we aren't, you can carry them however you want."

I sigh when Charlie finishes that sentence, so glad that I don't have to worry about arguing with him about this. I don't want to feel uncomfortable in my own home. In my own town. I'm going to be the queen and I deserve to be safe too.

Charlie directs me to the best place to run and get some target practice in, and then we go our separate ways so he can get some work done. While I'm running, Drake steps in front of me and I almost knock him over.

"Drake, what are you doing out here?" I ask him, breathing hard and wondering why he's out here instead of helping Charlie.

"I actually came out here to find you. Charlie told me about your trip back from town last night, and I wanted to check on you. Are you alright?" he asks me, concern lacing his voice.

"Umm, I think I'm alright. I just have high nerves, and don't want to be defenseless," I explain.

"Okay, well, let me know. And if you're worried, we can put a personal guard on you at all times."

"No. Please don't. I don't want someone following me around." I cannot imagine a guard trailing me all the time when I've always taken care of myself. "I can handle myself," I say firmly. "But I just don't want anyone to get hurt because of me."

While I know my new friends, Melanie and Stephanie, can handle themselves, I don't want to be the reason they need to. It's not fair to me or them.

"Okay," Drake says, though he doesn't sound like he thinks it's okay. "If you change your mind, or just want someone to train with, let me know." Then he turns and walks away.

"Wait!" I practically scream, making him stop and turn around with his eyebrow up. "I will take you up on that training offer." I laugh and then turn and go back to my run, waiting to see if he meets me at the field. It's way easier to practice hand to hand with a real person instead of a dummy.

When we get to the field I take the knife, hidden in a sheath, off my thigh and throw it in the grass where it stands at an angle in the dirt. Hopefully, we can practice hand to hand first. When I turn and look behind me, Drake is already in a stance to start practice.

"You coming, slow poke?" he asks with a smirk

I roll my eyes, then walk over and get in a starting stance.

"Don't cry when you get beat by a girl," I say with a laugh before reaching for him right as he dodges.

Chapter Twenty-Nine

Anna

TRAINING WITH DRAKE WAS a stress reliever. I got to brush up on my knife skills with someone who could actually dodge me. The hand to hand was harder, but he gave me pointers on how to use my small size to my advantage, which made it so much easier. I think after a few more training sessions, I'll be able to take down someone of any size, even without my dagger. We only train for a few hours before a rumbling stomach forces me to stop.

I tap out from our current battle before grabbing my dagger out of the grass.

"I'm starving. I could eat a horse." Drake motions toward the palace.

"Charlie probably hasn't eaten yet. We should grab him," I say.

Drake dips his chin in agreement, then without warning, blurts, "I'll beat you to the top!" He takes off, taking the stairs two at a time.

"Is everything a race with you?" I laugh and run to the top and race down to the study.

Busting the door open without even knocking first, I find Charlie sitting at his desk with his head in his hands. He looks up as I walk in and a smile spreads across his face. "How was training, my flower?"

"It's definitely easier to train with a partner. Thank you for sending him." I nod my head towards Drake as he walks in the door. "Even if I can beat him already," I finish saying with a laugh.

A sweet, elderly maid fetches us lunch while we tell Charlie about what we worked on today.

"I think we should all start combat training," Drake finally says looking between the two of us. "Just in case."

"I think that's a great idea!" I agree, before casting a glance at Charlie.

"I love that idea," he says. "Maybe you should invite Amy too?"

"Yes! And her fiancé is here, so I'll invite him," I say, setting my empty plate on his desk before I go find my sister. "Tomorrow morning then?" I ask Drake, wanting to make sure.

"Yup, same place as today."

I wander the hallways of the castle trying to find Amy and her fiancé. When I don't find her in the kitchen, sitting room, or her chambers, I try the garden as a last option. When I round the corner, I find them planting flowers while the gardeners are watering another part of the garden.

"Amy! You know we have gardeners for that right?" I ask while grabbing a pair of gloves to help them.

"I know, but I wanted to feel normal again. While I love living here and being with you, I miss doing stuff for myself," she says, sadness in her eyes.

"Yeah I get it," I say, thinking about home and a simpler life. "How about after the ball I get a garden for just you to work in?" When her face lights up and she starts nodding furiously. I know I made the right choice. I finish putting my gloves on and drop to my knees, helping her finish weeding and forgetting why I came out there to begin with.

Silently digging in the dirt, I let my mind wander to how we ended up here, then I remember why I'm out here. "What are the chances you both," I look right at her fiancé and then back to her, "would come and train with us? Like body strengthening and hand to hand fighting?"

"We'd love to! I think it's a great idea," my sister says, a smile spreading across her face.

"Perfect! I know it's not likely you'll need it, but just in case, I want you to know. We're meeting at sunrise tomorrow and starting with a run." I tell her, taking the gloves off so I can let Charlie know. After kissing Amy on her cheek, I turn around and head inside to look for him.

I head right to the study, assuming Charlie will be where I left him. I don't see any guards outside but check just in case and don't find him. *Weird.* I close the door and wander more of the castle, trying to think of where he would be. I check our chambers, and don't see him there either. The kitchen, dining room, and training areas are all empty as well. Finally, I hear laughter and follow it until I'm lead right to the sitting room. Charlie and Alex are sprawled out on the couch with a bottle of dark liquid between them.

"What are you two drinking?" I ask, crinkling my nose

"Something Alex brought back from his town. It is awful," Charlie says, taking another swig.

Rolling my eyes, I look between the two of them. "Are you sober enough for me to tell you about my conversation with Amy? It can wait until tomorrow if not." Despite my slight annoyance, I'm actually glad he's letting loose for the first time since we've been back.

"It should probably wait," he slurs, which makes me chuckle. "I am going to take a nap before dinner." When he tries to stand up I rush over, right as he starts to stumble. Thankfully, I catch him, yelling for Drake and Lucas so he can help me get these two to their rooms. I request for their dinners to be sent to them, since they definitely won't sleep this off in time.

I let Drake know my sister is joining us for training, then tuck Charlie into bed and head into the other room, ready for a hot bath. I slip into the bath and let my eyes fall closed, using the hot water as a way to relax my muscles. While I don't know how long I lay there in a trance, eventually, the water grows cold and my fingers become pruney. I finally crawl out of the bath and dry off, heading right to the closet to find something to wear. After digging through my closet, I find a flowy blouse in a beautiful light blue color that brings out my eyes. I grab my leather pants and my boots, getting dressed as quickly as possible and throwing my hair into a braid.

As I'm walking out of the closet, attaching my sheath to the thigh and putting my dagger that goes on my hip where it belongs, I see my handmaiden walking in. "Lady Anna, I came to get you ready for dinner, but I see you're already ready."

"Yes thank you..." *My mind blanked.* "What was your name again?"

"Abby! Do you need anything before dinner?"

"Abby, got it. Actually, if you don't mind redoing my hair so it's up more, that would be great" I sit down at the vanity, while Abby takes my hair out and brushes it before pulling it into a casual braided updo. Just like my sister used to do. "Wow.. it's just like how Amy used to do my hair. Thank you." I turn to her, startling her as I pull her into a hug.

"I asked her to show me some styles you like so we could make you feel more comfortable." She holds eye contact with me until I turn away from her. "I will be off now. Let me know if you need anything else."

"Perfect, thank you for everything, Abby!" She leaves me sitting there, wondering why I have such a bad feeling about someone who is so caring to me.

Chapter Thirty

Anna

AFTER A FEW DAYS of the same routine—wake up, train, eat, plan the ball, eat, sleep—it's finally the day of the day before the ball, the day everyone is due to arrive. I wake up more excited than I have felt in a long time. *It's almost time for the announcement. Almost time for the world to know.* There is also a knot in my stomach that I'm trying to ignore. Our plan will either go into motion today...or start a war, and we don't know which.

When I leave my chamber, I'm met with the hustle of servants and maids, hurrying to complete preparations. Heading to the dining room for breakfast, I light up at how busy it is in the castle. The more people arrive, the livelier the castle gets. The staff is running around to get people assigned to rooms. The chefs are making sure there is food on the tables at all times so no one goes hungry. Kings and queens who have already arrived are catching up with each other.

I wish the castle was like this all the time, full of life and happiness.

Charlie enters the dining room and takes a seat at the head of the table, and I walk over, kissing him on the cheek.

"Good morning, dear, how are you?" he asks, smiling at me before glancing around at everyone moving around the room. He looks like this is a normal day.

"Good morning, where are King and Queen Amorali?"

"They should arrive tomorrow morning, with plenty of time for a meeting before the ball," he explains to me, which makes the corners of my mouth upturn a little.

He knew exactly what I was worried about. I sit down to devour the delicious breakfast spread the chefs prepared, though even they can't beat mom's cinnamon oats.

When we're done with breakfast, I take my book about royal etiquette and head to the garden, hoping to get some reading in before preparing myself for the ball. I know the staff is decorating the ball room but they won't let me help. Apparently, manual labor isn't "queenly". They have requested that I come and approve the decorations later this evening though. I didn't grow up like this, so it's hard for me to sit around while people work, but I will get there.

After a couple hours of reading, I get up and head towards the ballroom to see how decorating is going so far. I walk in and my jaw drops. This looks like a whole new room. I never could have imagined how pretty this room could be. Every beam and column is covered in decorations, there are tables up with tablecloths ready to hold food, and the thrones are elevated.

"Why did you elevate the thrones?" I ask one of the maids as she walks by.

"Well, because once your engagement is announced, you get to sit up there milady," she says with a big smile before turning and walking away.

I didn't realize how real this would feel. I know we're engaged, but now it's going to be official. The whole continent will know, not just us. After the engagement announcement, we have to start wedding planning, then the coronation...I'm going to be the queen. My heart picks up along with my breathing.

I don't know how to be a queen. I don't even know how to be a princess. What am I going to do? Looking around the room, trying to calm my breathing, until I make eye contact with the one person in the room I can trust.

The room is crowded and loud, so I shout, "Abby!"

She jumps, startled, and rushes over to me.

With a wince, I calm down. "Oh, it wasn't that important. You didn't need to rush."

"Lady Annabelle, what can I help you with?" she asks, her face still flushed with surprise.

"Abby, can I tell you something? In confidence?" I ask, scared she might go and tell someone what I say.

"Of course! That's my job."

"I am kind of freaking out. I am supposed to be ready to step up and be queen in a few months but I don't even know how to be a princess. I need someone to teach me," I explain to her, glad I've calmed down a little, but still freaking out in my head.

"Oh! Lady Anna, that isn't something you should be stressing about. However, I will get something put together for you. I will find the royal tutor and between the two of us, we'll plan something to help you so you don't have to be stressed," she tells me, obviously able to perceive this is really bothering me.

"Thank you so much, Abby. We can start as soon as the ball is over. Is that alright with you?"

She levels a gentle gaze at me and holds up her pointer finger. "Lesson one, don't ask anyone's permission. *You* command people. *You're* in charge. But yes, I will get things set up for two days after the ball. You're going to want a day to rest, I promise." And then she turns and walks down the hallway, probably to go find the...tutor? Am I really about to get tutored on how to be a princess?

After I look at everything and approve it for the staff, I retire for the day, knowing I'm not going to get time to myself for the next few days. Plus, I still don't know which dress I'm going to wear tomorrow, so I need to decide that as well. I want it to be similar to the dress I wore the night I met the prince, but not the same. Deciding to look in my closet as soon as I get to my room, I swing the door open. I expect the room to be empty, but instead, I startle Abby who is pushing a drawer in my vanity closed.

"Oh, Lady Anna, I thought you were the prince," she stands up, leaning against the vanity like she's trying to hide something.

"What are you doing?" I ask, skeptical of all the staff still, but not wanting to accuse anyone of anything.

"I was making sure we had enough supplies to do your hair for the ball! I wanted to surprise you with a new hairdo," she explains, totally making sense.

I need to learn to be more trusting.

"Oh, well, thank you. Will we be needing anything for it?"

"No, ma'am. Would you like help to get ready for bed this evening?"

"No, thank you, Abby. You are dismissed."

She leaves my room, but the sinking feeling in my stomach won't go away. I won't accuse Abby of anything without proof, but I definitely am going to keep an eye on her. I change into my nightdress, forgetting completely about the fact that I still need a dress for the ball, before climbing into bed to get some sleep for the night.

I lay there staring at the ceiling when my stomach growls. *I should've asked Abby to send up a snack.* Right as I decide that I'm going to get up to get a glass of water and some fruit or something, Charlie opens the door, holding a tray. He sets it down on his bedside table to change, and I lean over to see fruit and two glasses of water on the tray. All the worries vanish when I realize how in love with me this man is.

"I wanted a late night snack so I figured you'd want one too," he explains when I grab my water and start snacking.

"It's like you read my mind," I say with a huge smile and then start giggling, so happy we found each other. Eventually we fall asleep, and that is the best I have slept in weeks. No worries about Minerva or the weird figure I saw in town. Just peaceful dreams about the future.

Chapter Thirty-One

Anna

I WAKE UP REFRESHED and excited. Today is the day of the ball, and tomorrow I start my princess training. I roll over to a cold bed, meaning Charlie has been up for a while already. Stretching and climbing out of bed, I grab a dress to wear for breakfast, since I have time before the ball. I know I need to bathe beforehand also, but I hear water filling the tub right now, so that will have to wait.

Right as I sit down in front of the vanity to do something with my hair, Charlie emerges, dressed but still drying his hair.

"Good morning, beautiful," he says, leaning down to kiss me on the cheek. "I'll probably be busy most of the morning, but we are going to be notified when King and Queen Amoreli get here, so I will see you then!"

"Okay, should I be ready for the ball at that meeting? Or will we have time after?" I ask, not really sure what I should be doing.

"That would be best! We don't want to be late to our own party." Laughing, he sets the towel down and heads out of the room.

I finish putting my hair up, not even having a minute to myself when a knock sounds on the door.

Today is going to be a busy day.

"Come in," I call, hoping whoever is on the other side of the door is a friend and not staff. Thankfully, Melanie and Stephanie walk through the door.

"Good morning, Anna! We were wondering if your mother and Amelia would like to get ready for the ball with us? I think it'd be a nice bonding experience."

My face lights up, glad they want to include my family in these things too.

"I love that idea! I will talk to them after breakfast. Would you like to join me? I think I'm going to take mine in the sitting room today for some peace and quiet before our crazy evening." If having friends means inviting them to do things with me, then this is a good start, right?

They both nod their heads furiously with huge smiles on their faces. It's contagious, and a smile spreads across mine too. After agreeing to meet in the sitting room, I head to talk to my mother and Amy and see what they want to do. They decide not to go to breakfast but agree to get ready with us in my room, so I give them a timeline for that.

Breakfast is set up already by the time I get to the sitting room, and it's calm and quiet. Melanie and Stephanie brief me on how the ball is going to be and how things will run. When we finally get back up to my chambers, Abby is standing there with a garment bag, and my mother and sister are sitting on the bed waiting for us.

The rest of the morning and afternoon is spent scrubbing and styling. When it's finally time to put our dresses on, Abby opens the bag to reveal the most beautiful dress I've ever seen. My gown is a light yellow dress with a corset top and a big skirt. It was white down the center of the top with little yellow flowers that just made it perfect. It's almost exactly like the dress from the night we met but just different enough to not bring up bad memories.

We go into the closet, and Abby helps me into it, cinching the corset up as tight as it will go. When I come out of the closet, all the girls are dressed, and they look beautiful. Stephanie chose a beautiful light blue dress while Melanie decided to wear a deep red dress, both of which made their eyes pop. Both my mom and my sister chose to wear emerald-colored dresses with lots of gold accents, which look beautiful against their skin tones.

"Wow, you all look stunning," I say. My heart flutters in anticipation and with gratitude for my family and new friends.

"So do you," Amy says, walking over to hug me.

We all take turns getting our hair done and our faces powdered. Abby surprises me with a beautiful half up bun with curls on the bottom. I've never felt more beautiful than I do at this moment. Spinning in a circle, I smile at myself in the mirror.

I feel like an actual princess.

Charlie walks in as I'm twirling.

"Wow, you look beautiful, my flower," he says. "As beautiful as the night we met."

"That was the goal," I say with a laugh, before grabbing his hand, ready to head into this meeting. "I'm nervous. What are we going to do if they say no?" I whisper, scared to look weak but also needing him to help me be prepared.

"The army is already there, and they started searching as soon as the king and queen left the country. We will find her with or without their help," he explains, putting his hands on my shoulders to reassure me. *Hopefully they just agree to the plan.*

After promising my mom and sister that we would meet them at the ball soon, Charlies and I walk to the study with our friends following behind. The closer we get, the more I wipe sweaty hands on my dress.

There's no way they won't agree.

As we stop at the study, I take a few deep breaths, slowing my heart rate before we enter.

"You ready?" Charlie asks, placing his hand on my lower back.

"As ready as I'll ever be," I tell him, taking one more deep inhale as he opens the door.

As it opens, King and Queen Amoreli stand, turning slightly to look at us. Charlie bows, so I curtsey, while they return the respectful gestures.

The queen is tall with dark black hair and irises that appear black but in brighter lights are actually a deep-hued brown. I have never seen anyone more beautiful. Flicking my gaze to the king, I notice he is almost as tall as Charlie. He has graying black hair and dark blue eyes with a soft face, like he's tired. As we straighten, Charlie and I walk around the desk, our friends filing into the room behind us.

"Thank you both for meeting with us," Charlie says, sitting down, the king and queen following suit.

"Your correspondence made it seem very urgent," The king says.

I watch the queen in an attempt to see how she reacts, hoping not to step on any toes.

"Yes, it is. Former Queen Minerva has escaped from our prison, and we believe that she has fled to your country. She tried to kill me along with Lady Anna, and we would like the threat back in our dungeon as soon as possible. We are requesting permission to come in and search for her in exchange for guaranteed military aid should you ever need an ally." While he's explaining to them, I am totally starstruck that he can stay so calm. "We also have reason to believe she poisoned the late king in an attempt to take over the throne."

I survey their expressions, and neither of them look like they believe us.

Then the queen *laughs*!

The nerve! We all glance among ourselves, confused about why they think this is funny.

Then the king levels a glare at us. "We would love to believe you, except that we identified a number of *your* regiments on the edge of our country when we left. Are you planning on raiding us either way?"

I start to panic. Trying to keep my face calm, I take a few shallow breaths, hoping to slow my breathing. *Everything will be fine.*

"Of course not," Charlie says, poker face still intact. "They are waiting for us to make a deal before we send orders to search for our prisoner," he explains. He doesn't even flinch at the staredown he's getting from the king and queen.

"You have our permission. Send word. However, if I suspect for one minute that you will betray us, know that we have people everywhere, including in this castle. I will not hesitate to go to war with you and take your country over as my own. Understood?"

Charlie stands, shaking their hands and thanking them for allowing us to hunt down Minerva. I wipe my hands on my dress before reaching over and shaking their hands as well. *I don't know how Charlie does this. They threatened war, and he's acting like they didn't.*

"I have a room prepared for you to stay this evening. Please follow our most trusted guard to the ballroom and enjoy the festivities. We will be there shortly," I say, hoping my voice isn't shaky with nerves.

"Thank you. We will stay. See you at the ball," the queen says with a curtsey. I curtsey back, and they head out of the study.

As soon as the door closes we all let out a breath of relief. "I can't believe that worked," I say. We celebrate for a minute before dusting ourselves off and making our way downstairs to the ball.

As we arrive at the ballroom entrance, Charlie squeezes my hand one more time while we wait for the announcement.

"You ready?" he asks, looking at me like I'm the only one in the room.

"Beyond ready," I say, squeezing his hand back.

We hear, "Regent King Charles Greystone," and the doors open. I stand there and wait until my name is called.

"Lady Annabelle Marie."

The doors open once again, and I step in, thankful that Charlie stopped halfway down the stairs. I focus on my steps as I descend so I don't trip and fall in front of all these people. As I reach Charlie, he grabs my hand to lead me the rest of the way. *It's show time.*

Reaching the bottom of the stairs, Charlie pulls me onto the dance floor, opening the ball. After a waltz, we move to the thrones, preparing to shake hands as Charlie introduces me to people. As everyone dances and socializes, I realize why some people enjoy being royals. Sometimes it's not about the money or the fame, or the title, it's about the people, and the relationships you make on the way.

Chapter Thirty-Two

Anna

THE BALL GOES ON well into the night. Hours of dancing, mingling, and eating, but it goes by much faster than I expected. As people start to return to their chambers, some decide to take a stroll through the garden.

Standing up from the throne and kissing Charlie, I whisper in his ear, "I need some air," before ambling out to our bench in the garden. My heart fills with joy, seeing all the work my sister put into the garden and observing everyone enjoying it. Looking around also feels like a slap in the face. I'm the only one who hasn't made the castle home. *It's time to make a change.*

When I start yawning, I decide it's probably time to head in for the night. As I rise from my seat and brush my dress off, a noise behind me make my heart jump.

I turn around. "Charlie? Honey, is that you?"

There aren't very many people that know about this bench, so it has to be Charlie. No one responds, so I shrug and step toward the path leading inside, but hear a noise behind me again. I open my mouth to call out again, but everything goes dark...

Charlie

As the last person leaves for the evening, I walk out to the garden to find Anna. The staff starts cleaning up the ballroom immediately, which I'm very thankful for. I make a beeline toward the bench where Anna usually sits.

She's not there. Odd. I wander around the pebbled paths a little more, admiring Amy's handiwork while I look for my fiancé.

"Anna, my flower? Are you out here?" I ask. When she doesn't respond, I realize she must have already gone to our room.

As I near the palace, I notice something out of the corner of my eye. A yellow ribbon lies on the ground. It's just like the one Anna wore in tonight.

The hairs on the back of my neck stand up, but I'm hoping it just fell out and she didn't notice. I grab it and take the stairs two at a time to reach our chamber.

But the door is already open and creaking on its hinges. I walk into an empty room.

"Anna?" I ask, heartbeat speeding up as my concern multiplies. *What is going on?*

I check the sitting room, closet, and bathing chambers just in case before glancing in the hall, only to be startled that Avery is standing just outside my door.

"Avery, has Anna arrived here yet? I didn't find her in the garden." I try to keep my voice calm, but fail miserably.

"No, sir, she hasn't. I'll have some guards search the castle," Avery says, turning around to go do that without an answer.

I close the door and pace the room, dread settling in the pit of my stomach. It feels like I wait for hours, until Avery finally bursts into the space, horror on his face.

"They aren't here." He says, hands on his knees, breathing extremely heavily.

"Who's they?" I ask. When Drake, Lucas, Melanie, Stephanie and Alex walk in behind Avery, my heart drops to my stomach.

"The Amoreli's, Abby, and Anna, we can't find them any-where." Melanie says, tears filling her eyes.

"Find them. Find them now." I say, trying to slow my breathing but not being able to. The last thing I see is Drake running towards me, right as my legs lose all feeling and the world goes black.

Chapter Thirty-Three

Anna

I WAKE UP, OR at least I think I'm awake. Everything is dark. My whole body throbs in pain, and for some weird reason, I'm lying on my hands. When I try to move them, I can't. Something soft but unrelenting twists around them, restraining me.

The whole evening comes flooding back to me. The ball, going to the garden, the sounds and shadow behind me...

Shit, I was kidnapped. I open my mouth to scream, but nothing comes out. Closing my mouth again, I feel cloth over my mouth. Suppressing the urge to panic, I slowly start trying to take note of what I already know.

I'm blindfolded, or at least I think I am since it's so dark. My hands are tied behind my back and I'm gagged. Thankfully, my nose is uncovered so I can still take deep, unencumbered breaths. I try to stretch my legs, and those are also tied together.

I quiet my breathing and listen as closely as I can. Horse hooves clatter nearby, but I'm lying flat, so I must be in a carriage or wagon of some sort. That means someone from high society kidnapped me.

You'll be okay, Anna. Charlie will find you.

As the hoof beats slow, my heart rate speeds up. *What's going on? Why are we stopping?* I do my best to make my breathing slow and shallow like I'm sleeping. That is until the blindfold suddenly gets ripped from my eyes.

"Wake up, *princess*" a voice I recognize sneers.

My eyes finally adjust to the light, and my eyes widen at the familiar face.

"Yeah, yeah, I know. 'Oh, no! I can't believe my own maid would betray me after I treated her with such respect!' And I have to admit, the respect did make it harder to do it, but I couldn't say no to the kind of money they offered me for you. Of course, they had to play into my plan and pretend like they supported you guys, or else it'd be too suspicious."

The longer she babbles on, the more confused I get. Who are 'they' and why do they want me kidnapped?

She rips the gag out of my mouth, and forces water down my throat. I cough it back up. My mouth is so dry that I can barely swallow the water fast enough though. She puts a slice of bread in my mouth, preventing me from speaking until I chew and swallow it. "Why?" I try to croak out but she doesn't hear me.

"I'll help you relieve yourself since I can't untie you. I was told to deliver you alive, and clean if possible," she says, scrunching her nose when she looks me up and down. She drags me to the woods by the rope and my wrists and gives me exactly one minute to relieve myself before dragging me back to the carriage.

I need to make an escape plan.

When she puts the gag back over my mouth, I black out once again, giving me no time to make a plan.

Charlie

When I regain consciousness, I'm in my bed, surrounded by all my closest friends. Confusion blurs my mind. I sit up as slowly as possible, until everything comes rushing back to me. Then I rush to get out of bed. Drake puts his hands on my shoulders, right as I get dizzy.

"Charlie, you need to slow down," Drake says, forcing me to lay back on the bed.

"I can't slow down. My fiancé is missing, Drake!" I shout, instantly regretting it when I see the hurt on his face.

"Charlie, we know," Melanie says with sadness in her eyes. "And we have everyone on it except for the people in this room. We need you to be at your best before you can do anything."

"What if she's dead by the time we find her?" I ask, tears welling in my eyes.

"We hope the army finds her first," Stephanie whispers.

I know they're right, but it takes everything inside of me to just lay down. I make them walk me through the plan with the army, which consists of them searching everywhere they can while they also search for Minerva on top of having someone discretely follow King and Queen Amoreli, just in case she's with them.

Thankfully, it only takes a few days for me to be back to my normal self, so we gather in the study to make a plan to get into the Shadowland's castle. We told all the armies to work towards the fortress, so everyone is there when we arrive. However, we still have small brigades placed throughout the country for emergencies. We also are digging through Abby's employment papers to see what her ties are, even though most of it seems made up.

As regent I have to be the one to arrive at the castle and bring up the issue. I still haven't figured out how I'm going to do it without being emotional, but that's part of my job. I'm going to tell them that we're searching everywhere, even if it is mostly within their kingdom, because the future queen was kidnapped. As long as I stick to the plan, everything will be fine...

Anna

I don't know what day it is, or how long I've been gone. It could be days, weeks, or even months, and I wouldn't know. We quit moving, and I'm in a dungeon somewhere, still being drugged somehow. If I was Charlie, I would have given up searching for me by now, so I'm sure he has. As long as he keeps my family safe, it doesn't matter. They're all that matters.

Part Two

Chapter Thirty-Four

Charlie

WHY DO YOU NEVER realize how far away something is until it's an emergency? That's how I feel about Veirda Shadow. The border doesn't seem very far, but the castle is in the middle of the country, so the trip is long. It takes a few days to get there, but when we arrive, we are shocked.

The castle is smaller than most. In fact, our castle is three times the size, and it's on the small end. This area is also very dark. I understand why people call it the Shadowlands.

Normally when a royal comes for a visit, there are people awaiting their arrival, but there is no one when we get there, which is also weird. I climb out of the carriage and walk toward the castle entrance, hoping to find someone inside, but the doors are locked. I turn to look at my friends, who all appear as confused as I do. *What the hell is going on?*

We decide to head to the stables, assuming there is someone taking care of their horses. Thankfully, there is a stable hand down there, so I wave, trying to get his attention.

"Hello sir!" I shout, as he starts coming towards me. "I am the Regent King from Weide Saliba, I'm looking for your king and queen. I sent word to them that I was coming." I try to stay as calm as possible but inside, the anger rises.

The stablehand bows when he finally gets close enough to be in speaking distance.

"Hello sir. I apologize, but they won't be back for a few days. Something political, I believe. I can have someone set up a room if needed, or we can send you to the local inn, free of charge, of course."

"I would love directions to the local inn if you don't mind." This whole thing feels suspicious, and I don't need prying ears listening in behind drafty cracks in the walls.

When I exit the stables, I give my footman the directions to the inn and climb in. We need to come up with a backup plan.

Once we're settled into our rooms, everyone meets in my chamber, so we can strategize how we want to get into the castle. We only meet for an hour before the exhaustion from traveling hits, and I send everyone off for the night, knowing we all need sleep for this mission.

We rise early , aiming to arrive at the castle before the king and queen do. After a restless night, I need a good breakfast to boost my energy. Walking into the tavern attached to the inn, I see a familiar face from across the room, one whom I haven't seen since Anna's first day at the castle. I find a table to sit at until all my friends join me, and point at Diane when they walk in. Drake's face instantly drops at the sight of her, sadness in his eyes.

"Diane! What are you doing here? I thought you've been traveling?" Melanie says to her, throwing me a concerned glance.

Jumping out of her chair at the sound of Melanie's voice, Diane whips around to look at us, knocking her chair over in the process. "Guys! What are you doing here? I am traveling, so I decided to check out the country when I was passing through!" The story seems rather suspicious, especially since no one travels to the Shadowlands, and it happens to be at the same time as Anna's disappearance. A suspicion forms in my head.

With a shrug, I say, "Oh, well, Anna went missing, so we're trying to find her. We believe the maid, Abby, had something to do with it, and she was seen going in this direction."

The faux shock on her face tells me everything I need to know. *She knows more than she's letting on.*

"After breakfast we are planning on heading back to the castle, would you like to come?" I ask.

"The castle?!" she repeats my words quickly, "do you think the king and queen have something to do with it?" If she's trying to pull the panic out of her voice, she's not doing a good job.

"No, of course not," I lie. "I just want to see if we can get some help locating her."

I hope she'll slip up and give something away.

"Oh, well, I don't think I can come along this time. As much as I'd love to meet them, I'm in a hurry. I'm hoping to be home by the time you guys do!" She rushes out, calling over her shoulder "I'll be off. See you all when I get back." Then she's gone barely glancing at the people she was eating with. I look over at them and make eye contact. Hatred slips through their stoic masks before they get up and follow Diane.

"That was weird right?" Stephanie asks behind me, definitely thinking the same thing I was.

"It was very weird," I agree. "Have someone follow her; she's up to something."

Lucas jumps up, immediately volunteering, which I'm grateful for since I know I can trust him.

After breakfast, we revisit the castle, planning to wait until the king and queen get back. Having a lead with Diane being followed is helpful for my nerves as well. If she knows something, Lucas will figure it out. We are greeted by a servant at the palace entrance this time, which is better at least.

"Hello, Your Majesty," he says with a bow. "We are sorry for the unwarm welcome, however the king and queen are very busy with political relationships, so they will not be back for a while. They have given me permission to house you in the guest wing as long as you agree to not wander the castle and only use it as a place to rest your head."

Their behavior makes me more suspicious of them.

I clear my throat before responding with a firm tone, "Will you be providing meals as well? If not we'd prefer to use the inn to rest. We are trying to find my betrothed, and I would like all the help we can get." I expect they will relay our message to the king and queen.

"I am so sorry she is missing, however we cannot offer any help until the king and queen return. Feel free to search for her while you are looking for Minerva, and if one of your trusted advisors would like to search the castle we can allow that, accompanied by our guards, of course. No more than one though," he says.

I look at Drake, silently communicating that I want that one trusted advisor to be him. He nods, and I know he won't leave one stone unturned.

"Drake will be the one to search the castle, please. Thank you for allowing this concession. We also wanted to know if one of my advisors, Diane, has come here before?"

"Diane? No sir. The only Diane we know is Lord and Lady Mortimer's daughter. As she advises our royalty, she couldn't possibly be the one you seek," he says in a tone far too haughty for my taste.

"Okay, thank you. We will wait out here until Drake searches the castle, and then we will be off back to the inn, thank you," I tell him, glancing at the rest of my party. Can they sense my concern?

Drake doesn't take long to search the whole castle given the underwhelming size, but it feels like an eternity. When he walks out shaking his head, I know that's a dead end. As Drake climbs into the carriage to head back to the inn, my mind swims with all the possibilities, the most likely one screaming at me.

You're probably too late. You won't be able to save her. What happened to her?

I don't remember the ride back to the inn, but we make it back, eventually.

Anna

The dreams stop coming eventually, and it's just darkness. Who am I waiting for? Where am I? Why is everything so dark? This can't be good at all.

Chapter Thirty-Five

Charlie

TRYING TO GO THROUGH what little information we have without freaking myself out is harder than I thought. I parse through the facts: Anna isn't at the castle, we think Abby took her, and we suspect Diane had something to do with it.

That's not enough factual insight to be helpful. And we definitely don't know where to go from here. When I finally get to my room, I black out. I don't know if it's from fear or misery, I just know that I don't remember anything until I see my friends standing there, staring at me like I have three heads. I look around confused.

Why is my room a mess? How did they get in here when I locked the door?

"What's going on?" I ask.

"We heard you freaking out and hurried over. I had to pick the lock." Alex says, concern written all over his face. *Well, that explains how they got in.*

"Did I do this?" I ask, gesturing at all the scattered papers on the floor. I lose all train of thought when I see *Diane* written in big bold letters on the top of a file. I pick it up and sift through it. Is there anything about Diane's parents in here?

I skim through it, flipping page after page, only seeing our former nursemaid listed as a parent, but she had no kids. "Hey, did any of you ever meet Diane's parents?" I ask, trying to figure out this puzzle.

Everyone looks at each other, wide eyes and furrowed brow betraying their ignorance. "No, I'm pretty sure she came to the castle as an orphan at twelve years old," Melanie says, tapping her chin as she tries to remember that far back. "I'm pretty sure our former nursemaid took her in, Lady Elizabeth."

"Why couldn't the guards find her parents, though? They couldn't have moved that far that quickly." I say, the pieces clicking together. "Unless they wanted her lost."

Understanding forms in my mind. Her parents are here. They were trying to infiltrate the castle, and she was their way in. "She has something to do with this. Send two more guards to find and relieve Lucas. He needs to report to me immediately with any information he has recovered." The tone of my voice leaves no room for argument and they jump up, prepared to follow orders.

I sort through papers, searching for anything I might have missed while I wait. When a knock sounds on the door, I continue digging before shouting "come in." I wait until the footsteps are right next to me before I finally look up from the papers.

"Hey Lucas, I know you weren't following her for long, but do you have any information?"

He glances at me, then the map, then back at me before he starts talking. "She met up with a couple after leaving here. They travelled east, I'm guessing towards their home as they didn't seem in a rush, and the guards you sent to relieve me caught up to us as they were arriving at a manor. It looked like a lord's estate in our country, but much darker. They also all seemed very familiar with each other, like they're friends or at least have met before. I'm unsure what they were saying since I couldn't get too close, but they were laughing and talking the whole way there, which seemed weird to me since they were so serious in the tavern." Lucas finishes up while I absorb and make sure to note everything he said.

"Do you think that you can point to it on the—" I ask him, just in case the guards don't remember. Before I even finish my sentence, he's setting a marker down at the manor's location. Nodding, I dismiss him, asking him to catch the others up before morning. I head to bed, knowing that I'm no good as a leader without sleep. Bad sleep is better than no sleep in most cases.

Chapter Thirty-Six

Charlie

WE WAKE UP EARLY the next morning, well before the sun is up, to figure out how to search the manor without being caught. Knowing Diane as well as we do, once she realizes we're suspicious of her, there is a chance she'll do something rash to protect herself.

Once everyone is gathered in my room, I nod at Lucas, giving him permission to take the lead. "Okay. here's what we know," he starts, getting everyone's attention. "The manor is here." He points at the marker he placed on my map yesterday. "There were three people, plus some staff. I only saw two staff members going in and out yesterday, so if there's more, they don't leave. No one guards the doors." He relays everything he told me last night to the rest of the staff, making sure everyone is listening. Picking the guards that have already eaten, I send them to replace the guards currently following Diane, and send everyone else to get eat.

"I hope these guards were able to get some more information," I mumble to myself before I start pacing. I don't stop until I hear a knock on the door. Running over to it, I whip it open to find my friends and the two guards standing there staring at me. Melanie holds a plate of food.

"You're just as hungry as the rest of us, and you're no good to us with an empty stomach." She shoves the plate of food into my hand and waves us towards the table so I can eat while we debrief the guards.

"I know you're right. But I'm also too anxious to eat" I tell her, looking at the plate she gave me.

"You at least need to try."

I nod at her in agreement because she is right. I'm no good on an empty stomach.

Thankfully, since everyone was sleeping, they were able to get us a better idea of the layout of the house, so we know what we're walking into. And they found the servant's entrance, which is how we'll sneak in. We just need to discover their schedule now to find a good time to do it.

After only a day of watching, we learn that all the staff except for one go on lunch at the same time. One individual is there to act as a guard, but they don't seem to be trained in any form of combat. As I get everyone gathered in my room, I raise my hand to silence everyone.

"Okay, we have one guard on watch duty in case anyone leaves, but we have a plan figured out. At about midday, the servants all go on lunch and there is only one guard in the manor because it is so small. So, if we send Drake and Alex in since they are the strongest and sneakiest, they can search the manor without getting caught. Then, if they find Lady Anna, they will come back to the service entrance and signal before rushing back to her. At that point, we will storm the manor to cause a huge distraction so they can get her out. Does everyone understand?"

I wait for everyone to nod before I continue. "Storming the manor may cause a fight, and if that's the case, lives could be lost. Are you all sure you want to do this? I will never force you to put your life at risk for my own personal gain." I wait and see if anyone wants to back out, knowing it's possible. I don't want anyone to put their lives at risk without knowing.

"Its not just for your gain," Melanie speaks first, ending the silence as everyone starts to agree.

"Lady Anna will be our queen, so it's for the country, and we will all put our lives at risk for that," one of the guards says, while everyone else grunts in agreement.

"Okay, then everyone get some rest tonight. Tomorrow, we get our queen back. You're all dismissed."

Everyone filters out, a weight leaving my shoulders knowing that we're taking another step closer to finding my flower. That night, the nightmares don't plague me, and the hope slowly comes back that, maybe, Anna still is alive.

Anna

I don't know how long I have been here, but I haven't been awake for most of it. They let the intoxicants wear off long enough to give me food and water, and then I'm drugged again. I briefly thought I heard someone mentioning needing to move me because the prince was here and suspicious of them, but I haven't been moved yet. At least, I don't think so. I hope Charlie finds me soon. I really miss him.

Chapter Thirty-Seven

Charlie

WE NEED TO BE at the manor by sunrise in order to search for Anna, so the stars are still visible when we approach the manor. Moonlight guides us. My guards spread throughout the village, prepared in case they try to make an escape with Anna. The rest of us get into position. Drake and Alex wait for the signal to sneak in while the rest of us watch for guards.

When we hear the low pitched whistle, we know Drake and Alex are slipping inside. The next few minutes feel like they're going in slow motion.

Drake and Alex rush out of the entrance, panic plain on their faces even in the dim light. They make eye contact with me, and I abandon all of my plans and sprint toward them. I need to save my girl.

Thankfully, Lucas is thinking for me and distributes the signal. Everyone storms the manor, creating the distraction I need. The blood rushing in my head is all I can hear by the time Drake and Alex lead me into the manor and down some stairs into the basement. When the door creaks open and I make it through, my heart stops at the sight. Laying there, unconscious and in chains, is my poor Anna.

I rush over and lift her limp head and fight back an enraged sob at her condition.

She is so pale, and her already petite form appears fragile from starvation. She's still wearing the ballgown from when they kidnapped her. How many days has it been? Fourteen? Fifteen?

My flower has wilted within this place.

I gently rub her sternum in an attempt to coax her awake. Her heart beats slowly...faintly.

"Anna, my love, please wake up," I whisper.

A metallic clink draws my attention to Alex picking the locks holding her wrists. "Please, my flower. Please be alright."

Stubborn tears run down my face. As soon as she's out of the chains, I pick her up and follow Drake up the stairs. I'm so focused on how thin she's become in such a short time that I barely hear the commotion of the fighting. As I get closer to the door screams pierce the night.

"Alex. Drake. I've got Anna. Go help them!" I command. They obey.

I continue to rush Anna away from this horrible manor, and toward the inn where I can help her.

I haven't gone far before I hear Diane's voice. A quick glance behind me reveals Diane flung over Drake's shoulder, struggling in his hold and yelling, "I don't know anything!" I can feel the anger radiating off him even from here.

Melanie catches up to me and I send her ahead to fetch a healer in hopes they'll be to the inn quicker. My arms ache not from Anna's size, but from the distance. When I finally get to the inn, and haul her limp body up the stairs and set Anna down gently on the bed. I collapse in the chair next to her, recovering my breath before the healer arrives.

Anna

I hear voices in my dreams, it sounds like Charlie. But Charlie can't be here though. He's not looking for me...Abby said he'd given up. I've been gone for too long.

"Anna, please wake up. Please be okay. Please, I need—I need you to stay with me."

My eyes slowly open as a warm hand touches my face. The most beautiful chocolate brown eyes I've ever seen stare at me. I'd know those eyes anywhere.

"Charlie," I croak. My mouth is dry as dirt and my words are barely audible. How long has it been since I last talked?

"Anna, oh my god, you're okay." He starts crying harder and just holds me. Tears gather in my eyes. I can't believe he found me. I can't believe he saved me and I'm not in that dark, damp dungeon anymore. When he finally loosens his grip on me, I look around the room.

We aren't at the castle. Is this an inn? I think that's where we are, at least. I can't really tell though. I also realize almost everyone is here. Melanie, Alex, Stephanie, Lucas, and Drake crowd the room. Confusion crosses my face. I would think since everyone else is here, Diane would be too.

"Water," I croak, simply because it's all I can get out. Someone I've never seen before rushes over with a glass of water.

"Lady Anna, I am Madeline, the town's healer. You went through some major trauma and you were deprived of water and food for a really long time. You aren't ready to travel yet, so you will be staying here for the time being while I keep an eye on you. I know this is a lot of information, but I have also told the prince this so you don't have to stress about it. I just wanted you to know. You're also going to want to eat very small portions and slowly work up your appetite so you don't get sick. Sip this water and I will be back in a few hours to check on you," she says, handing the water to Charlie, probably knowing I'm too weak to hold a glass right now. Charlie slowly helps me sip the water until I feel like I've had enough.

"Did you get Abby?" I croak as soon as Melanie leaves the room, itchiness still in my throat.

"Abby?" Charlie asks, concern lining his face. He glances at Drake and nods. Wordlessly, Drake turns and walks out of the room. "We'll look for her too."

"What do you mean, too?" I ask.

Charlie looks up at our friends, and then they nod their heads and leave the room. "My flower, Diane staged the kidnapping," he explains, with a solemn look on his face. "We were waiting until you woke up, but we have her locked in a room at the inn right now, and we will be sending Drake ahead with some guards to get her back to the castle for interrogation."

I start breathing heavily, almost panting, and feel like I'm going to pass out. This information is too much for me to handle. *Slow breaths, Anna. You have to take slow breaths.*

The fear in Charlie's eyes helps calm me. He saved me. I'm not allowed to worry him anymore. When my breathing is slow enough to speak, even with my heart beating out of my chest, I tell Charlie what I remember. "Someone paid Abby to kidnap me. She confessed that she couldn't pass up the kind of money she was getting. But I don't understand how Diane could do that to us."

I thought she was our friend. On our side. Not the enemy.

"I know, my love. We have her and we will get to the bottom of all of this. And we will find Abby. As soon as you are well enough to travel home, we can send a search party out for her." Charlie rubs his hands up and down my arms, trying to help calm my nerves.

"Did you at least find Minerva while you were here?" I ask, hoping when we get back we might actually get to experience our happily ever after.

"Not yet, my love. However, because we didn't come across her while searching for you, we don't believe she is here. Once you're better, we'll resume the search for her as well. Please stop stressing about stuff until then." he explains to me, "why don't you try to get some sleep and I'll send Melanie for some bread and soup for you from the tavern?"

When my stomach starts growling, I take that as a good sign. I nod my head at Charlie before laying down comfortably for the first time in a long time...

Chapter Thirty-Eight

Anna

NEXT THING I KNOW, I'm being lightly shaken awake. When I open my eyes and sit up, I'm met with the most delicious aroma. I look around and see Charlie in the room along with the healer, who is holding a bowl.

"What's in there?" I ask a little too enthusiastically, realizing how hungry I truly am.

"It's chicken broth. I also have some bread for you. We want to start you off with some easy meals today. How are you feeling?" Madeline asks.

"Like my stomach is eating itself right now." As if on cue, my stomach growls very loudly. "I feel more rested than I did, but I'm still exhausted." I feel slightly more refreshed after getting some sleep.

"Perfect, I'll leave you to eat this soup then and check on you in the morning. Keep resting and drinking water. Tomorrow, we'll try some more food, and if you continue to become stronger, you should be well enough to travel in a few days. That's assuming that you have a healer at the palace?" She looks at Charlie to answer her question.

"We do. Once we're home, Healer Adam will check on her frequently," Charlie assures her. She nods and turns to set the soup down.

"Perfect, I will see you both tomorrow. Goodnight." She leaves us with the delicious smelling food.

As soon as the door closes behind her, I rush over to the table she left the bowl of chicken broth. While dizziness made the room tilt, I didn't let it stop me.

"Woah, slow down Anna, I don't need you hurting yourself."

Charlie reaches for me.

"Sorry. I'm just so excited for real food," I tell him as I sit at the table. I pick up the spoon and start shoveling the savory liquid in my mouth, only stopping to take a bite of bread. Charlie sits on the other side of the table watching me. "Aren't you going to eat?" I ask him between mouthfuls of food.

"I ate while you were sleeping. Maybe we can eat breakfast together in the morning depending on how you feel, in the room of course," he tells me, making sure I know it's my choice.

"I love that idea. I know the healer said I need to rest after I eat, but do you think I can take a bath? I haven't been clean since I was kidnapped, and I would really like to feel like myself again."

"Of course, my love. I'll sit right on the other side of the curtain in case you don't feel strong enough."

I eat as quickly as I can, wanting both the nourishment and ready for a bath, but I don't want to make myself sick. When I'm done, Charlie puts the bowl outside the door and helps me draw a bath. As I sink into the tub, I realize how much I needed this. For a while I just lay there, eyes closed, letting the warm water relax my muscles. As the water cools off, I finally decide to dunk my head, needing to scrub the dirt and blood off of myself. I scrub my skin until I'm raw, but I need to feel clean again. After climbing out of the bath, I scrunch my nose at the brown water left behind. Drying off and wrapping myself in my towel, something dawns on me.

"Charlie, my love, did you bring any clothes? I was in a nightdress when I woke up, but it doesn't belong to me."

Charlie's face drops, "I was so worried about finding you I didn't even think about clothing. Let me grab Melanie and Stephanie." Then he runs out of the room, leaving me alone. I dry my hair off while I wait for him to return, and when he does, he comes with two different night dresses. "We weren't sure whose would fit you better, so both girls gave me one. Tomorrow we will send someone into town to get you clothes for when you start feeling better. Since we are not at home and it will be a few days' travel I told them to get you pants and tops like you wore when you first came home."

I smile at the consideration he took to make me happy.

"Thank you," is all I can say as I grab the night dresses and figure out which one fits. Then I climb into bed, exhausted already, waiting for Charlie to climb in next to me. He changes quickly before he joins me, rubbing my hair and whispering sweet nothings into my ears until I fall asleep.

Charlie

For the first time in what has felt like a lifetime, I finally get to hold my flower in my arms. I embrace her, rubbing her head and combing her damp hair with my fingers, until she falls asleep. Softly, I whisper how much I love and missed her, so she never forgets how much she means to me. Eventually, I fall asleep with her on my chest, finally able to rest now that I have her back.

Awaking early, with her still on my chest, I listen to her breathe for a while. After a few minutes of assuring myself that she's okay and alive, I quietly slip out of bed.

Running down to the tavern's dining area, I search for some things Anna will be able to eat, so we can eat breakfast together like I promised. I gather oats and some fruit, along with some thick unknown liquids that the owner swears is good. I head back up to the room and fear instantly fills me. Through the door, I can hear screaming and the shatter of breaking glass. Panic rushes through me as I burst through the door as quickly as I can. After practically throwing the food on the table, I look around the room Nothing is out of place except for the shattered vase on the floor. When my gaze finds Anna, I realize she's thrashing around in bed. Unsure what to do, I rush out to the hallway and call for Madeline's help.

Stephanie and Melanie jump out of their room, and stare wide-eyed at me.

"Get the healer!" I shout.

Stephanie races down the stairs. Melanie and I return to Anna and we try to wake her from whatever nightmare she's stuck inside.

Melanie rushes into the room with the healer Madeline in tow.

"Restrain her arms," the Healer Madeline instructs.

Stephanie and I both grab hold of Anna, and hold her as still as possible without hurting her.

"Hold this," the healer says, shoving a brown bottle and rags into Melanie's arms. The experienced healer takes a deep breath as she fills a syringe with liquid from the bottle. "I'm going to inject this into Anna to calm her. Keep this arm still."

"Sorry, Anna," I whisper as I obey the instruction.

Then Madeline stabs Anna's arm and pushes the liquid under her skin. Anna slowly starts to calm down. Finally, her body stops thrashing. Madeline pivots toward me with concern spread on her face. Stephanie and Melanie exchange relieved glances.

"Was she like this all night? Why didn't you call me sooner?!" the healer whisper-yells at me, trying not to wake Anna back up. "If she lives this nightmare in her head every time she tries to sleep, she's never going to heal properly."

"No, she was fine all night, I swear. I was in bed with her. And then when I came back from getting breakfast she was like this," I explained, not sure what happened in the time I was gone.

Realization dawning on the healer's face. "I'd recommend sending someone for food from now on. I think she dreamed she was back from wherever you rescued her when she no longer felt you beside her. She feels safe with you, so until she's healed more, you must stay with her at all times."

"Then I will," I say, meaning every word.

Chapter Thirty-Nine

Anna

WHEN I WAKE UP, all I can smell is oats. I smile, thankful that I get to try to eat something other than broth. I sit up slowly, still sore from the chains, and look around. The vase from the night table is missing, and concern fills me, causing me to search for Charlie.

Am I putting Charlie in danger? Did someone come in last night? Why would they only take the vase?

Finally, I lay my eyes on Charlie. He's sitting on a chair, hair a disheveled mess.

"Charlie, are you alright?" I ask, keeping my voice calm.

He jumps, realizing I'm awake. He jumps up and strides over to the side of the bed. "Yes, my flower, I'm alright. Just very worried about you."

"What happened to the vase? Did someone try to break in while I was sleeping? Are we in danger?" Words tumble out, concern for our safety obvious.

"Nothing bad, dear. When I got us breakfast a while ago, you had a night terror. It's okay now though," he explains to me.

My heart drops to my stomach.

"I...I did this?" I ask, unsure what to do. "No, I wouldn't do something like this."

"No, no, your dreams, or well, I guess nightmares, broke the vase. It's not a problem; the innkeeper doesn't mind. And the healer gave you medicine for the night terror. I promise you have nothing to worry about."

It takes a few minutes of him reassuring me that things will be alright before I feel comfortable enough to get out of bed. As Charlie helps me stand, my stomach growls loudly. We glance at each other and burst out giggling.

We sit down at the table and my mouth waters at the sight of all the food. I devour the fruit and oats first, but I even drink the weird liquid stuff he brought up because I'm that hungry.

Right as we're finishing up breakfast I decide to ask him what I've been thinking about all morning. "Charlie?"

"Yes, my flower?" He looks at me like I hung the moon, and am the only thing that matters to him.

"I'd really like to go and sit in the sun today. Do you think that would be alright with the healer?" I need the sun almost as much as I need food and sleep. Those who kidnapped me kept me in the dark for so long, I'm desperate for sunlight.

"Let's make sure breakfast doesn't make you sick first, and then I'll get the healer. For now, I want to soak up time with you while I can," Charlie says. He picks me up from the chair and carries me over to the bed, where he crawls next to me and wraps his warm arms around me. I curl into him, listening to his heart beat.

"Sleep," he whispers. "I'm not going anywhere."

Knowing my body needs the sleep to fully heal, I let my body relax and drift off.

After waking from the much needed nap, Madeline walks in as I'm stretching out, less stiff than I was yesterday. Melanie and Stephanie are also right behind her, holding piles of clothes. My face lights up with a smile when I glimpse comfortable pants and a slim corset. They place the clothes on the table where I'd had breakfast earlier. Before I can look more, the healer approaches me. "How are you feeling today Anna?" Madeline asks as she gently palpates my knees. .

"Much better, thank you," I say.

"Good," she says softly. "Let me feel your arms and neck and make sure they're healing properly."

I nod my consent and continue, "I know I still have a lot of healing to do, but I feel a million times better already. I was actually hoping I could go outside today and enjoy the sunshine? I think it might help." The hope in my voice is obvious when I ask.

"I think that's a great idea under two conditions. You stay close to the inn, and if you feel faint you tell somebody. I don't need you passing out and getting worse." Glad that she agreed, I nod my head enthusiastically. Unfortunately, that hurt a little, so I calm myself.

"Deal! Thank you so much." I'm beyond excited to finally see something other than walls.

As soon as she leaves, I slip off the bed, ready to go outside. I go through the clothes Melanie and Stephanie bought me until I find a good outfit to wear. Charlie helps me put on new boots and keeps an arm around my shoulders as he walks with me outside. Once we're in the fresh air, he staying close enough that if something happens, he's there, but still far enough away that I can feel independent. We walk around for a while looking at the shops, but not wandering too far so I don't break Madeline's orders. Eventually tired from walking, I find a bench to sit on and soak up the sunshine. Charlie plops down next to me and I lean over putting my head on his shoulder.

"Thank you for this," I say, closing my eyes and letting the sun glow through my eyelids.

"Of course, my flower, I just want you to get better."

We sit there in silence for a little while until eventually, my stomach growls once again, signaling it's dinner time.

For the first time since I was kidnapped, I sit in a tavern and eat dinner with my friends. It doesn't take long for me to get full, so Charlie and I head upstairs to our room long before anyone else does.

Charlie

I walk out of the bathing chamber, realizing that Anna is already asleep. As quickly and quietly as possible I sneak out of the room, intending to be back before Anna's night terrors start. When I arrive at Drake and Alex's room I knock furiously until they open the door.

"I need to be quick just in case," I say, turning to look at Drake, "I need you to leave first thing in the morning with Diane and get interrogations started." Then I turn and look at Alex, directing the conversation back to him. "Between you, Lucas, and the girls, I need meals brought up anytime we're not outside with Anna. She's also going stir crazy, so we need to take her outside as much as possible, and have as many eyes and ears out there as possible."

I know getting Diane away from Anna is the key to her starting to heal. We also need to get her strength up to get her home to her family.

I rush back down the hallway to get back, needing to know that Anna is alright. Thankfully, nothing seems out of place, so I'm assuming that she's too exhausted to be dreaming. Thank goodness. I check the room to make sure that everything is locked up and that we're alone. Once I'm sure we're safe, I climb into bed , curl an arm around my future wife, and fall asleep.

Chapter Forty

Anna

Everyday, I get better and better. It's been about a week since they found me. Drake left with Diane a few days ago, so they should be home by now. Madeline thinks I'm strong enough to travel home! Charlie has been busy coordinating the trip. I cannot wait to go home tomorrow. I miss my family so much.

Charlie accidentally wakes me up well before the sunrises by climbing out of bed. "Charlie, why are you awake? Is everything okay?" I sit up as I ask, wondering if we're supposed to be leaving already.

"Sorry, my flower, I just want to make sure everything is ready before I get you breakfast." I watch him get ready for the day, waiting until he walks around the bed and kisses me on the forehead before I curl into the blanket once again. "Get some more rest. We have a long journey ahead of us."

It doesn't take long for me to drift off, sleeping until I hear someone come into the room again.

"Good morning." The bed shifts as he climbs into bed beside me. "Are you ready for breakfast?"

I start to sit up right as my stomach starts growling. "Starved." I climb out of bed quickly, wanting to get ready before I eat. "Let me just get changed first!"

Charlie makes sure everything is packed up while I throw on clothes, then we sit down and eat our last breakfast together at the inn.

Doing one last check of the room, we fill up our water flasks and head out front. Thankfully, when I walk outside, I see a carriage attached to a few of the horses. *Thank goodness. I don't think I could handle riding a horse back.*

"The girls and I will take turns in the carriage with you. We want someone with you at all times in case you need to take a break. We also will be stopping at inns every night and not camping out just in case we need quick access to a healer," Charlie explains to me while I take everything in.

The inn owner was gracious enough to make sure we had enough food for the trip, and Madeline gave us all the medicine we could possibly need.

I turn to look at them both, standing in front of the inn to say bye to us.

"Thank you both for taking such good care of me this week. I wouldn't have made it without you." Glancing towards Charlie, the smile on his face gives me all the okay I need. "Hopefully once I'm healed I can come back and get to know you all better."

"I love that idea," he says looking at me then turning to look at them. "Like she said, thank you so much for your help and hospitality these past ten days We will send word when we arrive at home."

Then he proceeds to help me into the carriage with Melanie before getting on his horse.

After a few hours, the carriage slows. I look out of the small window. Everyone is dismounting their horses.

"Why are we stopping?" I ask Melanie. "Is everything okay?"

"We're just stopping for lunch! Don't be alarmed. Also, Stephanie will be with you for the next leg of the trip." She finishes her sentence before stepping down off the step, prepared to help me out of the carriage. I grab her hand and hop down, realizing in that moment how hungry I actually am.

"Oh good, I didn't realize it until now but I'm starving. How long have we been on the road?" I ask her, not recognizing where we were at. Did I doze off again? I must have.

"Umm, about five hours? The next town we reach will be our stop for the night, and then we'll get up early tomorrow and do it all again. We're hoping to be home in a few days," Melanie says as Stephanie comes over with two plates of food.

Charlie is right behind her, also carrying two plates of food. Assuming the plates are for us I reach out, grabbing one so I can start eating.

"We have about 30 minutes until we have to be back on the road to stay on schedule. Avery is checking the map and seeing how far the next town is so we know how much longer we will be travelling" Charlie tells me, making sure I stay informed for the whole trip.

"Thank you for letting me know."

We sit in silence, shoving food in our mouths as fast as we can. As we finish up and put all the dirty plates in the trunks we bought from a shopkeeper, Stephanie steps up into the carriage with me. Soon, the carriage jerks forward toward the next town.

The movement of the carriage doesn't put me to sleep this time as the terrain is much rockier. While the trip feels much slower when I'm awake, I'm thankful for Stephanie. She checks on me every half hour to make sure I'm not too sore or in need of a break. After a few hours, we finally make it to a town with an inn to stop at for the evening. Charlie heads in to get rooms, hoping there's enough for us, but comes out empty handed and disappointed. After a few minutes of Charlie talking to the guards he finally comes over and peaks his head into the window. "They only have one room. Everyone else is okay with camping out if you are?" He asks Stephanie, the look on her face pleading her to say yes.

"That works for me as long as Anna is in a bed!" The way she says it makes me feel loved and cared for instead of like a burden like it used to.

"Perfect, Anna and I will take the room then!" He turns and looks at me and says, "we don't want you sleeping on the ground unless necessary." He waits for me to nod my approval before turning back around and heading back into the inn.

Thankfully there is a good place for everyone to camp close by, and it's easy to set up a time to meet. We all eat dinner quickly and go our separate ways so we can get some sleep before the next leg of our trip.

Chapter Forty-One

Anna

I WAKE UP WELL before dawn, my brain ready to get back on the road. Knowing we still have time before everyone meets at the inn, I grab an outfit and head to the bathing chamber, needing to relax my muscles. Sitting in the bath, all I can think about is how excited I am to be going home. I know the journey will tax my still-recovering body, but I need my family to heal properly. A noise outside the door snaps me back to reality. Realizing Charlie probably had the same idea as me, I quickly scrub all the dirt off and climb out of the tub, giving him time to bathe as well.

I get dressed quickly before stepping out into the room, where Charlie is waiting with clothes in his hand. "You need a bath before we leave too?" I ask, my mind wandering to everyone camping that also needs a bath.

Knowing where my mind is heading, Charlie stands up, grabbing my face. "There is a hot spring not far from where they camped. The innkeeper told us about it before we set them up."

A sigh of relief escapes me, glad they're still getting taken care of. "I'll be quick so we can grab some food before we meet up." As he disappears around the corner, I do a sweep of the room, making sure anything we got out last night is packed away. After setting the bags by the door—wanting to be ready when Charlie is done—I hear voices in the hallway. Curiosity gets the better of me, and I press my ear to the door.

"I heard the Crown Prince Charles and his betrothed, Lady Anna, are in the country..." His words are muffled as they step farther away, but I overhear a woman say, "the rightful queen Minerva..."

The people talking slip around the corner, cutting off the rest of their conversation, but my mind races. *Do they know what happened to me? But they're on Minerva's side?*

"What are you doing?" Charlie asks. I scream and clutch my chest. He gasps and steps back.

I obviously didn't hear him come out of the bathing chambers.

"Just getting stuff around!" I answer once my panic is somewhat abated, I don't want him worried yet, so I hide what I overheard. So, I change the subject. "Are you about ready?"

"Uh, yeah," he says, a crease of confusion on his brow as he walks over to me and places a kiss on my forehead. "I love you. Let's get you one day closer to home."

Charlie grabs our packs and heads downstairs and toward the tavern to get food for everyone. We stuff them full with as much as they can hold, and give the innkeeper a hefty coin pouch in exchange. Walking out the front door, everyone is already mounted on their horses, confirming my suspicion that Charlie is riding in the carriage with me first today. *Perfect, now I can tell him what I heard.*

Thankfully, he sits next to me instead of across from me like the girls did, so once the carriage starts moving I lean in to talk to him. "I heard something really weird in the hallway while you were bathing, and I'm not sure what to do about it."

"Okay, what is it?" he asks. While his tone is calm, I know him well enough to notice the concern in it.

"I heard these people, I'm guessing a man and woman, talking about us, and the 'rightful queen Minerva.' But that's all I heard before they turned the corner to go downstairs," I explain.

Him staying calm is not helping my nerves at all.

He sticks his arm out the window, signaling something that causes everyone to speed up. "I'll up the guard duty once we get home. For now, we're going to travel at a faster pace as long as you can handle it. The sooner we're home, the better."

Knowing he's right, I try my best to calm my brain. Eventually my body gets used to the new pace, and my mind slows, lulling me into sleep. *Your body still needs a lot of rest after what you went through.*

Eventually, the carriage slows down, causing me to wake up. I look around trying to figure out what's going on when Charlie places his hand on my leg. Realizing that we're probably stopping for lunch, Charlie helps me out of the carriage. Thankfully, I need less help than yesterday, and we settle in to eat. While we're stopped for lunch Charlie gives everyone a brief explanation of why we needed to speed up and we get the map out to see how many more days of travel we have in the shadowlands. With our increased speed, we should be out of this dark kingdom by nightfall.

Charlie

The farther we get from the palace and the capital, the safer I feel, for mine and Anna's sakes. After overhearing those people talking in the hallway, she seems very shaken up, and I don't want to hinder her healing in any way if I don't have to. After briefing everyone at our stopping point for midday, everyone seems more on edge, and for good reason. Thankfully, we are on track to be out of this god-forsaken country by tonight. Once we cross into Weide Saliba, we don't have to worry.

As we near the border, a weight slowly lifts off my shoulders. We haven't run into any problems since we left. Riding is easy enough, even if it's long and exhausting, so I start listing the stuff we need to do once we cross the border in my head. We need to eat, hydrate, set up tents, and make a fire to stay warm all before dark, on top of making sure we get a decent amount of sleep to finish the ride home. I'm snapped away from my list making when I hear Avery shout my name. Glancing towards him at the front of our company, I see a group of guards dressed in all black, and behind them I see King and Queen Amoreli.

Riding up to the front of the group I call everyone to attention and take another look back to check on Anna as panic rolls through me. As we reach them, I finally speak.

"Hello Your Majesties, is everything okay?" I ask, worried about what they're going to say.

"No, in fact, every—" the queen says before the king puts his hand up, cutting her off.

"We were almost back to the palace when we got stopped by some guards that protect the lords and ladies of our country. We were told one of the lord's children has been kidnapped by your... friend?" the king says to me

What is he talking about?

"We didn't kidnap anyone. What is the child's name?" I ask, trying to figure out what game they're playing.

"Her name is Diane. We were told she was kidnapped and then taken through here on horse back. She had cuffs on," he explains, making everything click in my head.

Ah. Not a 'child' then.

"Well, Your Majesty, I'm sure you're aware that Diane is a fully grown woman and has been for a few years. And while she may be this lord's daughter, she is also a member of my court. One who committed a crime in my country. She was apprehended by my men and is being transported home to be dealt with properly, or would you prefer to harbor criminals from your neighbors?" I hope as a leader he understands where I'm coming from.

"Well that just won't do. She is also a citizen of my country and we will need her returned to us or it will be considered an act of war," he states, no waiver or question in his voice. I'm shocked by this statement because I would never treat another royal like this.

"War?" I say, tasting bitterness with the word. "She is also a political individual in my kingdom. This is an internal issue, and I will handle it the way I deem necessary. After we determine her guilt or lack thereof, she may choose to return if she desires."

"If you cross this border without agreeing to have someone escort her home, then we will be preparing for war against you. And while you may believe you have allies in the kingdoms surrounding you, you will see who really will stand by you if we declare war."

"How interesting you will go to war for this lord's daughter, but allowed my future queen to suffer in that very lord's dungeon. If anyone will declare war, it will be me. Therefore, I will take my chances, Your Majesty," I say, sarcasm coating my voice. "Now kindly move so we may exit your borders or we will have no choice but to attack. You might notice that I have more people than you do with you currently."

He scowls and a debate seems to run through his mind. The queen's face flushes red with suppressed rage. But after a moment, they step aside and allow us to pass while sending a signal to whom I can only assume is his general.

Wise. Even kings may not hold another country's royalty captive without the surrounding kingdoms rallying against them.

"You will see us soon, prince," the king says before turning and riding off, back towards his capital.

I blow out a tense sigh. We'll need to prepare in case he carries through with his threat.

Once they are out of sight, we cross the border and ride for as long as we possibly can so I know we're safely out of that country. When we finally stop it takes everyone working quickly to get camp set up before dark. "Get a few hours of sleep and then we will be back at it before dawn. We need to get as far away from that country as quickly as possible." I shout before walking over to Anna.

"My flower, I'm so sorry we had to push the traveling farther today. Are you feeling okay?" I ask, wanting to be sure she isn't going to get worse while we travel.

"Yes, my love, I am just fine. I slept most of the trip in the carriage, plus I'm just ready to be home," she tells me, smiling, which makes me feel much better about pushing her.

"Thank goodness. Let's go get some sleep so we can get home as quickly as possible. I'm estimating we have about two more days of travel, possibly one and half if we can push the days like we did today," I tell her and she nods. Then we climb into the tent while the first shift takes their places for the night. Sadly since we aren't in an inn we have to have guards posted always, just in case. Once Anna's breathing evens out, I finally doze off, sleeping as much as I can before dawn comes and we have to get moving again.

Chapter Forty-Two

Anna

THE CLOSER WE GET to home, the better I feel. When we finally pull up to the castle, my parents and sister greet me, relief courses through me. They trample me with so much love that I almost don't notice that my sister's fiancé is nowhere to be seen.

A warm voice speaks from behind them, "Now, now, I still have to examine her. Don't hurt her with too many squeezes."

"I think I know how to hug my sister," Amy responds sarcastically while our parents step back.

Adam emerges from behind her, and I smile when his kind expression surveys me. "We're glad to have you home, Lady Anna. Come with me, then I'll let your sister half-strangle you," he says, winking at Amy.

She rolls her eyes, but her twitching lips betray her amusement.

"I'm glad to be back," I tell him, wriggling out of my family's embrace and following him into the castle. "My muscles are still sore, so whatever you can do to help that, I'd be eternally grateful. But outside of that, I feel much better."

When we reach the infirmary, Adam looks over every inch of me to see how I'm healing and to check for anything that could be hindering my progress. "It seems you are in as good of shape as you can be considering what you went through. I'm going to give you a potion to help with your muscular pain. I recommend now that you are home and safe, to slowly get back to daily training. Don't push yourself, but you need to rebuild some muscle tone and gain more weight after your ordeal. Make sure you're eating your full meals, even if you aren't hungry."

As he piles the information on me I nod my head, hoping to remember it all.

"You have new maids to take care of you that I'm going to pass this along to as well. You do not have a new official hand maiden, as they will be going through a vigorous screening process. Please use your maids, Anna. I know you're a bit stubborn, and you don't *have* to rely on them, but you need as much help as you can get until you're fully healed."

Knowing he's going to pass the information on to someone else lifts a weight off my shoulders. *There was no way I was going to remember all of that.* "Okay, Healer Adam. Thank you for all the information. Can I go to my room and get some rest now? I'm very tired from traveling."

"Yes, of course. Get some rest tonight and tomorrow, then begin to start training lightly to rebuild your strength."

"Thank you. I will make sure to do that," I tell him, standing up from the chair. Arriving at my room, I find Charlie pacing and Drake sitting in the chair looking uncomfortable and nervous.

"We will finish this conversation in my study. Tomorrow. And you are *not* to go into the dungeon under any circumstances. Dismissed." Charlie's tone is oddly harsh.

Drake stands and leaves, barely glancing at me as he walks by.

"What was that about?" I ask, getting ready to change into my nightdress.

"Nothing, my flower. I will fill you in tomorrow after I talk to Drake more, I promise," he says before kissing me on the cheek and climbing into bed.

"I'm ready to get married. I'm ready for you to be king. And I'm as ready as I will ever be to be queen," I tell him, spilling what has been on my mind this whole journey. "We don't have to worry about any of these problems once you are crowned."

"Let's do it then," he says, a smile brightening his features. "You, Melanie, Stephanie, your mom, and Amelia can all start planning together. Set the date for next month, if you like. We have staff to help for a reason. I'm ready to be married too." The more he talks the more excited he sounds, which makes my chest warm. I can't help but smile as I climb into bed next to him.

"Okay, tomorrow then," I say, giving him a peck on the cheek.

Charlie

While Anna is getting checked out by the healer, I send for Drake. As I'm unpacking, a knock sounds on the door.

"Come in," I call.

Drake opens the door.

"Your Majesty, you asked to speak with me?" he asks, the formality in his tone causing me to lift my brow.

"Why so formal?" I chuckle. "Talk to me about Diane's interrogation. Has she confessed to anything?" He presses his tongue against his cheek before answering. "You're not going to like what I have to tell you," he says.

I pause before making eye contact. My stomach tightens. Drake is one of my best friends, and his behavior is throwing me off. I wave him to continue.

He clears his throat. "I cannot handle Diane's interrogations. I am requesting that Lucas or Alex take them over." Drake's words tumble out, even though he's keeping a stoic demeanor.

I raise my brow, trying to ignore the warnings flashing in my mind. "You're my best interrogator," I say slowly. "Why would I replace you?"

"Because, as you know, it is a long trip back. So obviously Diane and I talked about things on the way home. With the stuff I learned, I realized I cannot perform the interrogations without feeling guilty. I do not want to tell you too much until you actually have a chance to talk to her."

My composure snaps. "Drake. If you don't tell me what is going on you might join her in the dungeons," I growl, "She. Kidnapped. My. Wife."

He crosses his arms. "She isn't your wife yet, Charlie. And Diane was forced to do it. And I love her."

My jaw hits the floor. Did he just say what I think he just said? "You what?" I ask, hoping I heard him wrong.

"I love her. That's why I can't do the interrogation. I've loved her for a long time but I hated her for what she did. But now...now I'm unsure how to feel. However, I do know that I cannot interrogate her according to your expectations. I will not have that on my conscience. Do what you need to do, but I will not be the one doing it."

As he finishes that sentence, Anna walks in.

Chapter Forty-Three

Anna

THIS MORNING BEGINS WITH elation. Happiness. After following Healer Adam's orders to eat a big breakfast, I send for my friends and family so we can begin planning the wedding.

Right as I walk into the sitting room, Melanie and Stephanie come running in, my mom and sister not far behind them. "Are you okay? You're supposed to be resting!" my sister says, out of breath, but still concerned.

"I'm fine!" I say, grinning from ear to ear. "Charlie and I have set a date, so it's time to start wedding planning, between my training sessions of course!"

All of them just sit there staring at me, concern covering their faces. It feels like hours that they just stare at me, shocked, with no one saying a word. Finally, my sister starts laughing. Then everyone else follows.

"Whats so funny?" I ask, staring back at them like they've all grown another head

"You got us good! You can't get married in a month when you're still not even fully healed. And training? Are you *insane*?" Amelia asks.

"Healer Adam has recommended that tomorrow I return to my training sessions, modified, of course, to get my strength back up. And if I can do that, I can certainly get married," I tell them, hoping they get how serious I am.

As soon as I finish my sentence, they all look at each other, like they're trying to figure out if what I'm saying is true. "Go ask him yourself if you must, I will be here planning when you get back," I say, then proceed over to the coffee table and sit down with the parchment, getting ready to make decisions with or without their help.

Finally, they realize how serious I am, and slowly join me at the table. We are there for hours picking out wedding colors, cake flavor, and flowers. We finalize everything but my dress in a day, because of the excitement filling the room.

After the wonderful day of planning, I call for some tea and we just spend some time together in the sitting room, that is until I finally ask the question that has been bothering me this whole time. "What happened with Drake?" I ask, hoping someone knows the answer. When four sets of eyes snap to mine, confusion in all of them, I realize they know as much as I do.

"What are you talking about?" Mel asks me, concern dripping off her voice.

"Last night after I left the healers wing and got back to my room, Drake was in my chambers with Charlie. Charlie dismissed him very aggressively when I walked in, and then he was gone before sunrise this morning," I explain, bouncing my eyes between them all one at a time. "Seriously, none of you have heard anything?"

"No..." Stephanie says, mumbling something under her breath while shaking her head. "I might have an idea though."

Her and Melanie look at each other before looking back at me. "Before you came along, Drake was courting Diane."

That's all Melanie says before jumping up and heading out the door, Stephanie hot on her heels, leaving me there with my jaw on the floor.

Charlie

I'm up before the sun, not being able to quit stressing about Drake. I don't know what I'm going to do. Not wanting to wake Anna, I slowly slide out of bed and get dressed before heading to my study. As I sit there trying to wrap my mind around the news I got last night, I start making plans. Drake obviously cannot handle these interrogations. I make a plan to have Alex take over with Lucas helping him. I also need to figure out what I'm going to do about Drake since he obviously needs to be punished. Then, I sit there and wait. I also pace some. Then, finally, the sun had risen, and I send a guard to fetch all of them.

When they arrive in my study I have them all sit down at my desk. Alex and Lucas look confused, but obviously Drake knew why they were here.

"I'm glad you all are here. Alex, Lucas, you will be taking over Diane's interrogation. This is not up for debate. I need you to do it at Drake's level please. You are dismissed." I don't leave any room for debate or questions since I need to handle Drake. They both nod their heads, give Drake a look, and then get up and leave my study.

"What do you want to do about this?" Drake asks me, knowing that I'm going to punish him somehow.

"I still haven't decided. I know you were thinking about courting Diane before everything happened. What do you think is a fair punishment?" I ask him, hoping he's going to be honest with me.

"Honestly? I don't know. I can take kitchen duty if need be, cleaning everything. Or barn duty, cleaning up after the horses. I don't think I deserve banishment for this, especially since I was honest with you," he tells me, while I nod along listening to his argument.

"I agree that you don't deserve banishment. I'm probably going to assign you barn duty for the foreseeable future. And under no circumstances are you allowed to be around Diane until we get to the bottom of what happened. We don't need you helping her through interrogations or giving your opinion on things. And if I see you by Diane, you will go into the dungeon with her. Understand?"

"Yes, sir. Afterwards, if you decide to release her, we will be leaving together. We will leave the country, I would love to still stay in contact with you but I can also understand if you guys don't want that. I also am willing to subject myself to interrogations today, so that you can learn everything she told me, or I can write a report if you still trust me."

"Please just submit a report. I believe you can give us a proper report without inserting your opinion in it too much."

"Thank you, Your Highness. And I'm very sorry you have to deal with this," he says. Then, as he stands up, Melanie and Stephanie burst into my study, seemingly out of breath. Drake and I both stare at them with confusion on our faces.

"Can I help you?" I ask them, amusement on my face.

They just stand there and glance back and forth between the two of us. "You guys aren't fighting?" Melanie asks me.

"No?" Drake says, concerned why they would think that.

"We were worried about what was going to happen with you guys. Anna said there was a lot of tension last night," Stephanie says, still glancing back and forth between us.

"Nope. Everything is fine here," I say while Drake shrugs his shoulders and heads out of the study, I'm guessing to head down to the barn. "Drake knows his place, and we have new people handling the interrogations, nothing to worry about."

"Oh, okay. Whatever works. Wedding planning is going great by the way," they tell me before turning around and walking out of the study.

Chapter Forty-Four

Anna

CHARLIE HAS BEEN IN the study all day. He even missed dinner, so I decide to head up there and see what is going on. We need to come up with a new training schedule as well since Adam gave the okay. Arriving at the door, I hear shuffling on the other side, so I open it without knocking,

"Everything alright?" I ask him, eyes bouncing from the papers he's shuffling around, up to him.

"Yes, you can come sit down if you want, love," he tells me. So I step in and sit down, making sure to close the door behind me. "Did you need something specific or just coming to see me?"

As he asks, he comes around the desk sitting in front of me and placing a kiss on my forehead.

"I was wondering about training? I am planning on getting back into it tomorrow but I am unsure if Drake will still be my sparring partner or if I need to find someone else."

"I can see if Drake will like to spar with you. But because of his insubordinate behavior, he's been assigned to barn duty, so he'll need to train with you before he does his work for the day," he tells me, not giving me any more information.

"I see. What exactly did he do? I heard he was courting Diane before I came along?" I ask, hoping for some clarification.

"Yes, he was. And he has decided that he cannot do his job as my interrogator with her because his feelings are in the way. While I am glad he was honest with me, interrogation is an important part of his job, and his refusal is still considered insubordination. He also told me that it wasn't *her* fault, and he still loves her after she *kidnapped* you." His voice grows louder with every word. He's obviously still very angry at his best friend.

"Well... did he tell you why he doesn't believe it is her fault?" I ask him, curious for the answer.

"No. I didn't want to know. It is her fault because she set it up. And she has been lying to us this whole time."

"Charlie, honey. I want to know. I want to know why she did it. I want to know what I did wrong. I want to know why," I tell him, hoping he'll understand my plea for answers. When he just sits there staring at me in silence, doubt starts to creep in about the fact that I want answers. I still stand my ground, needing to know the answers to my questions.

"Okay," he says, and that's all he says before he gets up and heads towards the study door. When he gets there, he stops and turns to look at me, "Are you coming?"

"Yes." I get up and follow him out the door. "Where are we going?"

"We are going to get the answers you want. Directly from the source."

Charlie

As soon as Anna tells me she needs the answers I had refused to hear, I realize how selfish I'm being. I was so worried about her that I didn't want any explanation of why her kidnapping and negligent treatment happened. But she was the one who survived it. I should be asking her what she wants. Realizing that, I stand up from the desk, prepared to get the answers she so desperately needs and deserves. When I realize she's not following me, I stop and turn to look at her, "Are you coming?" I ask.

"Yes," she responds, jumping up and following me. "Where are we going?"

"We are going to get the answers you want. Directly from the source," I tell her, walking out the door and down the hall to the dungeon. As we're walking down the stairs I stop, turning to face her. "Are you positive this is what you want to do?"

"Yes. I need this," she tells me, ready to get her answers. We finish our trek and get to Diane's cell. As we reach her cell, she stands and bows, as if nothing ever happened.

"Your majesty, Lady An–" she starts to say before I cut her off.

"Do not say her name. She may be willing to talk to you but you don't deserve her name on your lips," I say, more aggressive than I intended. She slinks back against the wall and lowers her head, refusing to make eye contact.

"Charlie, calm down," Anna tells me before stepping up to the cell. "Diane. I come seeking answers. I can understand if you don't want to give them to me but I will either get them willingly from you or from your interrogations."

She sounds more queenly than ever, so I step back to let her handle this. Diane tilts her head up and looks at her, contemplating her answer before speaking.

"I will answer anything you ask me Lady Anna, but first I need to tell you that I am truly sorry for all the pain I caused you," Diane tells her, causing my anger to rise.

"Thank you for saying that," Anna says, holding her hand up to me knowing I'm about to say something to her again. "I just want to know why. Why did you do it? What did I do?"

"Well, it's a very long story, so I hope you have time." Diane says before sitting back down. Anna slides down the bars outside the cell as well. "When I was little, my parents dropped me off at the castle door as if I was an orphan, letting the king and queen take me in so I could infiltrate the castle. Obviously, when I was that young, I didn't understand what was going on. Twice a year, more if they could afford it, they would pay to transport me home, which is why I was always traveling, and they'd ask me all kinds of questions about the kingdom that I would answer because I didn't understand the problem. As I got older and started to connect with the people here I didn't want to do it anymore, but they blackmailed me. They told me if I didn't keep answering questions they would tell the king about my treason so I would get executed, so obviously I had to keep at it. Eventually, when the king got sick, they told me I needed to make the prince fall in love with me so they could take over the kingdom. I tried and tried but my heart was never in it because I am in love with Drake. Then, when you came along, I was hoping I wouldn't have to do it anymore. That's why I left as soon as you came back to court, so I could report back to them. But once I got there, they told me they already knew and paid someone to kidnap you. I was shocked and never imagined my parents would do something that cruel. Then they proceeded to blackmail me to stay, threatening to kill Stephanie and Melanie if I didn't obey. They planned on giving Charles time to grieve before sending me back to win his heart. Until he showed up and ruined their plan. Obviously, that pissed them off, so they blamed me at that time, hoping the king and queen would save me before we got out of the country. And now, here we are." She gestures to the dim walls of her cell.

As I listen to the story, I slowly realize why Drake feels the way he does. I start to feel bad for how I treated them both, because it really isn't her fault that she has shitty parents. I had zoned out at this point until I hear Anna's voice again, as if she had been processing just like me.

"Thank you for answering that. I realize that this has been a hard situation all around, and I appreciate your honesty. I will see about getting you a proper bath and some more comfortable arrangements, but you will still be a prisoner of the castle until further notice," Anna says before she turns around and heads back towards the door, not waiting for Diane to answer.

I look up and make eye contact with tears in both of our eyes, the sorrow conveyed on her face. I nod her way before turning around, and follow Anna out the door.

Chapter Forty-Five

Anna

AFTER WE GET OUT of the dungeon, I continue to walk. I walk so long that I lose track of where I am and where I am going. Eventually, I realize I'm in the garden, in the same place I got kidnapped. When I stop I just...scream. I scream so long that my throat becomes raw and my scream becomes silent. I feel arms wrap around me, and I start thrashing, scared that someone is kidnapping me again.

"Shhhh, shhh, it's just me. It's okay. Calm down." Charlie's voice, merely a whisper in my ears, shushes me while tears roll down my face.

"Charlie, I don't understand. Why must they do this to me? And why must I feel guilty for imprisoning her? *She kidnapped me!*" I can barely talk through my sobs.

"You have no reason to feel guilty. But if you meant it when you told Diane about wanting to get her better chambers, we can. You may have whatever you want, including full control over this situation, my love."

"I...I want her gone.." I tell him, doubting the words as they come out. "I don't want her anywhere near this castle, but I also don't want her punished. I want the people who caused this punished."

"Okay." he tells me, no question in his voice. "If that's what you want, then I will make it happen. But you need to know, if she leaves...well, then Drake will also leave. So we will have to figure out a new plan for your training."

I stare at him and blink, confusion on my face, and then nod as the pieces fall into place and I understand. I feel relief and dread all at the same time. "I'd like to tell Drake with you please. And I would like to tell him before Diane. He deserves to say his goodbyes."

"Okay, my love, we will make that happen. I'll send for him first thing in the morning."

Charlie

The next morning, I keep my word and send for Drake. Anna and I wait for him in the sitting room. She's ready to strengthen her muscles after this meeting, and she's wearing her training clothes with her hair braided back.

When we hear a knock on the door, I walk over and answer it. Drake stands there, waiting for me until I wave him inside.

"Good morning, Drake," Anna says with a smile.

"Good morning, Lady Anna," Drake says, "are you beginning training again today?"

"I am, once we find someone for me to train with."

"Oh, did you want me to train with you? Because I will," Drake tells us, looking back and forth.

"Actually. That's not why we called you here," I say, which causes his face to drop and concern to cross his gaze. He just stares at us, with nothing to say, waiting for me to continue. I glance at Anna making sure she is ready for this, and when she nods at me, I nod back. "Anna spoke with Diane last night. We believe her story and that she was forced to do this. She was moved to more comfortable rooms while still being prisoner. However, we have decided to release her. Under the understanding that she is never to return to the castle. She will be welcome in certain towns, but never the palace nor the surrounding towns. We will release her tomorrow morning, however we wanted to give you a chance to decide what you wanted to do. You will still be welcome here, of course, but I also know you love her, so we're giving you options."

When I finish, Drake proceeds to stare at me, unsure of what to do. "I'd like to go with her. As long as I am free to come home for a visit?"

"Of course you are. As long as she does not return with you."

"She will not. I swear. Now, I am going to go pack and say my goodbyes. Thank you both for your understanding." Then he walks out of the room.

"Thank you for letting me be a part of that, however, I must go find Avery now, I'm going to have him train with me for a while since he has to guard me anyways." Anna says before kissing me on the cheek and walking out of the room, leaving me standing there, feeling the pain of losing two of my best friends.

Chapter Forty-Six

Anna

AFTER MY TRAINING SESSION with Avery, he walks me back up to my room so I can bathe before tea with the girls. After we say our goodbyes and both go our separate ways for now, I turn and open the door, walking into the sitting room to put my daggers away. All I see when I walk in is the back of the blonde head I know so well. "Charlie my love, I wasn't expecting you to be in here." When I start talking I see him jump and wipe his eyes. I walk around to the front of the chair he's sitting in, and crouch down to his eye level. "Charlie, what's wrong?"

"Nothing, I'm okay," Charlie says, even though I can clearly see his eyes are puffy from crying.

"Talk to me, what's wrong?" I ask again, hoping he'll tell me this time. I need him to tell me.

"I'm just processing love. Two of my best friends are leaving. And I know Diane tried to hurt you, but I still never grieved her loss, and now I'm losing them both. But this isn't manly, so I'm going to clean myself up." As he turns around, I reach for his hand and pull him in for a hug. When I pull back, I grab his face and make him look at me.

"I don't want you to pretend around me. You're allowed to have feelings just like I am, and you have every right to cry over your friends. I'm just sorry I wasn't here to hold you. Take all the time you need. I can skip tea. And I think we should let Diane join us for one last family dinner. I'll have Avery come down with us so I still feel safe, and you guys can feel normal," I tell him, trying to make up for what a bad fiancé I have been. I didn't even think of how he has felt through all of this, only what I have felt. I lower myself onto the couch and tap the seat next to me. When Charlie finally joins me after a few hesitant minutes, he cuddles into me and lets the tears flow again, releasing the suppressed emotions until he physically can't cry anymore.

Charlie

I don't realize I've fallen asleep until I hear Anna whispering. "Yes, thank you. Please set that up and we will be down in about twenty minutes."

Someone mumbles words I don't quite understand

"Did you get Avery set up?"

More mumbling.

"Yes, thank you."

The door clicks closed, and I sit up right as Anna walks into the room.

"Oh!" she says, seeming as if I startled her "I was just coming to wake you up. Dinner is soon so you're going to want to get ready." She kisses me on the forehead.

"Thank you," is all I can say to her, my mind still not wrapped around what happened earlier. All she does is smile back before walking into the bedroom to finish her hair. I realize at that moment we haven't started finding her a new handmaiden yet. "Anna?" I ask as I walk towards the room to bathe before dinner.

"Yes?" she questions back, already at the vanity.

"Do you have anyone that you'd like to be your hand maiden? Someone that's already in the castle?" I ask her, hoping to make both our lives easier.

"I haven't thought about it, honestly," she says as she stops braiding her hair to look at me, then proceeding to turn back to what she's doing. "I'll think about it, though."

And with that I walk into the bathroom, hoping to feel normal one last time.

`As I walk into the dining room, a small smile creeps across my face. Everyone is sitting at the table, not in formal attire but sitting there together like friends. Diane and Drake sitting next to each other, looking more in love than I've ever seen them. Melanie sits next to her, looking guarded but happy. Across the table Alex, Stephanie and Lucas line a bench, chatting away. Further down the table are Anna's family, her mom and dad on one side of the table and Amelia on the other, no fiancé in sight once again. And next to Amelia sits Avery, fully on guard but not in uniform, which makes me smile a little more knowing he is always prepared to protect my fiancé. Anna and I sit down at the heads of the table, my way of making her feel like my equal, and dinner gets served rather quickly after that. As we all eat, I hear more chatter than I have in months and it makes my heart feel full.

As dinner comes to an end, I start to feel sad all over again. This time tomorrow Diane and Drake will be who knows where, and although Diane betrayed us, it is still sad after having grown up with her. After a few minutes of processing the way things are going to change, I rise, tapping my knife against the glass.

"I want to say something."

Everyone stops and looks at me, waiting for me to continue. My mind reels about all the things I want to say. "I have never been prouder to have a group of friends and family quite like this. Diane, I know this has been a wild road, and I'm sorry it has come to an end. I wish you the best in whatever you do, as long as it's far away from my future wife. Drake, we will miss you more than you could ever understand, and I hope you both have the best life together. Drake, please make sure you come visit, and bring whatever little scoundrels you two end up having together with you." I hear a round of cheers coming from around me before I set my cup down and turn to leave, not wanting to cry in front of everybody. After a minute, I hear footsteps coming up behind. I turn expecting to see Anna but find Drake standing there instead.

"That was a terrible speech, you know?" Drake says, a smirk on his face while he tries to hold back laughter.

"Yeah, well, I'm still trying to process my thoughts," I tell him, trying to stop the tears from rolling down my cheeks.

"Are you sure you're okay with me leaving? I won't go if you say no right now."

"Why? So you can resent me forever? I will never prevent you from being happy Drake. I just wish it was with someone else. I can see how much you love her though. You always have, even when we were boys."

"I really do. I promise I'll visit,' he says before hugging me. This embrace didn't feel like previous ones, though. This was goodbye.

Chapter Forty-Seven

Anna

As Charlie finishes his speech and walks out of the room, I stand to follow him, but Drake beats me to it. The pleading in his eyes causes me to sit back down and let him handle it. Glancing around at everyone, I realize the friendships I'm breaking up and the things I'm making Charlie lose and I can't stand it. I push my chair back in a hurry, knocking it down in the process, before practically running out of the room and to the garden. When I get outside I take multiple slow deep breaths, trying to calm myself down. When I hear two sets of footsteps approaching behind me I startle and whip around, only to find Melanie and Stephanie are walking towards me, worry on their faces.

"Are you okay?" Melanie asks when they're close enough for me to hear them.

"I'm alright. This is just very overwhelming," I say, trying to mask the pain in my voice. Stephanie grabs my hand and walks me over to a bench in the garden before sitting me down.

"I know you feel guilty. I can see it on your face," she says. Melanie sits down and grabs my other hand at the same time.

"I'm forcing you guys to lose two friends who are like family to you because of my fear, even though my own family is sitting right there next to me. Of course, I feel guilty," I choke out, tears filling in my eyes. "I should just let her stay."

"Anna, look at me," Melanie says, causing me to jerk my head up. When I make eye contact with her, I see Diane walking up behind her. I wipe away my tears refusing to let her see the conflict in my eyes.

"It's okay to be selfish sometimes," Melanie says right as Diane reaches us. As Diane crouches down my heart beat speeds up and my hands get clammy, fear surging through me.

"You shouldn't have to have this reaction to someone in your own home, Lady Anna," Diane says, regret and guilt coming out in her voice. "No matter how guilty I feel or how great of friends we might have been, you will never feel safe in your own home as long as I'm here. And if one day you feel like you want to take that chance you can send me a notice, and I will be back here as quickly as I can. But until then, this is *your* home first. I messed up, so please don't feel guilty for that. If everyone else chooses to forgive me, they can always come visit, and Drake can come back here and visit you guys. For now, I came to say goodbye and tell you that you deserve nothing but happiness." Diane stands up and walks back inside, and tears roll down my face harder than before.

Charlie

After Drake and I have our heart to heart, we walk back in to see all the girls and Avery gone. I look at Anna's dad, and he just shrugs at me. Of course, that's the moment they all choose to walk back inside. Diane and Avery walk in first and then a minute later everyone else comes in. Anna's face is beat red from crying. I stand up attempting to rush to her but Melanie shakes her head to tell me it's alright. We all gather up to say goodbye to Diane and Drake one last time before they head to their rooms to finish packing. They plan on leaving before the sun is up. Anna and I stay in the dining room, sitting by the fireplace and watching the flames. It feels like hours before she finally says something.

"I'm sorry I'm being selfish. I just want to feel safe walking around the castle," she all but whispers, causing me to strain my ears to hear her, while refusing to look at me.

I grab her chin and pull her face, forcing her to look into my eyes. "This is your home. It is supposed to be your safe place, and I want *nothing* more than for you to be selfish," I tell her, wanting her to know that she needs to be happy here.

After staring at the fire for a little longer I push myself up and grab Anna's hands to pull her up with me and we walk to our bedroom in silence, dreading the changes to come.

Chapter Forty-Eight

Anna

I WAKE UP THE next morning and ready myself for training, needing some type of normalcy in my life. I do my best not to wake Charlie up and sneak out the door, knowing Avery is awaiting me in the training ring. When I get there we warm up, running laps around the ring until I physically can't anymore, and then stretch, which is a new thing for me that Healer Adam insisted on while my muscles are still healing.

"So, Avery, how are you feeling about everything going on?" I ask him, hoping it'll make me feel less selfish.

"Honestly? I never really liked Diane, but Drake leaving this morning is unfortunate. At least they'll both be happy though," he says, standing up since he's ready to get to work. I finish up my stretches and get up off the dirt floor.

"You ready to get your rear kicked?" I ask him, taking him by surprise.

"Yeah, yeah, princess, we'll see about that," he says before he lunges, causing me to have to dodge him multiple times. Once I get my footing back I lunge for him, but of course he dodges like the professional he is.

"As fast as you are, you're staying too open, Anna. I could take you down in two moves. Get smaller, use your shorter height as an advantage."

As soon as he says that, I crouch down and make myself smaller. Preparing to go for his legs, I lean forward like I'm going to and he goes to jump over me, but can't because I didn't actually attack. I grab his legs on the way down and pin him down.

"Thanks for the tip," I say before standing up and dusting off my pants. I walk over and take a gulp of water just as Charlie walks in, looking ready to train. "Hi love," I say as I kiss him on the cheek. "Come to join us?"

"Yeah, I'm hoping training can get my mind off of everything. Lucas and Alex are on their way down. I invited Melanie and Stephanie as well. And I left a note under Amelia's door but they didn't answer when I knocked. I hope that's alright with you?" he asks, realizing that these are usually quiet training sessions.

"That's perfect! I've been meaning to invite everyone back down but things have been so crazy I forgot," I say with a smile. "Want to watch me kick Avery's butt again while we wait?" I smirk at Avery.

He laughs and rolls his eyes.

Charlie laughs and shakes his head. "Always," he says, making himself comfortable against the wall while Avery and I take our spots in the middle once again. After a couple more rounds of sparring, some that I win and some that Avery wins, we take another water break. That is when everyone decides to walk in.

"Perfect timing," Charlie says, standing up and dusting his pants off. "Who wants to go first?"

After a few hours of training we head up for lunch, everyone hungry and exhausted. "I vote we all go to sleep after those sparring sessions." I say with a laugh, knowing that we all made sure that we had no work to do today.

"Tomorrow we go back to wedding planning?" I ask, turning to the girls.

"Please?" Melanie says, a smile stretching across her face.

"Perfect," I say with a giggle.

Charlie

"I'm going to my study to set up a plan for tomorrow and to check on the staff," I tell Anna.

She quietly responds, "Okay."

I walk out of the dining room. When I make it to my study, I am very surprised to find the King of Vierda Shadow.

"Guards," I yell, preparing myself for a fight.

He towers over me.

"That won't be necessary, I'm not here to fight."

"When I was leaving your country, you declared war, remember? Forgive me if I assume that would mean you're here to fight," I retort with as much attitude as I can muster. The guards come rushing in behind me, swords drawn and ready to defend me at all costs.

"That's why I'm here. As I'm sure you know, news travels. We hear that you released Diane under the stipulation that she is never to return to your court. We would like to offer that if you tell us where she is planning on going, we will collect her and bring her home, no war necessary," he says, trying to sound like it's a compelling deal.

"I apologize, Your Majesty, but we told her that we would never force her to return to her country, and I am nothing if not a man of my word. That information is not your concern, and if she chooses to come home then that is on her. However, we do have proof that the lord and lady you seem to be trying to protect so hard conspired to kidnap my future wife. What are you going to do to handle that?"

"Well, since it did not happen to someone in our own court, we cannot do anything about it."

"Then war it is. My guards will escort you out of the castle, and should you try anything, I will kill you myself. Now go." I tell him, moving out of the way of the door. The guards surround him, swords pointed at him from all angles. Sadly he doesn't try anything while being escorted out of the castle. I start preparing my armies to stand at all sides of the castle, because we need to be ready for whatever is coming.

Around dinner time, Anna comes up to get me. "I thought you were going to be fast. You've been in here for a few hours. Is everything alright?"

"King Amorali came for a visit and wanted me to tell him where Diane went, but he's refusing to give up her parents. So now I'm trying to prepare for a war on any and all fronts," I explain, hoping she understands why I've been up here for so long.

"Can you take a dinner break? Then I can send Alex and Lucas up to help you strategize?"

"That sounds like a great idea," I say, getting up to head down with her to the dining room. "I definitely could use their help."

After dinner Alex, Lucas, and I head up to the study, needing to come up with a plan to protect our country. We realize the weight of losing Drake in this moment. He was our best strategizer, but we know we need to figure this out on our own. We stay in the study until well after the sun goes down, however we get a plan finalized before we leave. Part of the army will be at all parts of the border prepared for attack. Notices are going out to all of our allies, calling them to send in reinforcements if necessary. And we have upped conscriptions to help make the army bigger. Following the recruitment rules, I will enforce the statute that anyone over eighteen in a household who isn't the man of the house must report for military duty. We need to get our armies as big as we can without causing unrest in the country.

Chapter Forty-Nine

Anna

THE NEXT FEW WEEKS are spent in different ways for Charlie and I. I spend my days in the sitting room, finalizing wedding plans and giving tasks to the staff to make sure the castle is ready. Charlie spends his time in the study with Lucas and Alex making sure we're ready for an attack that we're not even sure is coming. We wait and wait but no attack seems to come. Until our wedding day finally comes...

Smiling and looking at myself in the mirror, I look like a proper princess. Immediately after our vows we both have to get crowned so we will officially be king and queen. I'm wearing the most beautiful white dress with a pale yellow belt and yellow flowers braided into my hair. My makeup makes my blue eyes stick out more than they ever have before. Sitting on top of my head (for easy removal) is the princess tiara. The queen's crown waits for me at the altar. I know I am not ready to rule a country, but I am as ready as I am ever going to be.

I hear a quiet knock on the door and I turn to my mother walking in.

"Good morning, my beautiful daughter," she says, stopping to sniffle half way through.

"Mom, you can't cry. Then I'm going to cry and ruin my makeup," I tell her, tears forming in my eyes.

"Okay, okay. I'll try not to cry. But you know your dad is going to right? You're the first of his daughters to get married!"

That reminds me... "Speaking of, I haven't seen Amelia's fiancé around as much. What's going on with them?"

"Oh nothing to worry about, dear. When you were...gone..." she says, skirting around the fact that I was kidnapped and imprisoned, "they were fighting about leaving the castle. She wanted to be here when you got back, and he wanted to travel. So he decided to travel without her and since then there has been a lot of, um, tension. I don't know if they're ever going to get married at this point," she finishes explaining.

It makes sense why he isn't around. If he's traveling then he wouldn't be in the castle as much as normal.

"Will he be here today?" I ask, hoping I can talk to him and convince him to make up with her.

"I'm not sure, dear, but let's not worry about it today. You're getting married!"

As soon as she says that, Amelia walks in with Stephanie and Melanie right behind her. All three of them have the biggest smiles on their faces. "Are you ready for this?" she asks.

Just as I'm about to answer her, a storm of guards rush into the room. Avery leads them, dressed for the wedding but fully on duty.

"What's going on?" I ask in a panic, never having seen the guards this worked up before.

"There's been an attack, just outside the castle. We don't know how they got through all the armies. We need to get you to safety," Avery says, sounding more serious than I have ever heard him.

"But what about the wedding?" I ask, letting the tears roll down my face. Why did this have to happen *today* of all days?

"We think that is why they're attacking today, to catch us off guard. We need to get you out of here before they breach the castle walls." Avery grabs my arm to me to safety.

"I can't go," I argue, pulled against his firm grip. "I'm supposed to get *married* today, Avery. And I refuse to let them ruin that!" I yell, angry that they won't let me make my own choices. "Just increase the guards on duty and it'll be fine."

"Princess, I hate to do this. And I'm sorry in advance," he says before picking me up off my feet and carrying me out the door, ruining what is supposed to be the happiest day of my life. Between Avery's running and me crying, my hair and makeup get ruined. My dress gets covered in dirt from trailing on the ground, by the time we get to the secret room in the dungeon for safety, I look like a disaster. Charlie is already there with my dad, Alex, and Lucas, waiting for us to get in there. Once inside, Avery shuts the door so it transforms back into looking like a wall, and I collapse to the floor. Charlie slides down the wall next to me, letting me put my head in his lap.

"I'm sorry this is happening today, flower," Charlie murmurs, rubbing my hair, trying to soothe me.

"I just want one day. One day that we can all be happy," I get out between sobs, trying to stop the tears, but unable to. Why can't we, for once, be together with no problems?

"I know. I know. We will get our day. One day, I know it. Today just can't be that day," he tells me, trying to calm me down as best as he can.

Charlie

When Avery walks in carrying my bride, anger rises up in me before despair can. Her dress is covered in mud, tears stream down her face along with her makeup, and her tiara is falling off her head and about to take strands of hair with it. She shouldn't look like this on her wedding day. Everyone tried to talk me out of getting married, knowing that we had a looming war, but I was selfish and wanted nothing but for Anna to be my wife.

"I'm so sorry, my love," I say softly, running my hand on her head while she falls asleep on my lap. I look up at Avery who is standing by the door, guarding it, but also glancing at Anna as often as he can. I can see the worry on his face; he is just as worried about her as me. "Avery," I say, forcing him to look at me. "Thank you for caring about my bride as much as I do."

"Always, sir, it is my job to protect her.".

"It is your job to protect her, not care for her. You do that all on your own."

"Its hard not to care about somebody that cares about everyone else, sir." he says before turning back to the door with his sword drawn.

I continue to stroke her head, thinking about how things should be now. Right now I would be standing at the altar, waiting for her to walk to me. When she walked down the aisle, she'd look like the princess she always deserved to be in this beautiful dress, not covered in mud. Then we'd officially be crowned king and queen, ready to take over the country. As much as everyone listens to me now, they would respect me more with the official crown.

I don't even realize that I've fallen asleep until Lucas is forcing me awake. "Sir, we need to move." The way he says it forces me to jump up, everyone including Anna is already awake.

"What's going on?" I ask, looking around, seeing nothing to cause concern.

"They left. The armies left the castle and we need to get you and Anna to safety before they come back." Avery says, slowly opening the door looking for anyone still lingering in the castle.

We're rushed to our respective chambers, packing clothes and things for however long we might be gone. We load everything up into our carriages, heading for the north. We have a secret house in the very north of our country that is not on any maps, but the one I currently hold in my hand. We rush all of the family up there along with multiple guards, Avery and my guard Milton are among them. Along with their small companies charged to protect us. I force a set of guards in every carriage with at least four people in each carriage. Amelia, her parents, and Lucas in one carriage. Anna, Melanie, Stephanie, and I in another. With Alex refusing to ride in any carriages, needing to be prepared to fight at all times.

After hours in the carriages, we finally reach the mountains in the northern part of the country, the house in the mountain range. We hurry out of the carriages and into the house, hoping not to be seen and send the carriages away as quickly as possible. We need to keep a low profile so it is harder for them to find us. We have to use staying hidden to our advantage. As soon as we're inside, I head right into the study ready to come up with an attack plan. We need to survive this war.

Chapter Fifty

Anna

As soon as we get to the safe house, Charlie, Lucas and Alex disappear into the study. I'm guessing to discuss their military strategy. One of the few maids that is stationed in the house shows all of us to our rooms, where I bathe and proceed to climb into bed, hoping the bed sucks me into the sleep I so desperately need.

The next morning I find Charlie's side of the bed still cold. After I change, I wander into the hallways, hoping to find the study. We were supposed to come here after our wedding for a few days, and now we're here as an escape from war, still unmarried. When I eventually discover the study's location, I knock before opening the door. Lucas and Alex are asleep sitting up on the couch, and Charlie is passed out with his head on the desk. I clear my throat as loudly as I can, and they all jerk awake.

"Good morning. You should probably all go get baths and maybe sleep in a proper bed for a few before you try to continue planning."

Lucas is the first one out the door with Alex not far behind him, obviously more exhausted then they thought they were.

"Charlie that goes for you too," I say, looking at him sternly when he still refuses to move. "Charlie."

"I have to come up with a plan first," he mumbles, looking over the map like he's trying to come up with an idea.

"My love," I say, walking around the desk, sitting on his lap. "You need sleep. You're no good to us half dead."

"I have to make sure you're safe," he says, the exhaustion seeping through his voice.

"I know, my love, but you can do that after you get some sleep, I'll be safe for a few hours while you're sleeping." I stand up and grab his hands, dragging him toward the room. When we get there, I draw up a bath for him and get him into it. I wash his hair for him while he scrubs his body. He's barely able to keep his eyes open. Once he's done, I help him dry off while trying to not stare at how handsome he is, and force him into bed before climbing in next to him so I can make sure he actually sleeps.

"Last night was supposed to be happy. We should be married and on our way here as king and queen and instead we're here, hiding! From a war that we shouldn't be in," Charlie says, while he slowly falls asleep.

"I know, love, but for now, we stay safe. Then, when we get to go home, we'll be happy. Forever," I tell him, rubbing his hair until he finally falls asleep. Then I climb out of bed and go get Charlie some hot tea and something for him to eat as soon as he wakes up. When I get to the kitchen, I see my mom behind the counter with a giant smile on her face.

"Honey!" she says, excitement in her voice. "There are no cooks here!" She's back in her happy place, the kitchen.

A huge smile spreads across my face. It's been so long since I got to be normal, I almost forgot what it was like. I grab an apron and put it on before stepping behind the counter with my mom. We spend hours in the kitchen baking bread, making soup, and cooking whatever we can find in the kitchen. I realize how much I missed being a normal girl, and not having a country to take care of.

Amelia walks into the kitchen only for a shocked look to take over her face. "You guys have made a huge mess in here," she says, trying not to laugh.

"Would you like to join us?" I ask.

She grins and immediately grabs an apron and joins us, making our giant mess even bigger. Not long after, Melanie and

Stephanie walk into the kitchen looking for food. Concern furrows their brows when they see us covered in flour. Then they start laughing.

"I never thought I would see my future queen covered in flour and wearing an apron," Melanie jokes.

Stephanie shakes her head in the doorway. "Anna this is widely inappropriate," she scolds gently, looking around for the maid.

"We only employ one maid for the house, and no one to cook. We need food, and I need to feel normal," I tell her. "Besides, I'm your future queen." I wave a messy spatula at her as if it's a royal scepter and raise my voice higher than normal. "So, please don't tell me what is inappropriate." I end with a giggle, not being able to take myself seriously.

Laughing at themselves, they both get aprons and join us. "I need to send food and tea up to the boys at some point," I say before I turn back toward the counter and see Charlie leaning against the doorframe. "Never mind, there Charlie is. Come, sit."

As he climbs onto the chair at the counter, I grab a slice of the bread fresh from the oven and some hot tea, and place it in front of him. A smile lights up his face when he reaches for it. "You know, bread isn't going to fill me up," he says with a laugh.

"I know, that's why we made soup," I say with a smirk. I stir the steaming soup before ladling it into a bowl and placing it in front of him with a smile.

He picks up his spoon and moans with the first sip.

"This is the best soup I've ever had," he says, finishing it faster than I've ever seen someone finish soup before. I laugh before scooping him some more. "You might have to cook more when we're home."

"Honestly? I wouldn't mind that." I say, sadness seeping through while I think of how fun today has been. I wish I could be more like myself in what is supposed to be my home. "I would love to do the things I used to," I tell him, a hint of sadness in my voice.

He seems to be pondering what I'm saying until he finishes his soup. Then he stands up, kisses my cheek, and walks out of the kitchen without a word.

Charlie

As I walk back to the study, I think about all the things Anna said to me while I was sitting at the counter. I wish she could be comfortable in the castle, but I know deep down she isn't. She loves me, so she pretends to be, but I need to make it so she actually is. That is my next project. Once I deal with this war, I must make her comfortable before I marry her.

I make it to the study in record time and find Lucas and Alex sitting on the couch already. "Have you two eaten?" I ask, "Anna and her mother made the best soup and bread in the kitchen, if you have not."

"Anna is cooking? I wasn't aware she could, but is that appropriate sir?" Lucas asks, glancing between me and Alex. "Should our future queen overwork herself simply because we didn't bring enough staff with us?

"It usually is not, but I will make some changes once we deal with this war." I tell them with a stern nod.

And with that, we discuss defense strategy and where our enemy might attack. We're protected up here, but we cannot underestimate Veirda Shadow. We spend the rest of the day and well into the night trying to come up with a plan. The problem is their armies are at least twice the size of ours. Eventually we can barely keep our eyes open, but this time we take a break and head to our chambers, making sure we get rest so we can do this again tomorrow.

When I get back to my room, Anna is already asleep in bed, looking as peaceful as ever. I change and climb into bed, and enjoy being next to her. The way her chest rises and falls. She's so beautiful.

The next morning Anna and I both wake early.

"Do you think it is safe for me to go outside today, my love?" Anna asks me, while she is braiding her hair in front of the mirror.

"As long as you stay by the house, it should be alright," I tell her, proceeding to explain to her where she needs to stay to remain unseen from any spies that could potentially be in the area. I make sure to walk her through every spot that spies could hide as well, so she doesn't go too far. The chance of her getting kidnapped again is low, but it bothers me and I have to make sure she's careful. As Anna and her mother head outside for a short walk and some fresh air, I get up and head to the study once again, wishing I could be done seeing the inside of these walls.

"Alex, Lucas, maybe we could all use some fresh air?" I ask them, in hopes that they'd be up for it. Some sunshine and crisp mountain wind might help our brains function better.

"I think that is a great idea," Alex says.

Moments we sit outside in the fresh air, taking a well deserved break, until the sun is right above us, indicating mid-day. That is when we decide to head back into the study and try to come up with a solid plan.

"Alright, they have taken out all of our allies, they're twice our size. We have to come up with our own advantage," I say, repeating what we're facing for perhaps the hundredth time. I stare at the map and the little figurines of my armies and rack my brain as if thoughts alone could fix the disadvantage we're stuck with. We are silent for what feels like hours, then all of a sudden Alex jumps out of his chair.

"I got it!" he yells.

Lucas and I just sit there and stare at him, trying to figure out what he's talking about.

"What if..." He starts moving things around on my map before he continues. When I glance at what he's arranging, I see small infantry and cavalry companies, very spread out.

"What if what, Alex? We can't separate companies like this. It's too dangerous." I tell him, trying to figure out what he is thinking of.

"What if we set up small companies as decoys? Obviously we will have to up the draft as best and gather as many new soldiers as we can. Then we can send in most of our armies to attack, along with our spies. Look," he points to several small tokens that represent military units. "We send them separately. So these men sneak into Veirda Shadow and attack them from the inside while the others can be stationed within Weide Salibe where we mentioned yesterday, here and here." He jerks his pointer finger toward two positions we'd discussed yesterday. "So while they are attacking us in different parts of the country, we defend and attack them where they aren't expecting it. How will they protect themselves when they're getting hit from both sides?" I tap my fingers against my lips, absorbing everything he just said. Is this a viable strategy? I do the math for how many spies we have already on the inside and how many more we have here that we can send in. Then I try and figure out if we can adjust the draft, which would be pushing it but possible.

"I think we can make this happen. It'll just take a lot of work. And I need you to send for messengers, at least three." I push my chair out so I can move things and see if this plan will be the best way to make things happen. And I genuinely think it will...

Chapter Fifty-One

Charlie

I RUN OUT OF the study and, as soon as I see that the messengers are here, we have three letters going out to different companies. We wait for their response before starting our official plan. Anna stares at me like I've lost my head when I run outside and then come back inside. Once I catch my breath, I stop sit down on the couch next to her, and laugh.

"What is so funny?" she asks, staring at me like I've lost my mind.

"I think we finally have a plan. But I needed to send orders to my generals first in order to put it in motion. And now that's done, so we have to just wait for notice that word has been received. Until then.....we do this."

I lay my head on her lap and stare up at her. She goes back to her book, and I just lay there watching her giggle and read.

I'm happy to get one day with nothing to do. Then I have an idea.

"Let's go dance," I tell her.

"What do you mean?" she asks. "There is no music, so we can't dance."

I sit up and pluck the book out of her hand and set it on the table, pages down so she doesn't lose her place, and then I stand all the way up and grab her hands, pulling her to a stand.

"We don't need music," I say before pulling her into a dancing position. I spin her around the sitting room, avoiding the middle where most of the furniture sits. The fireplace gleams in the background. Then I start shout-singing the most random melody, giving her the music she said we wanted. Our smiles are the biggest they have been in months. For a few minutes, we have no worries, no ex-queen, and no war; we just get to be ourselves here. After a few minutes of dancing, we fall onto the couch laughing. When Anna lays her head on my shoulder, I pull her closer to me.

Anna

The next morning I wake up, lying on the couch with my head on Charlie's chest. I sit up, stretching my muscles, but giggling at the fact that we slept in the sitting room. I pat Charlie on the shoulder trying to wake him up.

"Charlie, my love, you need to wake up. We fell asleep in the sitting room."

He opens his eyes and begins to stretch, then winces at his sore muscles. Immediately I start giggling and then so does he. We're both laughing when my mother walks into the sitting room.

"What are you two doing?" she asks, looking between us.

"We fell asleep after dancing last night," I tell her, noticing the smirk on her face and the slight sparkle in her eye. She just shakes her head at us sitting in the chair across from us.

"Do you both want to come cook with me this morning? I thought I could go collect some eggs from the chickens outside and then maybe we could make some more bread since we ate most of it yesterday." I jump up off the sofa, a smile spread across my face.

"Let's go change and I would love too," I say. Then I run up the stairs, excited to cook with my mother again. It's been so long since we cooked together.

Charlie

Standing in the kitchen and staring at Anna and her mother seamlessly moving around and never bumping into each other is never something I'd thought I would do. However, the sight of them cooking together is so magical I never want to stop watching.

"Are you going to help?" Anna says, breaking me out of my daydream.

"Uhh." I just stare at her, trying to figure out how to say I've never cooked a day in my life. I am a prince after all.

"Get in here and we'll teach you. No reason you can't learn." Her mother beckons me over with flour-covered palms. I smile and grab an apron, preparing to learn how to cook breakfast even if it kills me. *It might.*

Chapter Fifty-Two

Anna

AFTER A LONG TWO weeks, we finally hear back from the generals in charge of the armies and companies we sent orders to. The plan is in motion. Alex and Lucas ride out early the next morning, offering to be part of the company sneaking in, much to my dismay. In the two weeks we've been here, we all have grown increasingly closer, and the thought of one of my family members going into war is not something I want. After they leave, I stay in my room all day and cry, hoping for their safety. Eventually, my mom drags me out of my room.

When I go outside and see that the sun is shining and everyone is sitting in the grass, I smile a little, trying to appreciate the people still here. However, as soon as I sit down, we hear horses hooves clattering down the road. Everyone jumps into action, assuming it's the worst case scenario since no one should be approaching this stronghold. When I look up, I meet the eyes of Amelia's fiancé as he's dismounting, and my blood runs cold, then instantly it's boiling.

"You disappear for months on end and have the nerve to show up here of all places when you know we're in the middle of a war?! You almost got stabbed! And not only that, but how did you even know where we were—"

He cuts me off by putting his hand up to stop me which only pisses me off more. "Who do you—"

"I ran into the royal guards, and they told me how to get here. Amelia, we need to go. I have bargained for refuge for us in Vierda Shadow since we were not there when these Royals"—he spits at us—"kidnapped one of their citizens. And until the war is over, you are not allowed back in this country."

My jaw drops. Amelia rises to step inside like she is going to pack her things, and I grab her arm to stop her.

"You're not leaving. You won't be safe there. They know you're mine and Charlie's family." I say, hoping she understands why I can't let her choose in this instance. I turn to deal with him as heat floods my entire body. "And you," I say through gritted teeth and jabbing up at him with my finger. "You do not get to come here, interrupt your future *queen* and then order my sister around. You are not her keeper, and you are not mine."

When I finish talking, he turns to Charlie and looks him in the eyes "Keep your wife on a leash before I—" I don't even let him finish before walking up and smacking him across the face.

Amelia gasps, but doesn't defend him.

"I hope you have a good life being a refugee, but you are done here. And if I ever see your face around here again, I cannot promise you will make it out alive." I turn, meeting Charlie's eyes. When I see the smirk on his face, I start to walk away and my family follows closely behind. Charlie however stays outside long enough to make sure he leaves.

My mother makes us a delicious dinner in an attempt to get our minds off of what just happened while Amelia twirls her ring around her finger.

Guilt gnaws in my gut. "I'm sorry, Amy. I should've let you make your own decisions. But I couldn't risk losing you. That place..." I'm trying to hold back tears, while the regret and memory of what I survived eats me alive. While I believe I protected my sister, I should have at least given her some choice in the matter. She shakes her head and her voice is gentle when she responds, "No, don't apologize. You were right, but I was so blinded by what could've been that I refused to stand up to him. He was controlling and manipulative soon after we started seeing each other, and I should never have put up with it."

I sniff and outstretch my arms to hug her. She falls into my embrace and I squeeze her as if loving her can make up for my mistakes.

"When we get home we'll host a ball and find you a proper fiancé" Charlie jokes with a wink.

She chuckles. "I appreciate that Charlie. I hope one day to have a love like you and Anna do," she says before turning to my mother. "May I be excused?" My mother nods her head and my sister gets up and rushes to her room, tears looking like they're about to fall. I sit there staring at my plate, pushing my food around it but not really eating. After a few minutes of silence I stand up and excuse myself heading upstairs, Charlie close behind me.

"I'll never be a proper queen. I can't be quiet and let you deal with issues, and I can't be trapped in a castle. I don't like maids and staff serving me. I can't do it," I confess as hot tears slip down my face. "A proper queen would've never let her emotions get the best of her out there."

"I don't want everyone else's definition of a proper queen. I want you," he tells me, grabbing my chin and forcing me to look at him. "You are beautiful, kind, smart, funny. And honestly watching you win that verbal battle was astounding. I would've stabbed him for talking about you that way. Hell, I still might," he finishes with a laugh, making me smile just a little. "If I wanted a proper queen I never would've come and found my little assassin and asked her to marry me. I never would've courted you. And I sure as hell wouldn't be here right now."

The tears start flowing harder, this time with a smile on my face. "I love you, more than I ever thought I could love anyone. I can't wait to marry you." I tell him, then a wicked smile stretches across his face.

"Why wait?" he says, "get dressed."

"We don't have anyone to marry us!" I say, confused as to how this is going to work.

"Your sister will marry us. Your dad will walk you down the aisle. Everyone we need is here. Let's make sure one good thing comes from having to hide out here," he says, changing into his nicest clothes he has.

I run to my closet while he leaves the room to fill everyone in on the plan. I find my favorite dress, the pale yellow one that sits at about mid calf, and grab my slippers. Then my mother heads into the room with all the girls behind her. They start pulling at my hair and doing my makeup before they spin me to look in the mirror. I look beautiful, all done up like this. The smile on my face is bigger than it has been since my wedding got interrupted. I stand up and step out of the room, seeing my father who instantly starts crying and my sister runs ahead to where Charlie waits outside. *I guess this is happening.*

Charlie

When the idea comes to me, I make it happen at full force. Within an hour I am in my best clothes with Melanie standing next to me and Stephanie on the side of the aisle where Anna will be. All of our guards make up the crowd and Amelia is standing at the end of the aisle ready to marry us. I look up when I hear the guards gasp. I make eye contact with my favorite set of eyes and smile. She looks beautiful in her yellow dress. It makes her eyes pop. And as she approaches on the arms of her mother and father, the biggest smile brightens her face. The walk from her to me is only a couple feet, but it feels like eternity when I'm waiting for her. Tears fill my eyes as my bride makes it to me, and I reach out and grab her hands, her mother and father stepping to the side.

"You are the most beautiful girl in the whole world," I whisper.

Then Amelia starts with the typical wedding speeches.

"Hello everyone, we are gathered here today to wed Prince Charlie and Lady Annabelle. If anyone has any objections, then it's too bad because they're perfect for each other."

Anna giggles and I hold back a chuckle.

"Did you guys write your own vows? I don't have those memorized," she whispers loudly enough for those closest to us to overhear. A snort and a couple muffled laughs later, and I nod my head.

"Anna," I start, looking her in the eyes. "I know this isn't everything you imagined it to be, and I promise to make sure you have the wedding of your dreams when we get back, however, I am so happy to be able to marry you today. You are beautiful, kind, caring, and everything I could look for in a wife. You've stuck with me through a lot, and today is finally our day. I love you so much, and I cannot wait to spend the rest of our lives together."

When I finish, she smiles, tears rolling down her cheeks.

I lean close and whisper, "Stop crying. You're gonna ruin your makeup."

She somehow sniffs and giggles at the same time. I make a new goal to make her do that again whenever I can.

But I could listen to her laugh forever.

"Charlie, I'm never going to top that. But I'm going to do my best to try." She wipes her eyes, smudging her makeup a little. "When we first met and I didn't know who you were, I was smitten. The night we spent together dancing made me fall for you, then when I found out who you were and that I was going to have to kill you, I couldn't bring myself to do it. And I tried, multiple times."

As she's reminding me that she was an assassin, my heart twists. She loved me even then?

She continues, "My heart knew long before my brain did that you were my forever, and I wouldn't want it any other way. So thank you for loving me despite my flaws."

Tears roll down my very masculine face as I remember how we started and where we are now.

"I now pronounce you husband and wife," Amelia says with a huge smile. "Now kiss!" she screeches.

I flinch at how high-pitched her voice was. When I lean in to kiss Anna, I realize it's our first kiss as husband and wife. Our beginning to forever.

"You're officially stuck with me," she whispers in my ear, pulling me down to kiss me again.

"Good. I love you," I say. My cheeks ache with how much I'm smiling. "Tomorrow we have to go back to the real world but for the rest of today we stay in this bubble. Deal?" I ask, looking into her eyes.

"Deal," she says, before I bend down and pick her up princess style, and carry her up to our room. I'm determined to make our wedding day the best day ever.

"Here's to the start of forever," I say, closing the door behind me.

Chapter Fifty-Three

Anna

THE NEXT MORNING I wake up happier than ever before. I'm a wife, and I get to enjoy that before officially becoming queen. However, as I climb out of bed, I hear a noise that I haven't experienced out here before, and it instantly ruins my mood. It sounds like an army of thundering hooves, and I'm pretty sure it's coming our way. I dress in my best fighting outfit, strapping my dagger to my thigh before I run out of the room.

Charlie isn't in bed anymore. When I make it outside, I see him and the guards already there, swords in hand. Something is coming, but I can tell by their faces no one knows what.

"What do you want me to do to help?" I yell towards Charlie.

"I want you inside, but I know that's not going to happen so stay toward the back until we know what we're dealing with."

Avery grunts in agreement. I nod and stand in the back, waiting for the cavalry to come over the mountain so we can see who is approaching us. After some time, and a lot of tension, we finally see horses peeking over the skyline. Alex and Lucas ride at the front of the army. When I see them I take off, running faster than I've ever ran in my life.

"Alex! Lucas!" I yell.

They both laugh when they see me running. They continue on past me–*rude*–on the horses causing me to stop, pivot,, and run back toward the fortress. When I get there, I'm out of breath, but it's worth it to hug the two men who've become like brothers to me.

"I'm so glad you guys are okay," I gasp in between breaths.

"So are we, and we are beyond happy to see you. But we need to debrief before we catch up okay?" Alex says.

I nod and let them head to the study, glancing at Charlie when he walks past me.

"Are you coming?" Charlie asks me, and I smile.

Yes, I am.

I follow them all into the house and up to the study, glad I get to hear what's going on in the war. When we all sit down at the desk, Alex speaks first.

"Firstly, we're only staying today. We're heading back first thing in the morning. But we wanted to give you a slight update. We were able to infiltrate the castle and find out that they've offered all of our allies a lot of money to not back us up for this war. And we also found their plan of attack, so we relocated some armies to the places they think of as holes. And they knew about the wedding which means we still have a spy in our midst, and it wasn't just Diane." As he explains, his eyes never drop from mine and Charlie's.

"It was Amelia's fiancé," I say, looking at Charlie and realizing he came to the same conclusion I did. "That must be how he bargained for refuge in Veirde Shadow."

"I was just thinking the same thing. I'm glad she stayed and cut things off with him," Charlie says, glancing back at Lucas

Why are Lucas' eyes lighting up? This is heavy subject matter. Suspicious.

After they catch us up on the rest of their time in the shadow lands, we all head down to an early lunch, but I grab Lucas' arm and have him stay back.

"Do you have something you need to tell me?" I ask, giving him the same look my mom used to give me when I was hiding something from her.

"Um, nope, don't think so," he blurts in a rush, trying to step past me.

I block his path and raise an eyebrow. "You like my sister, don't you?"

His face turns red, and he refuses to make eye contact with me.

"Yup, that's what I thought," I huff. "Well, don't pursue anything yet. Her fiancé just left her, and you need to let her heart heal But..." I eye him up and down. "I do approve," I say before unblocking the hallway and heading to the dining room. Everyone else is already at the table when Lucas and I walk in.

Charlie shoots me a questioning glance, and I wave him off, planning on telling him later. We all sit down to eat, and we are joking around with each other. After a peaceful day of bouncing back and forth between eating and going outside until the sun goes down, we retire to our rooms. We all say goodbye to Lucas and Alex, making sure to give them our well wishes and hopes of safety. When everyone is done with their goodbyes we head to bed. Now, we prepare for the months before we see our brothers again...

Charlie

After spending the day with my best friends, the dread of them leaving again fills me. I have a restless night of sleep, tossing and turning through my thoughts. Realizing that this is the longest any of us have been away from each other, so being away from all three of them for this long is hard. Eventually after tossing and turning for long enough I decide to get up and head to my study, hoping to get some work done. When I walk into the study, I get the biggest shock of my life. Drake is sitting in my chair with his feet on my desk. I stop at the door and just stare, assuming that I'm hallucinating from lack of sleep.

Finally, after staring at each other for so long, Drake speaks, "Are you just gonna stare at me or are you going to come over here?"

"Drake, what are you doing here?" I ask, stunned into silence.

"You thought I wasn't gonna fight in a war that affects my country and my best friend? I'm only sorry I couldn't get here before the wedding," he says with a laugh. I pull him into a hug, happier than ever to see him.

"You're supposed to be off living your happily ever after," I say, "not solving my problems."

"Someone has to be here to help Anna solve your problems. Now tell me what's going on so I can help." He gets out of my chair and settles onto the couch, waiting for me to join him. I sit down in my chair, and start giving him the updates from Alex and Lucas along with the plan. "So, you're taking them down from the inside?" he asks, curiosity filling his voice.

"That's the hope, but it's going to take months," I tell him.

"Not if we send Diane in. And she's already volunteered," he says, while I stare at him like he grew a second head. Not sure how to handle this, I continue to just stare.

"We can't send her in. It's far too dangerous."

"It's not dangerous for her, though. They want her there," he reminds me.

I sit there, debating what he's saying. If we send Diane in and she's actually on our side, that would be an advantage on our part. The biggest advantage we have. But if she betrays us again, then we would most likely lose this war. It would devastate our country. So I just sit there for a few very long minutes before I get up and exit the study. I wake up Anna and then bang on Alex and Lucas' door until they yell, "We are awake! Stop knocking!"

They all know if I'm interrupting their dreams like this that it's something important. They all get dressed and head to the study. When they walk in, they have the same reaction I did to Drake being there.

Anna is the first one to break the silence. "Drake!" she exclaims before planting her hands on her hips. "Don't get me wrong, I'm glad you're here. But also why are you here, exactly?"

"Diane and I have an idea that you guys will either love or hate, so I'm here to give it to you," he says, looking between all of us. "We need to send her in."

They all stare at him, debating what he said.

Alex is the first one to speak. "Okay."

"Start talking then," Lucas says.

Everyone sits down, and we start adjusting our plans.

Chapter Fifty-Four

Anna

AFTER SPENDING THE REST of the night catching up, strategizing, and figuring out the safest way to slip Diane into the castle, we have the perfect plan. First, we need to get her here, so we send Drake to get her. He said it's about half a day's ride to where they were staying, so they should be back first thing tomorrow morning. With that information, we all head down to breakfast, causing a ton of confusion since Alex and Lucas weren't supposed to be here anymore.

"Good morning," I say when we walk into the dining room. "Change of plans! Everything is put on hold until Drake returns with Diane tomorrow morning!" I proceed to sit down, causing everyone to look at me like I grew a second head.

"Wait what?" Melanie finally speaks up, looking between all of us.

"Drake and Diane came up with a fool proof plan. The only problem was that they didn't know where the troops were, so now, we have the perfect plan and Drake is on his way to get Diane," I explain. "Just trust us, please. We'll explain it all as soon as they get here." I give everyone just enough information to soothe their anxiety so they can go back to eating. The tension from the night before is gone.

We spend the day laughing and pretending like everything is normal. We know eventually we're going to have to find our new normal, but we aren't ready for that yet. Drake and Diane arrive the next morning. They decided to ride through the night since there were no good inns to stop at. So, I get them set up in Amelia's chambers, deciding that she can bunk with Melanie and Stephanie for now. Then, after they get a few hours of sleep and a bath, we agree to meet in the dining room to iron out plans. That way, we can eat and work.

I talk to my mom and see if she needs help cooking breakfast or lunch for everyone, since she's been cooking meals for us. I find my dad and Amelia helping her in the kitchen.

"I'm guessing you guys don't need help then?" I say with a laugh before I glance over and see Lucas walking out of the pantry with a bag of flour.

"No, Your Majesty, I think we got it covered," he says with a wink. Alex and Lucas were really upset yesterday morning when we told them that we got married without them but they understand.

"I'm not 'Your Majesty' yet. I still haven't been crowned," I say, laughing as he trips over his feet and makes a mess of flour everywhere. I go to help him up but Amelia beats me to him.

"Let me help you clean that up," I say, stepping between him and my sister to get the broom. After Lucas and I clean up the kitchen, I grab his hand and drag him out of the kitchen into the hallway, giving him a dirty look.

"Why are you mad at me? You literally said you approved!"

I shush him. "That was before I knew you were staying!" I whisper-shout, hoping Amelia isn't eavesdropping. "She just got left. Give her time before you try to court her. Please."

"Anna, I'm not dumb. I'm just trying to get to know her better first. That's all, I swear."

I nod my head, contemplating what he's saying. "Forget it for now. Lets go see if they're ready for us in the dining room."

"Okay," I say, looking back at the kitchen and my sister one more time before following Lucas into the dining room. When we get there, everyone is already around the table with the maps spread out. Lucas and I grab our seats, and just as we do, my family walks in with the food they were making and set it on the table before sitting down too. I look at them, shocked, before glancing at Charlie. He shrugs his shoulders like I shouldn't be surprised before everyone dives into the food. After we all eat, I half expect my family to get up and leave with the war talk going on, but instead Melanie stands up and clears the dishes from the table before sitting back down.

"Are you sure you guys want to be here during the talk of war? It's not necessary."

"You're our family, which makes them—" my mother swipes her hands towards my put together family, "—family too. So it is necessary," she says before turning to Charlie and nodding her head.

He smiles and nods back before saying, "So what we figured out last night is that sending Diane across enemy lines is our best bet."

Hands lift in protest before Charlie holds a finger to his mouth to hush them "Hear us out before you interrupt me, please. Our enemies want Diane. That's why they started the war—or that's their excuse. So, sending her over there should also be the end of the war on their side, but not on *our* side. Diane is going to infiltrate the palace and learn their weak spots since we can't seem to figure them out. They should be withdrawing their forces at this point. If so, we can go back to the castle while we're doing this.

Then, when Diane learns their weak points, she will send word to us and we will send Drake in to get her. Once again, this will cause a war, but they won't be prepared this time, because we'll already be attacking before they have their armies formed. The key to us winning is that Diane gets in and out without them realizing she's on our side until it's too late. If we attack their weak spots then we can win."

"What if they don't retreat when Diane returns?" Melanie asks.

"Or more importantly. What if this has all been a long scheme to once again take down my sister?" Amelia asks, glaring right at Diane when she says it, the disgust dripping from her tone.

"I deserve that," Diane responds softly. "But, I promise you it's not. And to show you it's not, I'm going to tell you something I've never told anyone. My parents weren't born a lord and lady like everyone in their town thinks they were. In fact none of our lords and ladies are. They were all placed in their positions by the queen so the royals can control what's happening in their land and still have spies in the area to prevent any uprisings that might happen," Diane explains, looking right at Amelia.

My heart refuses to trust her, but my mind understands we have to. I glance at my sister and dip my chin to let her see that I believe her.

"So we're all good now?" Charlie asks. "Perfect, to answer your question Melanie. We have no plan if they don't retreat so we're just hoping this works. But we don't have a better plan. We have our troops stationed where Lucas says they will attack, and sending Diane in is our best, and possibly only, hope of winning this war. Is everyone in agreement on that?"

A unanimous *yes* goes through the room signaling that everyone understands the plan and will do their part. We make sure that Diane and Drake have enough food to make it to the border, and that Drake has everything he'll need to stay close until Diane sends her signal. Then we just have to wait until morning to start.

Charlie and I need to see Drake and Diane off. He tossed and turned most of the night, and I notice dark circles under his eyes.

"You're worried," I say softly.

He purses his lips before answering, "More like I'm really nervous about this plan not working, but I'll be alright," he says, even though I know he's lying.

He's just not ready to talk about it, but I suspect we both worry about everything falling apart. As we head downstairs, we stop a few steps up, Charlie scanning the room like it's the last time he's going to see them all together. My heart clenches. After a moment, we step down to the bottom of the stairs, and

Charlie goes right for Drake, so I head over to say goodbye to Diane.

As I pull Diane into a hug, she looks at me like I've lost it before I whisper in her ear, "Come back in one piece, and come home. You'll be welcome back at the castle if you can pull this off."

Shock registers on her face before she puts on a mask of indifference and nods at me, giving me one more squeeze before pulling away and pushing me towards Drake. In that moment my heart shatters again. He was my first companion at the castle, the first person to see who I was and embrace it instead of trying to change me, like the maid and servants did. "Thank you Drake, for everything. Come home," I say, blinking back the tears forming in my eyes.

"Always," he promises before pulling away and turning to head toward the door. We all watch them leave, and I wonder if anyone else is nauseous with anxiety.

Waiting is the hardest part, but it will take time for Drake and Diane to infiltrate Veirde Shadow and implement the plan.

After a few hours of sitting in silence, finally Alex breaks says, "I know the waiting is hard, but we can't just sit here and stare at the wall. There has to be something we can do in the meantime." He looks at all of us, trying to get someone to agree with him.

"There isn't anything we can do to help them. But we could have someone go scope out the castle and see how things are panning out there. We also could clean up around here so it is ready to go when we leave, yeah?" I tell him, looking at Charlie for confirmation.

"Yes, that's a great idea! Who wants to go to the castle?" Charlie asks, glancing towards Alex.

Stephanie is the first one to stand up and volunteer, Melanie not far behind her. We get a guard around to go with them before sending them off. Stressing about two more friends leaving, but I brush it off, and move on to assigning projects around the fortress. Knowing we should be able to head back to the castle soon means that we have a lot of stuff that needs to get done here. I give everyone an assignment before heading off to do stuff I need to get done first. I have my mom and Amelia cleaning up the kitchen and making a list of things that need to be restocked, Alex and Lucas are in the barn cleaning up and seeing if anything needs to be restocked out there, while Charlie my dad and I are going through the house to clean up and make sure everything is organized.

We work on things for a few hours before we settle down for dinner, everybody has their list so we send it with a guard to town in an attempt to get a head start. Melanie and Stephanie should be back at some point through the night, so tomorrow we can get a status report on the castle. After dinner we all head up to bed, exhausted from the day, especially knowing all we can do is wait and hope until something happens.

Chapter Fifty-Five

Charlie

AFTER A FEW DAYS full of pacing, scouting, and organizing, we finally get word that the Vierde Shadow troops are retreating from the castle. After Melanie and Stephanie returned from their first scouting mission, we agreed that they would go out on scouting missions every other day with Alex and Lucas, taking the opposite days to keep us informed on what was going on. However, we also thought it would take a few weeks before scouts started retreating, not days. The fact that they started moving so quickly is suspicious. Either Diane really convinced them that she's not on our side, or she's really not on our side. We still wait a few days before we think about heading back to the castle. We need to make sure that there isn't a trap being set before we officially go home. We continue our scouting missions before it's finally time. We wake up super early and finish packing, taking one last look around the room.

"Are you ready to go home?" Anna asks me with a smile.

"Let's do this." I say, turning and heading towards the door. Once we get downstairs everyone is already at the door with whatever they brought with them, pleasant expressions on all their faces. The tension of the last several weeks is fading, even if slightly. I smile, only a little disappointed to be leaving this peaceful sanctuary. We all head outside and the horses are already tacked up so we can leave immediately. We load up the carriage, and I help Anna's mom and dad inside and we start the journey back to the castle. It takes a few hours but soon, we are riding up to the castle, finally home.

The damage that was caused by the armies is extensive, but nothing that we can't fix. First things first, we need to eat something. We head to the dining room where the chef already has food set out for us. I smile at him, but feel my heart breaking a little, knowing that Anna's mom didn't make this meal like the meals we've had for weeks. After we all eat, I head right up to my study, needing to make the plans for repairs. While I work on that, Alex and Lucas start cataloging what got ruined so we have a record. I make a list of supplies we need, and send it with a messenger to town and to collect them. After doing all the tasks I need to do, I head to bed, finding Anna already there.

"I know I should be grateful to be home, Charlie, but I miss the quiet," she whispers, almost as if she doesn't want me to hear.

"I was thinking the same thing. Once we get through the coronation and our big wedding for show, we can make some changes. I promise," I say gently as I climb into bed with her. We spend the next few days gathering supplies and assigning tasks to fix the castle. We have every member of the castle staff working harder than I've ever had them work before. We make a list of tasks that need to get done before our second wedding and the coronation. Everything must be impeccable so we appear strong. After a few stressful weeks between preparing the castle and hearing nothing from Diane and Drake, finally we get our first letter.

I walk out to the hallway from my study, and turn to look at my guard that's outside. "I need Lucas and Alex. Quickly please." I say before going back to my desk and reading the letter again.

A headache begins to form behind my eyes. Concern is creased on my brow when they walk in the door.

"What's wrong?" Alex asks, not even bothering to greet me. All I do is shove the letter towards him. He picks it up and reads it, his face dropping just like mine did. "This isn't good," he says as he glances up towards me. Now lines of worry burrow into his features.

"Something is wrong. We don't have a date picked out for the coronation yet, so why would she put a date on there like that?" I look between them, the realization dawning on their faces before it hits me. "That's when they're going to attack." I instantly jump into action, needing to get companies prepared.

Lucas reads over the letter again, trying to glean more information. Using the intel from the letter and what Alex and Lucas uncovered when they infiltrated the castle, we send companies to all the spots they were planning on attacking before. We spend the whole night writing messages and sending them with our fastest messengers, so when they attack in a few days we're prepared. I send for Anna, Melanie, and Stephanie.

"I wanted to update you all and let you know that we got a letter from Diane. She gave us a date, which we're assuming will be when they attack, and using the information that Alex and Lucas gathered, we have also determined the three spots they are most likely to attack. So we are sending extra companies there in order to have a counter attack prepared. We just finished giving all the all letters to the messengers. We also need to prepare a few small companies in case they attack anywhere else." I pause, taking in their serious expressions. "How's that sound?"

"I think for the sake of the staff, it sounds great. But for us, I need more information," Anna says. Melanie and Stephanie nod in agreement.

"Well, that's how I'll address the staff then. We are pretty sure that they are going to attack by water, at our border, or through the mountains," I say. "That's all we know."

"Okay, and you have companies there already?" Melanie asks.

"They will receive their orders tonight and be on their way. We diverted two companies to each area while leaving one here at the castle and we have an extra one prepared to move to wherever soldiers are getting hurt the worst at," I add, trying to give them all the information I have.

"Okay, let's end this war then," Stephanie says, standing up. "What do we need to do?'

"Let's gather the staff so I can update them, and then we will just have to wait and see what happens," I tell them. They get up and start gathering the staff for our announcement. Anna and I wait patiently, practicing my speech until Alex comes back to get us.

"They're ready for you," he says. We approach the bottom of the stairs in the great hall where everyone gathered. They need this hope as much as we do.

"I'm sure you are all wondering about updates in the war. We have received our first letter from our spies, and we have a date on the big attack. We have redirected companies to the three places they are most likely to attack while also leaving a company here at the castle so we can be prepared and remain safe. I understand if you would like to leave the castle and return to your families, you will be granted leave with no issues. We are leaving this up to you all," I tell all of the staff, giving them options to decide what exactly they want to do. "Now you are all dismissed. If you would like to be granted leave, please see Melanie or Stephanie and they will get your information passed onto me." All of the staff heads out to decide what they want to do for the time being.

After a few hours we only have two staff members that are asking for leave, and it is people with family close to places that have been affected since war. We grant them leave, and I stay locked in my study until dinner, making sure that we have nothing else to deal with, and then I head down to dinner with the family, needing some sort of normalcy in my life.

Chapter Fifty-Six

Charlie

IT FEELS LIKE MONTHS while we wait for the attack, but it is merely days. We have someone ready to send updates while we wait for them. Finally, we receive a letter. They can see the armies moving in from the water side. So the information Diane sent was accurate.

We dispatch our extra company of people to the attack site so they have the numbers they might need. I continue to lock myself in my study, day in and day out, waiting for something, anything. Until one day I get awoken earlier than normal...

"Your Majesty!"

The yelling jolts me awake, making Anna stir next to me. I look out the window and see the sun still isn't up in the sky. They bang on the door, so I climb out of bed and yank it open, wondering what is so urgent.

Standing at the door is a servant, sweaty and frantic, waving a letter above his head. I yank it out of his hands with a mumbled thank you, and close the door, heading to the sitting room to read it. I open the letter, and a smile spreads across my face as I jump back up, needing to wake Anna up.

"Anna! Anna, you're never going to believe this!" I shout as she starts to stir, slowly sitting up and staring at me, exhaustion on her face. "I know it's early, my flower, and I'm so sorry, but you need to read this." I pass her the letter, giving her a minute to read it.

"Does this mean what I think it means?" Anna asks, a smile stretching across her face.

"I think it does, we need to go tell the others!" I rush to get dressed, Anna not far behind me. Heading to each room individually to wake everyone in the castle up, servants and maids included. Once everyone is gathered at the bottom of the stairs, Anna and I stand before the crowd, smiles on our faces. "We have received word from King and Queen Amoreli. They have decided to remove the troops and surrender. The soldiers began their retreat first thing this morning. They also have agreed to allow Diane to go wherever she pleases, so Drake should be coming home soon."

As soon as I finish, an uproar of cheers start. Everyone is ready to be done with this.

"I will need volunteers to go to the cities affected by the war, and find out what they need so I can get them supplies. And then we will be able to celebrate!"

I collect volunteers, assigning them with different towns to go check on, wanting to make sure my people are taken care of. Information trickles in over the next couple of weeks and we get supplies sent out so no one is in need. After all the towns and people are taken care of we start planning our big wedding and our coronations, needing things to be official. Even though we are already married, we have to do a wedding for the people to see us as a united front, and for the people to see Anna as their queen. The day we sit down to start making our plans, the people we've been waiting for walk into the castle.

"Diane! Drake! We're so happy to see you both," Anna says, walking up and giving them both a hug. "Perfect timing, too. You get to be a part of planning the big day!"

"Oh yay," Drake says sarcastically, even though I know he's joking and is very excited. Anna smacks him in the arm before grabbing Diane's hand and dragging her to the dining room where everyone is getting ready to eat breakfast, Drake and I not far behind. As soon as we walk in everyone jumps up and rushes to greet Diane and Drake.

"We were wondering when you all would get home," Alex laughs, grabbing Drake's hand before pulling him into a hug.

"Yeah it took you guys long enough, must have been sight seeing," Melanie laughs, hugging Diane.

We all sit down for breakfast, chatting and catching up on things. I smile, glad things are slowly going back to normal.

It takes a few weeks but we get everything planned and invitations sent out. For a show of good faith, we also decide to invite King and Queen Amoreli, in hopes maybe we can start forming an alliance. We set the wedding for a month from now so everyone has time to get here and we have time to get things set up. I make sure Anna gets a new dress, one for the wedding and one for coronation so she doesn't have to stay in white since she's not a fan of white dresses. As the day approaches, she seems to be more and more on edge.

"What's the matter, my flower?" I ask her one night as we're climbing into bed. "You haven't seemed like yourself."

"I think I'm just nervous. I'm scared of being queen. I'm scared of something happening at our wedding, again," she tells me, staring at me like she doesn't know how to feel.

"It'll be alright. Anything that gets thrown at us, at least we'll be together," I tell her, pulling her in close to me.

"It's not just that. Something feels wrong. I don't feel 100% like myself," she says softly, laying her head on my shoulder. "I just feel...off."

"Should we call a healer in the morning? Just to check you out."

"That's probably a good idea. Can you send for Adam? He's the only one I really trust."

"Absolutely, my love. For now, let's get some sleep." As we both doze off my mind is going a million miles a minute. What could possibly be wrong with Anna? I hope she's okay.

Chapter Fifty-Seven

Anna

THE NEXT MORNING I sleep until I hear a knock on the door.

"Lady Anna, it's Adam. May I come in?"

I slowly sit up and blink the sleepiness from my eyes.

"Yes. come in," I say, not moving to get out of bed. "Thank you for coming on such short notice. I'm sure you're busy."

"Anything for you, my lady," Adam says, walking over to me. "Tell me what's going on."

"Well, you see, I haven't been feeling like myself. When we're training, I'm getting exhausted more easily and I feel like I'm dragging. And I'm sleeping and eating a lot more than I was before. I think something is going on since I wasn't able to heal fully." As I finish talking I look up and see Adam smiling. "What's so funny? Do you know what's wrong with me?"

"Oh Anna, I think I do. I'm fairly confident you're pregnant," he says.

My jaw hits the floor. "That's not possible. We were careful. We wanted to wait until after the coronation," I ramble, trying to make him understand that there's no way.

"I hate to tell you this, but it's very possible. I want you to keep to your regular routine for now. After the coronation in a few days, we'll run some tests to be sure. Until then, drink a lot of water. I'll see you in a few days," he says, standing up and leaving me sitting there in shock. It just can't be possible. After I sit there and process what he told me I get up and change, heading for Charlie's study first. I knock on the door and open it before he tells me to come in, finding Drake in there talking to Charlie already. As soon as the door opens, they stop talking and look up at me.

"Sorry to interrupt. I can come back." I say, turning around to leave.

"No, it's okay. I was just leaving," Drake says, standing up and walking out the door, nodding his head at me as I walk by.

"What did Adam say? Are we okay to do the coronation and wedding still?" Charlie asks me, concern dripping from his voice.

"Umm, he actually encouraged it. I have to go see him the day after for some testing though," I tell him, trying to hint at what I need to tell him without blatantly saying it.

"Did he say what he thinks it is that's causing you to feel off?" he asks again as he stands up. "I can call a different healer if I need to."

"No, no, it's fine. He did great. You should sit back down for this," I say, which makes him sit down and look at me full of concern. "Adam thinks I'm pregnant."

Charlie just sits there, blinking at me.

After several minutes, I finally break the silence. "Charlie, please say something."

"I'm gonna be a dad?" he asks, eyes lighting up when he looks at me. I nod my head, tears filling my eyes which causes him to jump up and run around the desk. "We're gonna be parents?" He says again, picking me up and spinning me in a circle.

"I know we wanted to wait. But I feel like it's destiny for us to have this little one," I say, tears forming in my eyes.

"It is. Now let's get you back to bed."

"No. I'm going to training. Adam said it's best to keep up my daily routine," I tell him. "I just needed to tell you first."

"Okay," Charlie says, sounding hesitant. "Just be careful please." he says, placing his hand on my belly before he leans down and kisses me. "I love you."

"I love you too, Charlie. I will be careful. I promise," I say before heading out of the study and down to the training ring, happier than I have been in a long time.

I continue my normal routine for the next few days until I'm awoken by knocking on the door. When I open my eyes, Charlie isn't in bed next to me. I get up and head to the door opening to find all the women that are supposed to help me get ready for my wedding and coronation.

"Please come in!" I tell them, stepping aside before I realize that I'm still in my pajamas. "Let me go change."

"No" they shout before rushing me over to the vanity. "Let's get you ready first." my mom says walking into the door with a huge smile on her face.

I sit down at the vanity, and the maids do my hair, placing it in an intricate braid before wrapping it into a bun at the crown of my head. They place my tiara on top of my head, then apply my makeup, including giving me a beautiful nude smoky eye, before I head into the closet to get changed.

My dress is even more exquisite than my first wedding dress. It is a beautiful white ballgown with flowers sewn into the bodice. The maids help me into my dress before my mother laces it up, making a comment about it not going as tight as the other one did. She gets my coronation dress ready before stepping into her own gown. When I walk out of the closet, I find Amelia, Stephanie, Melanie, and Diane all in very beautiful dresses, waiting to watch me remarry the love of my life.

After the wedding, I have to immediately come back to change and do the coronation, since I can't be crowned until we're married. My dress for the coronation is a light floor length dress that's made of silk and covered in embroidered flowers.

Melanie takes the lead, and we head down to the garden. The men are waiting for us right inside the door that heads out to our makeshift aisle in the garden. When Melanie and Stephanie move out of the way, I make eye contact with my dad, who immediately bursts into tears. I wrap my arms around him, squeezing him harder than I've ever hugged him. "I love you, dad."

"I love you too, baby girl," he says, kissing my forehead. "Are you ready for this?"

"Beyond ready." I smile at him, tears close to falling. "I can't cry. I'll mess up my makeup."

Chapter Fifty-Eight

Charlie

As I'm waiting at the altar for Anna to come down the aisle, I realize how nervous I am. I wipe my face off again when the doors open and my friends come down the aisle, Drake walking with Diane, then Stephanie and Melanie with Alex between them, then lastly Lucas and Amelia. I smile at all of them as they find their seats in the front row. I look into the crowd and see that everyone has shown up. As soon as I do a sweep over the crowd, the violin players start, and a smile spreads across my face.

When the door opens, Anna and her parents step out. Everything vanishes but her. She looks absolutely stunning in her dress with her hair done perfectly for when she becomes my queen. As she reaches me at the end of the aisle, I reach out for her hand, pulling her up onto the altar with me. Her parents kiss her on each cheek before letting go of her and hugging me.

"Take care of my little girl," her dad says before pulling away.

"I will," I promise before turning and looking back at Anna, my cheeks already aching from how huge my smile is.

Once the officiant starts the ceremony, it's pretty quick. We exchange vows, then kiss, and we're officially married. At least in the eyes of our people. Then Anna's mom rushes her off to change for the coronation and the ball after the wedding. Once again, when she comes down, she is the most beautiful woman I've ever seen in her yellow silk floor length dress. We walk over to the dais hand in hand and step up to the thrones.

"We are all gathered here today to crown our newly married king and queen!" the priest says, and a roar goes through the crowd. First he turns to me. "Prince Charlie, do you vow to do whatever you have to in order to protect your country and your people?"

"I vow," I say, bowing down as he lifts the crown onto my head.

"Princess Anna." He turns to Anna, ready to ask her the same question. "Do you vow to do whatever you have to in order to protect your country and your people?"

Anna glances at me and smiles before turning back to the priest. "I vow." Then she leans down, getting the crown placed on her head.

"Then by the power of this country and the law, I now pronounce you, King and Queen Greystone!"

Another roar goes through the audience at the announcement. I glance over at Anna and seeing her with the crown on her head is everything I needed.

"I love you, Queen Anna," I whisper, leaning over before kissing her.

"I love you, King Charles," she says back, smiling.

We soak up the happiness of the night, dancing the night away, knowing tomorrow we find out if we'll actually be parents. We spend hours dancing, eating, and mingling. Melanie and Stephanie keep refilling Anna's wine not noticing the fact that she's been dumping it out every chance she gets. As the night winds down and guests start heading back to their rooms, we have an unexpected visitor...

The doors burst open as Anna and I get ready to head up to the room, the one person we thought we wouldn't have to deal with walking in the room.

"Guards!" I shout, pulling Anna behind me.

"No, no. No need for that, Charles," Minerva says with a smirk as the guards start to surround her. She swoops her hand and sends them all flying backwards. I stand there in shock.

Magic used to exist, but I believed all magic wielders were extinct outside of healers and potion makers. The closer she gets to me, the farther I push Anna back, not sure what to do.

"I mean you no harm, stepson. I'm just here for the one in her womb," she says pointing a slender finger at Anna's middle. I hear gasps from all my friends around, and they all look at us for confirmation.

"I don't know what you're talking about. We have nothing confirmed yet," I say, looking at the guards that are trying to sneak up behind her.

"But you knew there was a suspicion. I just need some of its blood to heal me, there is a sense of magic in it that I need.'

"No!" Anna shouts, pulling into herself more. "I will never let you near me or my baby."

The guards jump on Minerva, moving to arrest her, but before they stand up, she's gone. Disappearing into thin air.

I turn to Anna who is pale as a ghost. "I guess that's all the confirmation you need?" I ask, hoping she says no and that we can still go see Adam.

"We have to do something about her. And our baby doesn't have magic," she says, turning toward the door. "I need sleep and then we're going to see Adam first thing in the morning."

"Okay, my love." I follow her to the room after saying good-night to everyone, telling them we'll explain more in the morning.

First thing the next morning we go see Adam and he confirms our worst fear. There is a sense of magic in the baby, and Anna is definitely pregnant. Now, we need to come up with a plan to protect us and the baby while also giving Anna the most stress free pregnancy possible.

After a few days of planning we decide our best option is to have Anna leave the castle. We just have to figure out where to send her so that Minerva can't sense the magic. We also need to figure out what we're going to do with a new magic wielder. We call our family into the study for a private meeting to explain to them what's going on.

"Thank you all for meeting with us. We have met with Healer Adam and determined that we are expecting a baby, and the little one has a sense of magic. We have to figure out what to do in the meantime so Minerva cannot get to the baby or Anna. And we also need to figure out how this happened, because we thought magic was extinct."

When I glance at Anna's mom, I notice she looks super fidgety, like something is wrong.

"Mom are you alright?" Anna asks, picking up on the same vibes I did.

"Well you see. I have something to tell you guys. And I don't know how to tell you," she says, looking between Anna and me. Then she opens her palm and a leaf appears. "We have magic."

Acknowledgements

To my mom and dad, thank you both for supporting my dreams and ambitions. You have supported me every step of the way and I am so grateful to you both for always encouraging me to follow my dreams. You guys are the best parents I could ever ask for, thank you for being in my corner, always.

To MOP, thank you guys for being the best internet friends a girl could ask for and believing in me always. I have never felt more loved by people I've never met in real life than I do by each and every one of you.

To Alex, without you this book would not have happened, seriously. Your encouragement and help have been more than I could have ever imagined from some stranger on the internet. The way you have gone from an internet friend I just talked to about books, to not only my closest friend but also my biggest cheerleader means more to me than you will ever know and I am so so grateful to you.

To Kier, thank you for being my publishing partner in crime. From making the cover, to answering my marketing questions, to reading my story when I was crashing out, and everything in between, I would not be here without your support. YOU are truly the angel that I needed.

To Mak, I don't even know where to start. From an internet stranger I randomly messaged because I loved your vibes, to my best friend in less than a year. Getting to be on this journey with you has been incredible and I don't think I could have possibly done it without you being there for me. Even when you were deep in the editing trenches you were offering to help whenever I needed you and I will forever be grateful for that.

To Sky, thank you for always pushing me, even when I didn't believe in myself. Thank you for reading a hundred drafts and dealing with me constantly stressing out. Thank you for being the angel that you are and helping me whenever I needed it. I appreciate you more than I could ever put into words.

To Sanikki, before even reading my story, you helped nurture it into being what it is today. If it wasn't for you telling me that you can't wait to read it I wouldn't have kept pushing some nights. Your heart is so big and the love you give is never ending, thank you for letting me be on the receiving end of it.

To B, if it wasn't for your crazy group chat I never would've followed my dreams and for that I am forever grateful. On top of that you are an amazing friend, hands down one of the best. Wherever we go from here we do it together. Thank you for supporting this journey from the jump and not thinking I'm crazy.

To my ARC and Street Team, thank you for taking a chance on this debut author and jumping on the bandwagon as soon as I asked, I'm forever grateful for your love and support. I hope Anna and Charlie's story finds a place in your heart like you all have in mine.

To Sarah D, this journey has been a wild one and I couldn't be more grateful to have you be a part of it. Asking you a million questions I already knew the answer too, giving me advice whenever I needed it, or simply being in your DMs bothering you for fun, you've been there every step of the way and I am forever thankful for you.

To Sarah E, thank you for being the best editor I could've asked for. You jumped in to save me when I felt like my ship was sinking and you stopped it. You have been the biggest helper and an amazing friend. I am beyond grateful to have you be the one that edited my book and made it perfect for readers.

Lastly to Rae, I am forever grateful to have my built in google search in your brain. You have been a lifesaver when it comes to research for this book and I don't

ACKNOWLEDGEMENTS

think I could've found these answers on my own. You're an irreplaceable friend and I'm so glad your traumatic little novels brought us together. Thank you for your immeasurable help.

About the Author

Jazmine, also known as J. Gillman, is a 26 year old cat mom whose love of writing started in high school. She loves all things fantasy and pretending she lives inside of her books. During the day Jazmine is an Author PA and business owner who loves helping Indie Authors make their dreams come true. Growing up in Michigan her whole life you can typically find her enjoying the scenery in the warmer months or curled up with a book and her laptop in the colder months.